Fade to blue

An Otter Bay novel

Fade to blue

JULIE CAROBINI

PUBLISHING GROUP
Nashville, Tennessee

978-0-8054-4874-0

Published by B&H Publishing Group
Nashville, Tennessee

Dewey Decimal Classification: F
Subject Heading: ROMANTIC SUSPENSE NOVELS
\ WOMEN ARTISTS—FICTION \ DOMESTIC
RELATIONS—FICTION

1 2 3 4 5 6 7 8 • 15 14 13 12 11

To everyone in need of a second chance,
and to the Good Shepherd who provides them.

In loving memory of Alice M. Carobine,
beloved wife, mother, and grandmother.
Thank you for leaving such a rich legacy of love.

Chapter One

 The fumes had overtaken me. There could be no other explanation. Of all the people I might have imagined seeing today through the windows of this graying warehouse, Seth Russo hadn't made the top ten. Not even the top ten *thousand*.

A ladder stretching two stories high cast a long shadow across the workstations, and over my heart. Memories of the life I once led and the one I longed for still—stable, nurturing, and uneventful—flashed onto the screen of my mind as sure as that man on the ladder resembled Seth. And yet I knew it wasn't him. It couldn't be. If it was, how could I face him again after all the mistakes I'd made?

"He'll be done soon enough, Suzi-Q." My mentor's voice startled me, and I forced myself to refocus on the job before us. Fred's round eyes peered over his wire rims, "All those northerly windows are a blessing to the artists, but when the sea winds kick up sand and dirt, they can be a curse too."

I nodded before flicking another glance toward those windows. Maybe I was hallucinating. Maybe the stranger only resembled my first love. Surely the aromatic swirl of oil paints and glossy finishes could have such an effect on a person. I drew in a shaky breath and tried again to focus on my boss at my side.

With his cherry red cheeks, featherlike white hair, and round spectacles, Fred Abbott, art conservator and my new boss, reminded me of jolly old Saint Nick. Considering the array of raw materials spread all around us on every shelf and tabletop, this drab building could pass for a toy shop too. Without all the elves and hilarity, of course.

"Now see these here?" He pointed to a tray of metal tools in varying degrees of size and sharpness. "Each one has a purpose all its own." He placed a cold strip of metal in my hand. "Go ahead and roll it around in your palm."

I glanced at the object, trying to memorize its size and shape while also predicting the type of work I might use it for some time. "It's heavy."

He nodded. "That it is. You'll want to use that mainly for wood. If you try to wield it across anything lighter, you'll be in danger of damaging the piece."

Heavy. Has its own purpose. Got it. There was something decidedly comforting in knowing and understanding one's purpose. After what felt like a lifetime of anguish, I had determined mine and taken the steps necessary to see it through.

I would not—could not—stop until I provided a safe, uncomplicated life for my son. And for myself.

Outside, the ladder scraped across metal, sending out a high-pitched screech. It took all my willpower not to turn and gawk at the man again, the one who carried a bucket and wielded a squeegee. A turn in my stomach made me want to bolt, but I fought it off. If I didn't turn soon, though, I might continue the notion that the man I left in haste all those years ago had found his way to Otter Bay. The idea was . . . well, it was crazy.

My nose tickled. "Ah . . . achoo!"

A whirling concoction of fuchsia-colored fabric and cinnamon-laced perfume lofted into the studio and landed next to me. Letty and I had met less than a week before, yet who could tell? She was blunt and honest, too much so to mess with surface pleasantries. She had given me the two-minute version of her life story—thirty-five, of Spanish descent, and devoted to her art—then assessed me in one long, flowing stroke.

"You are a people pleaser. And you have stars in your eyes." She reached over and thumbed through my portfolio, the one I'd pulled together in a valiant effort to acquire a job restoring art at the famed Hearst Castle. "Mercy, you can paint, though."

I let her believe what she wanted. No need to tell her the gritty details of my past. In the brief time we had known each other, Letty made biding my time here as a restoration artist apprentice much easier. Failure to move to the next level—which included permanent employment and the loss of the word *apprentice* behind my job title—was not an option.

Now Letty stood close, her black hair wrapped in a chocolate-tinted scarf, the spiciness of her perfume tickling my nose. "You do sushi?"

I sniffled. "I can honestly tell you I do not."

"Do not *what*?"

"Do sushi."

"Well. It is a shame."

I owed her a snappy comeback, but my attention stood divided. How stupid. What was I thinking? That man could not be Seth. Seth's hair had length and wave and, well, it was always rather moppish. A trademark look for him. But this man wore his hair short in soft spikes.

To better highlight his eyes.

I swallowed my own gasp and flashed Letty a stilted grin. "But I'm happy to give sushi a try. For you."

She puckered her nose and mouth. "Don't put yourself out on my account."

"Come on, Letty. You angry with me?"

She plunked herself into a chair and twirled the fringed edge of her scarf. "Me, mad? No, no. I just like to see you squirm." She rested her chin on curled fingers. "You are such a Goody-Two-shoes. I will break you of this yet."

I laughed and slid a look at Fred, who only offered a brief shrug and no comment. "Oh, brother. Who says 'Goody-Two-shoes' anymore? And what does that have to do with eating sushi anyway?"

"Was that a spark of fire that crossed your face?" she asked, her voice nearly-taunting me. She turned to our boss. "I think I may have finally offended our Suz here."

Fred scratched his head, leaving a plume of feathery hair to stand aloft on his crown. "Doesn't look offended to me. Did you *want* to offend my newest apprentice?"

Letty leaned back and laughed into the rafters before jerking herself upright. "Okay, you and I are going to do some sushi. Tonight. I know the cheapest dive in town. The only place I can afford. Well, it is the only place I ever dine out."

Fred's mouth quirked downward in defeat. "I think this would be a good time for a break, Suz. I'll return in twenty minutes with a picture of the cabin, if you're interested." He shuffled off.

Letty's dark eyes narrowed. "Cabin?"

"I'm hoping to move soon, and Fred mentioned that he and his wife own a cabin they rent out."

"The one in the woods?" Letty's voice rose. "Isn't that occupied?"

"The renters are leaving soon. A job transfer, I think."

I set down the tool I'd been rolling over and over in my hand until every bit of its cold surface turned warm. Letty watched me in silence for once, her eyes piercing, as if wanting to know more about my desire for new digs. The reason was simple, but I wasn't about to divulge it. Not now.

"Tell you what. I promised Jeremiah I'd take him to the Red Abalone Grill tonight. Not so sure about sushi being on the menu, but everything's good. Want to come?"

She hesitated, her usually expressive face a mask. "Sure he won't mind me butting in on your date?"

"He's four. He'll get over it."

She sighed, the lines of her face softening. "The elbows on the table, the toothless grin, the eating with the mouth open . . . Hmm, it has been a long time since I have had dinner with a man." She smoothed a hand across the surface of the workbench. "I will take it."

"Hey, thanks for all the compliments on my parenting skills." Even as I said it, a slight twist tugged at my insides. "See you at six thirty?"

A thump against the wall drew our attention to that expanse of windows. Seth's look-alike stood at the base of the extended ladder and slid it sideways, his eyes drawn upward. Shadows played down the length of his arms exposed at the elbows by upturned sleeves, his muscles moving reflexively. I remembered the strength in Seth's arms when he held me in his embrace. He was always a hugger, the kind of man who'd pull you close and hug like it meant something to him.

A shiver of warmth traveled through me and I flinched. *What am I thinking, letting my mind wander back like that? Those days lay buried—as they should.*

"My," Letty said without answering my question. "I think I need to call a man about some windows."

"Really?" I almost didn't recognize the breezy, distracted tone of my own voice. "Thought your landlady had the whole house done last weekend. Or did they miss your room?"

Letty's black eyes flashed. She pushed her chin forward. "I do *not* rent a room. It is a cabana, Suz. A *cabana*."

Letty felt embarrassed about her rooming situation. Check. At least she could say she paid her own way and didn't have to rely on a generous older brother to provide shelter for her. *And* her child. "It was a joke. Sorry."

Letty batted a hand. "No apologies. Just consider yourself lucky. If I had not committed to dinner with you and that little one of yours, I might have turned to a handsome window washer instead."

"Well then, I must live right." I stuffed down rising alarm over Letty's interest in the man who reminded me of my past.

She fixed her eyes on the windows again. "Then again . . ." Letty gaped at me. "Can you explain why that guy is ogling you?"

Until now I had been toying with thoughts from the past the way a cat bats at a ball of string. I'd been musing about the man outside the window, wondering if he could be my old love yet unwilling to garner his attention, examine his face, and come to a conclusion. Were my wanderings brought on by a life not working according to plan, not to mention the finger-numbing hours spent in this stark warehouse? Or had Seth somehow managed to land in the same small town as I had just a few months ago?

The man stopped his work and peered through the window, one strong arm still propped against the ladder, the other pressed against clean glass. And I knew . . . it was him.

THE DINER BUSTLED FOR a Tuesday night. As usual, Mimi wove in and around booths, swinging a coffeepot, but both Peg, the diner's owner, and her niece Holly, who helped run the place, still hung around.

Holly pulled up in front of us at the hostess stand, gathering menus. "The three of you tonight? Then follow me." She whisked us to an open table along the side wall where windows offered a glimpse of the bubble and churn of the sea. Though fall had begun, the sun had yet to make its descent.

"Hey there, Jeremiah. Bet you'd like some hot chocolate with marshmallows on top."

Jer looked at me for quick approval, and when he received it, he nodded vigorously at Holly.

She laughed. "All right, and for you, ladies? Suz, you usually like chai about now, am I right?"

"Perfect, thanks."

"I've seen your friend around town but never in here before." She smacked her order pad on the table and reached out a hand. "I'm Holly. Welcome to my home away from home."

"Thank you. Letty. And I will have a cup of your strongest coffee. Black."

Holly nodded, then picked up her order pad again, drawing my attention to her unusual clothing. I was glad for the distraction. Since spotting Seth this afternoon, I'd thought of little else. "You're not wearing your uniform tonight, Holly. Pretty dress. Going somewhere?"

A blush crossed her face and she dropped in a minicurtsy.

"Thanks for noticin'. Yeah, I've got a date." She glanced over toward the kitchen. "Tryin' to get out of here, but my aunt Peg's got a bee up her bonnet tonight for some reason."

"Sorry to hear it."

"Eh. It's less and less these days so you won't hear me complainin'. I already went home once but she called me back. Anyway, I hope to get to the back office soon." She patted her head. "Have to do somethin' with this mess of hair."

Letty leaned forward, her face animated. "Tell me you are kidding! Don't you know how much women pay to have hair like that? No, no, no, do not give in to the comb and brush. Just leave that tousled look as is."

Holly smiled. "You think?"

"I do not think—I know."

"Well, then. Thank you. Considerin' he's pickin' me up here any sec, I'm relieved to hear it." Her smile brightened. "I'll be back in a New York minute with all your drinks."

Letty glanced at me. "That was fun."

"She's a character. With that bubbly personality of hers, Holly's known for snagging all the eligible surfers in town, but she's too precious to resent." I tipped my head to the side. "Not like I'm into chasing surfers or anything."

Jer bounced on the vinyl booth. "She's nice. She makes good pancakes—with whipped cream!"

Letty's eyes flashed wide. "Whipped cream? Maybe I will have to order that for my dinner."

Jer dropped his head in an avalanche of giggles. "You can't have whipped cream for dinner." He poked me with one tiny forefinger. "Tell her, Mama. Whipped cream is only for dessert."

"And breakfast?" Letty asked.

Jer smacked himself in the face with his hands. "Oh yeah. For breakfast!"

Holly appeared with three drinks on a tray. "Here we go. Jer, your chocolate is just the right temp'rature for you." She served us our drinks. "I'll be takin' your orders now, and Mimi will be bringin' them to you. But don't you worry, you'll be in good hands."

After scribbling down our orders, she took off in a hurry. I played with the handle of my mug but didn't take a sip. Jeremiah ate two marshmallows off the top of his drink.

Letty stared. "You want to talk about the window washer with the sizzling eyes?" She leaned into the table, zeroing in on me. "The one who ran off like a wounded buck after taking one long look at you?"

Jer slurped his chocolate. "What's a buck?"

Letty patted his hand. "A wild animal. Drink your chocolate, honey."

I took a sip, allowing myself time to answer, but I knew she wouldn't let up. "He's . . . he was an old friend." I sighed. "We didn't part on very good terms, though."

"But I thought you weren't from around here."

"I'm not."

A coy smile raised the corner of her mouth. "So, perhaps he followed you."

I shook my head. "Not possible. He didn't know I was here. It's all just a . . . a fluke."

Jer had already emptied half his mug of chocolate, much of it on his upper lip. "What's a fluke?"

Letty thrust out her chin. "There is no such thing, young Jeremiah. Everything is part of the plan with a capital *P*. The man upstairs—he knows what he's doing."

Jer scrunched up his face. "What man's upstairs?"

"I meant God, Jeremiah. He knows what he is doing. And he has his mother, Mary, and all his saints to help him. You know that, right?"

My son furrowed his baby soft brow. Fluke or chance, it was a deep concept to explain to a four-year-old, especially when mixed with theology. "She means that God is in complete control of our lives and that we shouldn't worry about things that happen." The words fell off my tongue like a rote prayer, making me wonder if I believed it. I looked to her. "Isn't that right, Letty?"

"Yes. Amen. Make sure you always believe that." Letty watched me. "So. Will you be talking to him?"

"You mean like make amends?"

"That is one way to break the ice, I guess. I would stick an olive branch in my teeth if it meant I would be invited up close and personal to a handsome one like that."

I allowed myself a brief smile but shook my head. "It's been too many years. We were kids who fell in love before our time, and that look you saw on his face told me all I needed to know."

"And what might that be?"

"That of all the places he could have landed in this great country of ours, why'd he have to pick the one with the most wretched woman from his past?"

Jer's empty cup fell over. "What's wretched?"

Mimi blew toward us with a full tray of steaming food. "Here we are." She placed the food before us. "Can I get you anything else— Oh, looky here."

We all turned. Seth had just walked into the diner, alone, looking tall and sharp in dark pants, a denim blue shirt, and a casual blazer.

Letty reached for my hand. "Invite him to sit with us."

I jerked my hand away and dropped my gaze to the chopped Cobb salad in front of me. Twice in one day? What was he doing here?

Lord, I've prayed for you to show me the transgressions that have gotten me to this place in life, but I never expected this. I had my reasons for choosing another man over Seth. What about those? Or have you chosen this public place for me to make amends with a man I once hurt?

Letty's sudden, deflated "Oh" pulled me from my thoughts.

Holly greeted Seth. They exchanged some words, and although I tried, I couldn't make them out. Then he held the door open for her. Just before leaving, Holly turned her head toward us and, with a wide smile, mouthed the words: *This is him.*

Chapter Two

 The waves rolled in layers toward me. The pages of my diary flapped free, like sweet memories, like the days I longed to recapture when life was at its simplest.

From this spot on the beach where the tide rushed free and exposed undersea lands, I turned to glimpse the towers of Hearst Castle extending above the clouds. I'd chosen this spot between my two favorite worlds—one undulating and peaceful, the other meticulously planned and stalwart—as the place to unleash my long-locked-away thoughts onto the page.

The only thing that had made its way onto the page, however, was an image I'd sketched as hastily as it appeared in my thoughts: a spattering of glowing sea anemones, similar to the ones I bravely touched soon after moving west. I found them easy to sketch, especially with a mind preoccupied by the sudden, unexpected appearance of an old flame on an otherwise uncomplicated day. Seeing him again had not only washed me in happy memories, but also dredged up the reasons for our parting. My heart beat as if a battle waged within.

The morning sun's brightness dimmed and I peered upward, my left hand shading my eyes.

"You're out early. Glad to see it." Fred stood above me wearing a rumpled cotton button-down shirt, tails out over his faded Dockers, and hiking sandals.

I dropped my hand to my diary, laying it across the page. "Too beautiful of a day not to spend some of it outside." I cringed after saying it. Would he think me ungrateful for my apprenticeship at the warehouse?

"'Course it is. That's why I'm out here on a jaunt myself." Hands in his pockets, he crooked his head toward the castle. "When's the last time you took a good look around?"

My face burned. "Haven't actually been up to the castle in person, Boss, but I've read all about it. And I've studied some of the art pieces online. Fascinating history."

"I suppose you're right about the history and all, but now I understand."

"I'm sorry?"

"No apology necessary. I understand now something in you. There's curiosity in your eyes, and while that may be dandy and fine enough for some folks, no one can get work done that way. You need a tour to cure you of your wonder for the place."

Cure me of my wonder. Wouldn't climbing *La Cuesta Encantada*, "the Enchanted Hill," and seeing the castle up close do the opposite? I gave Fred a smile, forcing any perceived look of curiosity from my face. Not that I'm not *dying* to walk every hall of that magnificent castle. But more than the castle's elusiveness had been on my mind. It was far more likely that on this particular morning, Fred witnessed the sting of Seth's sudden appearance in Otter Bay darkening the circles below my eyes. And just as I had taken steps to put old failures behind me too.

"We'll do it tomorrow." Fred's statement came tinged with hope and a helping of pride, as if he'd solved a problem and felt quite good about himself.

I stood since there'd be no time this morning for jotting down freewheeling thoughts. "Thank you, Fred. I can't wait to see it."

As he continued down the beach, I jogged up the stairs and hopped onto the cotton-candy pink bicycle my future sister-in-law, Callie, had given me when the camp where she worked replaced their equipment with new wheels.

At home Jeremiah wore his favorite train pj's, the ones with frayed and browning edges, and ate sugary corn flakes at the kitchen table. My brother had the coffee waiting. He turned to me holding out a cup. "You timed that well."

"It's a gift." The coffee burned its way down my throat, as if making sure that every nerve ending had fully awakened. "Thanks for letting me slip out this morning. I appreciate it."

He smiled and slipped one arm around my shoulder. "My pleasure. Did you accomplish what you set out to do?"

Not yet. How I wished I could tell my big brother that we no longer needed his charity. Unannounced tears welled behind my eyes. For now, Jeremiah and I needed his help, and for how long was anyone's guess. I cradled the cup in my hands. "I ran into Fred."

Gage's brow lifted.

"My boss."

Understanding lit his face and he nodded, turning back toward the sink to slosh running water into his coffee mug.

"He's going to arrange for me to take a tour of the castle tomorrow."

Gage looked over his shoulder and winced.

"What?"

He set the mug into the sink, grabbed a towel to wipe his hands, then reached out and rubbed my shoulder. "Sorry, Sis. It's been on my list to take you there myself, but with the new project I'm on and, well, all the costs I incurred on the old one . . ." He paused. "Anyway, I really should have done that for you before you started the apprenticeship."

A fissure fractured the dam of emotion swelling within me. "That wasn't your responsibility," I snapped.

He sighed and leaned back against the sink, looking very much like a father ready to scold his wayward toddler. Could I blame him? At thirteen years my senior, he'd often drifted into the parenting role. "Something going on I should know about?"

I poured Jer a cup of apple juice. "I'm just saying I'm a big girl and it's time I act like one. As soon as possible, I plan to move out and give you your privacy back."

He crossed his arms. "When have I ever made you feel unwelcome?"

"You haven't. But you're engaged. Don't you think Callie would prefer to marry a man without so much baggage?"

"Callie loves you, and she's never said—"

"Of course not, and I wouldn't expect her to. But she's not marrying all of us—just you." I let out a harsh breath. "Look, I can't do it yet—we both know it—but it's my goal to get out of your hair. And hers."

He stared at me, his forehead creased. "Feels a little unfair of you to say that."

I swallowed the sharp lump in my throat. Jer climbed down from his chair and picked up his bowl and spoon, as he'd been taught. As he padded across the kitchen floor, his spoon flipped out of the bowl, landing with a clatter and spraying milk on the tile.

"Uh-oh." He watched me with moon eyes.

I took the bowl from his hands and set it in the sink. "Go put on your school clothes, Jeremiah. Mama will be right up."

He scampered away.

Gage grabbed a wet rag and crouched down, scrubbing the droplets and puddles from the tile floor.

"See? This is what I mean. You shouldn't have to deal with things like this until you have your own wife and kids underfoot." An overreaction, maybe, but everything inside me stood poised to burst.

Gage grunted and threw down the rag. My big brother, who took us in and had never uttered a negative word about it, glared up at me. "What's gotten into you? I thought you liked living here with me. Have I done something to offend you?"

I clenched my fists. "Stop being so nice to me! I'm the one who's screwed up, and I'm just trying to set things right for the first time in my life."

He reached out for me. "I haven't seen you like this since . . . since . . ."

I wrenched away from him. "Since you found me in a sobbing mass—like a fool—the day Len sent a letter telling me he wanted a divorce?"

He pulled me into a hug. "Stop. Whatever it is, I can help you. You haven't screwed up your life. Sometimes, it's just plain hard, but you and I, we've always been in this together."

Maybe it was his crushing hug, or maybe the years of mistakes raining down on my head, but I couldn't breathe. The weight of my predicament, of living a life that looked nothing like I had dreamed, had a way of draping itself about my shoulders like a steel cape.

He released me, concern creasing his brow. "Right, Suz?"

I nodded, still unable to speak. I had no real means of leaving soon and had been frivolous to suggest otherwise. "I'm sorry. You're right."

"Don't apologize." He rubbed my shoulder somewhat

awkwardly. "Just go back to being the dreamer you've always been, squirt. Always admired that in you."

I pulled away. *Dreamer?* Seth used to call me that too. I shut my eyes a moment. It unnerved me to have him showing up in my thoughts with sudden regularity.

Gage eyed me. "Promise me you'll tell me whenever something's bothering you—before it overtakes you. Will you do that?"

I pushed the image of Seth greeting Holly in the diner right out of my mind and gave my brother the best conjured-up smile I could. "Sure. Of course."

He smiled back. "Good. I'll take Jer to school for you this morning so you can have more time to get ready for work." He paused a full three seconds. "Before I go, though, I have to tell you something." He pulled an envelope out of his back pocket and handed it me. "You received a letter yesterday from Heinsburgh. The guy's got lousy timing, as usual."

Heinsburgh Valley Correctional Facility. The return address shone, emblazoned in lyrical black script. Why would they bother? "Thanks." I took the envelope and stuck it in my purse on the counter.

He quirked that eyebrow again. "You gonna open it?"

I shrugged. "Maybe."

"I could open it for you."

I glared at him.

He shrank back. "Your divorce is final so whatever that guy has to say, he should be saying through a lawyer."

"He's Jer's father."

"And a criminal." My brother raked his hand through his wavy, brown hair. "Look, he chose a path that's unhealthy and dangerous. You couldn't possibly want Jer to have that kind of influence in his life." He paused, his eyes unwavering. "Tell me I'm right, Suzanna."

I stared back at him, knowing I needed to take control of my life again. It was the only way I'd find what Gage and I'd had as kids: a stable, God-loving home unmarked by upheaval until, well, until both our parents were gone. Still, I knew better than to toss out my faith in the process. "Our marriage may be over, but I pray every day that he will come back to God and that he can be the father—*the person*—he was created to be. God hasn't given up on him, so I have no right to."

Gage blew out a long, measured sigh. He watched me in silence.

"What?"

"You're our mother all over again. She had the hardest time saying anything against anyone."

I paused. "Is that so wrong?"

"That's a hard one to answer, squirt. Just do me a favor."

"What's that?"

"Be careful."

"Aren't I always?" I said the words, knowing I needed to be more than careful. I needed to be smart.

Chapter Three

Letty's perfume tickled my nose as she hissed into my ear, "How did you manage to get a private tour so soon?"

I shrugged, because I hadn't a clue. One minute I sat on a lonely beach peering up at the over sixty-year-old castle, the next my boss gave me the day off to see the architectural treasure up close. We bumped along the winding path toward the castle in an old Jeep, Fred and the driver up front, Letty and me in the back.

She leaned toward me again, her voice still a whisper. "I can't believe he wasn't going to invite me to go along too." She paused. "Thank you for saying something."

I nodded as we hit a bump so hard my head grazed the ceiling. I gripped the seat in front of me, pulling myself forward. "Is this okay? Going up privately, I mean?"

Fred stared straight ahead, but his jowls shifted, the grizzled whiteness of his cheeks rising into a smile. "All protocol has been followed. Sit back and enjoy the scenery."

I sat back. Letty's whisper took on a hisslike quality. "I have been *training* for more than two years, and all I've gotten is a ride on one of those tourist trams with piped-in music from the forties."

I patted the back of her hand that also gripped the seat in front. "I'm jealous. If I could have afforded to, I would have done the same months ago."

She was quiet for a moment. We both took in the rolling hills, listening as our tour guide and driver, Clem, yarned on about Mr. Hearst's former collection of wild animals.

"And over here's the area where they roamed free over two thousand acres. All kinds of wild critters—water buffalo, yaks, emus, ostriches, elk, zebras, llamas, oh and deer. Lots of deer of all types."

Letty clutched her purse closer to her body, as if protecting herself should a dangerous animal charge our open-air ride.

Toward the top, Clem pointed toward some vague spot on the other side of the hill. "They say he even kept polar bears over there, where it was cooler. Made concrete pits to keep the ground cold and to hold ice hauled in on hot days."

Her mouth fell open. "Polar bears in California? That is loony, if you ask me."

Different, maybe, but I was charmed. The higher we climbed toward the romantic castle on the hill, the more I let my worries and stresses melt away. No ex-husband to worry about or old flame who bolted at the sight of me, just a fairy tale of a day walking the halls of history. If I shut my eyes, I could imagine the castle in its heyday, the merry images playing out on a drop-down screen. "I wish I could've been here."

Letty bumped my shoulder. "Why? So you could risk seeing your flesh torn right off your bones when some wild animal decided it was feeding time?"

"You're gross."

"No, I am realistic. All I can say is that it is a good thing those roaming animals were sent away to the comfortable confines of an upstanding zoo somewhere."

"Oh, brother."

Letty shook her head, an expression of feigned disgust on her face as she repeated my words, "I wish I could've been here . . ."

I laughed. "C'mon, Letty. Aren't you the least bit excited about viewing the castle again, seeing all those famous art pieces up close, walking the halls where political dignitaries and Hollywood's biggest names once partied?"

"I have said it before—someone has stars in her head all right."

I shrugged. "Well, I'm excited." I held up my notepad. "This is a learning experience for me and I intend to treat it as such. My degree has been put on hold, so I consider this an important part of my education. So much fine art from all over the world in one place!"

"Yes, it is rather like a museum, is it not?"

"The castle's too romantic to be thought of as just a museum. Not that I don't love a good stroll through an art museum, of course. It's just . . . oh, I don't know."

"Ah, I see where this is going. Suz has romance on the mind, and dare I say, I did not notice this about you before that irresistible window washer appeared in your viewfinder yesterday like some wounded cowboy."

I bumped her shoulder harder than she had mine, and then glanced at the men bouncing along in front of us. "Stop it. Seeing Seth was a shock, yes, but then again, why should seeing an old friend from the past be that way? And besides, didn't you see him run off with Holly last night?"

"They were not exactly *running*, my dear. They had a simple date. The whole scene was rather old-fashioned too—he with his overcoat, she in her sparkly dress."

"Jealous?"

Letty glared at me. "Ever notice that it is always the blondes who have all the fun around here?"

I began to comment, caught sight of a loose strand of my long chestnut locks, and then flapped my gaping mouth shut when we crested the hill. I took in the grandeur of this castle that took almost thirty years to build. The cloudless, azure backdrop served to heighten its magic. Peace continued to drape itself over me. I felt lighter, as if weights floated off of me and into that great expanse of blue above.

After we parked, Letty and I followed Clem and Fred to the entrance where we climbed the stone steps. Standing in front of the mighty castle, I took in the patterned tile at our feet, the soaring edifice, but strangely enough, the rush of water from the marble fountain and sounds of calling birds enchanted me as if I'd just stepped into the pages of *The Secret Garden*.

Letty fished around in her bag and handed me her compact mirror. "Take a look, Suz. That angelic swoon on your face reminds me of Snow White. I am half expecting to see your prince storm by on a white steed followed by bouncing bunnies and happy little chipmunks."

I ignored her. "Wow. It's . . . it's even more magnificent than the pictures."

Letty watched me, then whipped her gaze to the castle entrance, shielding her eyes from the rising sun. "Well, it was designed by a woman, you know."

True, architect Julia Morgan had supervised the construction of Hearst Castle and the surrounding buildings. It had been said that she was hired to create "something that would be more comfortable" than tents. Talk about creative interpretation.

I stood there, thinking about the freedom Ms. Morgan must have enjoyed. This place cost millions and took many years to build. I pictured her at the top of this hill, sketching away, inspired by the high altitude and forever views of the West Coast and beyond. We were sojourners here, but at the moment, nothing felt so temporary.

The groan and growl of a four-wheel drive climbed the road below us, interrupting the fantasy. A truck carrying three men pulled to a stop next to our Jeep. Two hopped out, their hiking boots landing with harsh clomps against the roadway.

Seeing Seth among them, my lungs contracted. Letty swiveled her pointed chin at me, her mouth agape. "Are you asking me to believe that this is all one big coincidence? That, my friend"—she pointed one French-manicured nail at the man who had become familiar to us both—"is a sign from God himself."

I slid a look her way. "I'm not blaming this on God." Although even I had to wonder why, after all these years, Seth had turned up three times in less than twenty-four hours. And how I'd managed to avoid speaking to him . . .

Clem greeted the men as they approached. "Good to see you." He stuck out a beefy hand to the one in a park ranger uniform.

Seth didn't seem to notice me, his eyes roaming over the castle's entrance. Of course, I didn't help, hiding behind Letty and Fred as I did. The awkwardness of the moment threatened to derail the magic of this impromptu tour of *Casa Grande*.

I shifted sideways, pretending to examine the flowing fountain, the one with water cascading in a soothing rush. Letty would have none of it and moved away from my side as Seth took a step in my direction. When I turned back around, our gazes collided, nothing between us but oxygen—and the memory of time.

"Hello, Seth. You look good. It's been a long time."

He nodded and opened his mouth, as if to return my hello. Instead he let it shut again.

Heat reached my cheeks. I swallowed the lump in my throat and a little pride too. "Well . . ."

"Suz."

"You remember."

His eyes pierced me. "Some things are harder to forget than others."

I mulled over his words—and the way he delivered them. Everything about him was familiar and yet different at the same time. The same diamond-shaped face with a dimple at the southernmost point, penetrating gray-green eyes, and high cheekbones that gave him that chiseled look. Yet something was missing. The warmth he once exuded so richly had vanished.

The park ranger tapped Seth on the shoulder. "Ready to go?"

Seth gave the ranger a quick nod, and then turned back to me. His gaze seemed to hover for the slightest moment, then he gave me the same businesslike nod he'd given the ranger. And then he left. Just like that.

I watched his back and exhaled slowly, fighting off the compulsion to lower myself to the ground in a crumpled mess.

"That had to hurt."

I didn't look at Letty, unwilling to let her see in my eyes what she already knew.

FOR THE NEXT HOUR we wandered around the castle, through the same areas designated for tourists. Occasionally we would come upon a group of people crammed into the various rooms, their gazes traveling over the walls and floors and priceless furnishings while a patient tour guide filled them in on details and offered anecdotal tidbits from the Hearst days.

My energy for exploration had dulled since we arrived, my mind occupied with meeting Seth again and his quick dismissal of me. When we found ourselves ushered into Hearst's old movie theater, relief flowed through the taut muscles of my neck and back. I sank into one of the old padded seats, hardly listening as our guide told us about the ornate screening room. Hearst, he said, treated many guests to private showings of black-and-white films, many featuring his girlfriend Marion Davies.

I winced. Wasn't Hearst married at the time?

A large gray screen dropped before us, imprinted with the ghosts of movies past, and I tucked away my thoughts on Hearst's past. Vaguely I recalled Fred turning to me and whispering something about his knees aching and would I mind if we took a respite and enjoyed a Hearst-era film?

The music started, a piano piece, jaunty and light. My mind wandered to the past, but not the yesteryear portrayed on the screen. One I knew. Seth's face appeared before me. Only this time instead of a cold gaze, his eyes radiated warmth. We both had reached for the same sad-looking Christmas ornament at a church bazaar.

"Excuse me," he said.

I laughed. "No, excuse me. You take it." While other booths were overrun with customers, this sparsely decorated one had been passed over again and again. I noticed from across the gymnasium and couldn't stand it, determining then that I would march over and reach for the most hideous item I could find and buy it.

Apparently Seth decided to do the same thing.

The woman behind the table beamed. Her salt-and-pepper hair fixed with a velvety red Christmas bow hung near her cheek as she bobbed her head. "You don't need to fight over it. I've got more where that came from." She reached behind her and brought out a box nearly full of the homemade ornaments: golf balls with the eeriest smiles painted on their pock-marked surfaces.

I bit back a smile until my lip ached, especially after noticing Seth wince at the appearance of so many of the awful things.

"I'll take them all," he said.

I gasped and they both looked at me, so I faked a cough. A harsh, wracking cough.

The woman patted my back. "There, there. You really should see a doctor about that."

Seth paid for the items—including one for me—and thanked the woman, offering her liberal praise for her artistry.

"My compliments." He handed me one as we scooted away from the booth.

"I really should pay you."

"Don't bother. That show you gave over there was payment enough."

I giggled as we strolled through the crowd. "She's so sweet . . . I couldn't bear the thought of her not getting any business, but if these aren't the ugliest things I've ever seen."

"Fine way to talk about my first gift to you."

I stopped and looked up at him. "Well, then, I suppose if you're planning to buy me fine gifts, we ought to officially meet."

He grinned, his ocean-green eyes making it difficult not to stare. "I'm Seth. Nice to finally meet you. I've seen you in church."

I leaned my head to one side. He noticed me as I had him? I reached out my hand. "Suzanna, but most everyone calls me Suz. Good to meet you too, Seth."

The music drifted off and another voice caught my attention.

"And . . . fade to black!"

I whipped my chin to the side to see Letty watching me. "What?"

"The movie. It's over already. And if you ask me, it was much too long anyway." She nudged me. "Were you sleeping or something?"

I shook my head. "No, not at all. Just thinking." I picked up my purse from the seat next to me and set it on my lap.

Letty pointed at the envelope sticking out of my purse with *Heinsburgh Valley Correctional Facility* emblazoned in the corner. "What's that?"

I sucked in a quick breath. "Something I'd like to forget." I stuffed it down into my bag and snapped it shut. "Have you ever wished you could have penned your own life story, Letty?"

"Now that is a thought. But I do not believe so, no."

"Why not?"

"Because I believe the good Lord can come up with something better than I could on my own." She touched my arm. "Not that he's done all that much yet, but I'm sure he will. Someday."

Her words humbled me. "You're right." I batted the air. "I was just being silly."

"We all have our pains from the past, Suz, and though I can't imagine writing my own life story, I've got nothing against asking God for a rewrite!"

I laughed at this, the sound of it working to dislodge any lingering sadness. By now, Fred and our tour guide stood by the exit, hands shoved in their pockets, their gazes flitting around while waiting for us.

I followed Letty out, thinking about meeting Seth all those years ago and how quickly our relationship blossomed from its random beginning. I wasn't sure how appropriate it would be to ask God for a rewrite, yet in this moment, I decided one thing: Although my romance with Seth had long ended, our friendship deserved a second chance.

Chapter Four

At twilight, I ventured toward the steep cliff at the end of our block of colorful cottages with second chances on my mind. I maneuvered down the wooden stairs before hopping onto the pebblelike sand that made a muffled *whoosh* upon landing.

Several beachcombers made their way along the shore, and part of me wondered if the soothing ripple of the ocean would prove to be a distraction rather than the aria I longed to experience while sketching.

Breathing in the briny, moist air, I found a dry spot on a smooth rock to settle on for a while. Despite a less-than-hopeful start to our castle tour this morning, I had managed to fill more than eight pages of my sketchbook with images from throughout Casa Grande. I hoped to study them more closely and perhaps write through some of the angst that had attempted to disrupt my day.

A girlish laugh caused me to raise my head.

"Hey there, Suz!" Holly's long, blonde, spiral hair bounced when she walked.

Seth trailed behind her, slowing when Holly spotted me. If facial expressions could be translated into story, I'd have to say Seth's took on the air of mystery, with a dark draw to his eyes and a gaze that darted around.

I snapped shut my sketch pad. "Hi, Holly. Seth."

Holly froze and sucked in a breath. "Glory be! You two know each other?"

I stood. "We're old friends from back East."

Holly cast a glance at each of us, oblivious to the cold front put forth by Seth. "If this world isn't smaller than a pea pod. When's the last time you saw each other?"

"This morning. Up at the castle. My boss was giving Letty and me a tour, and Seth breezed by on a private tour of his own. Although I never did learn how that came about."

Holly hugged her sides. "It's so excitin', really. Seth may take over the window-washin' duties for the castle. The park service contacted him directly—that's how good his company's reputation is. Can you imagine? Washin' windows high up on that bluff for weeks on end? There are worse things that could happen in life!"

She had that right. Unfortunately, I had experienced some of them.

Seth stuffed his hands into his pockets and looked around,

one muscle in his cheek twitching. That cheek muscle always twitched when he fought back the urge to say what he felt. Like that last night we stood on the porch of my parents' house.

"So that's what you came out here to do." The words flew out, as if condemning his long-ago decision to move out west. I regretted phrasing it that way but said nothing else, figuring that what I said wouldn't matter to him anyway.

As if proving me right, Seth frowned. "I came out this way for a lot of reasons."

Holly either pretended or didn't notice the thickening air between us. "Seth bought a company with just one employee, and in no time he's already got fifteen people working for him. Isn't that great?"

"Yes, it is. Really great. I'm glad for you, Seth."

He glanced at the toe of his hiking boot, his mouth screwed up in a pucker. "It's worked out all right."

Holly pressed a fist in her side. "All right? I'd say you're doing mighty fine, mister." She dropped the hand from her side and playfully rubbed Seth's shoulder.

He glanced at Holly. The grin he'd been fighting appeared, and seeing it caused my heart to drum in my ears. The sea swirled and churned beyond us, and for a moment I wished to get caught up in it. Instead I pulled my attention back to Seth and Holly. Holly and Seth. Absurd as it may seem, a middle school vein of something—jealousy, maybe?—wriggled its way through me, as if awakening feelings for him long believed dormant.

The thought horrified me.

For his part, Seth showed little sign of interest in me anyway—friendship or otherwise. But what did I expect? I married another man and had his baby. Jeremiah's dimpled face dropped into my thoughts. My sweet baby. Every pain from the past was worth it, if only because of my son.

My eyes took in Seth again, and I pushed away wayward thoughts that dredged up our past. I intended to keep living in this town, and it appeared that Seth did too. So it made sense to smooth over the cobblestones of yesterday. "Wild seeing you here in California, Seth."

He considered me, leaning his head to one side. "I would agree with that. Pretty wild."

Silence fell between us. "I saw you working on that wall of windows at the art studio. It's not the castle, but that's a big job in itself."

"Can't complain. The contract has been a boon for us, and I appreciate the work."

"He always personally takes on jobs that are really important." Holly patted his shoulder. "Isn't that right?"

Seth shifted from one leg to the other and offered a quick nod. Or maybe more like a shrug. More memories of my time with Seth rolled in. A master of brief, quick answers and long pauses, he always drove me crazy. Worse, when I would rephrase questions and ask them again believing maybe he hadn't understood my meaning the first time, he'd crinkle his brow and say, "I was thinking."

Holly leaned forward. She couldn't handle empty airspace

either. "That old warehouse often contains priceless works of art. He can't be too careful just letting anyone work there."

"Uh-huh. I see."

"I mean, there's more than the art from the castle being run through Fred's studio. Isn't that right, Suz?"

"Absolutely. You'd never know from its termite-ridden exterior that one of Elvis's guitars was recently in for repairs."

"No!"

"You didn't hear it from me," I whispered.

Holly crossed her heart. "Your secret's safe here. Wow, the king's guitar, and you're working on it."

I flipped my palms up. "Not me, well, not yet anyway. I'm still learning, still following Fred around. It is exciting, though, getting to work with new media in ways I'd never imagined." I paused. "I am very blessed."

Seth eyed me. "Weren't you always more of a freehand artist?" He looked at Holly. "She had raw talent and could paint anything."

"Well, not *anything*, Seth."

His gaze brushed across my face. "You're modest. I remember your way with a brush and the way you could conjure up designs in your head."

Holly smiled, not showing the least hint of jealousy over Seth's compliment. "I'd heard about that. Didn't you make over Callie's place? And your brother's too?" She turned to Seth. "Her brother, Gage—he's engaged to Callie—comes into the diner a lot. He's mentioned Suz's talent bunches of times. He's so proud of her."

Seth's eyes shifted, breaking contact with mine. "I remember Gage."

"She and Jer live with him," Holly added.

He pressed his lips together, and his eyes flickered over my ring finger. "Jer? What happened to—?"

I cut him off. "Jeremiah is my son." Seth might not have information about the years between now and then. I had chosen Len to marry over him, and because of that, Seth had left town earlier than planned, destined for big adventure across this country of ours. If we had not run into each other in this small town of Otter Bay, chances were he never would have learned the rest of the story.

"I see."

Holly's brows bunched and she looked from Seth to me. "Wow, it really has been a long while for you two. Jer looks just like his mama. 'Cept the hair color. He's a real blondie and cute as a bug's nose."

Seth shifted again. "So he's what, four years old?"

My boy's face beamed in my mind. "Nearly five."

Seth grew quiet again. He had questions, obvious by the way he shifted and paused. He probably wouldn't ask them now, not until he formulated them, and certainly not in front of Holly. If ever.

The sun sat atop the horizon, as if playing a game of chicken. Jer and Gage would be wondering about me, so I picked up my journal and sketch pad. "Enjoy your walk, you two. Time for me to head back and fix dinner."

Holly linked an arm through Seth's. "We will, Suz. Nice talkin' to you."

Seth nodded, as was his way, although this time he looked as if he might have something to say. Still, he held his words, and the two began down the beach only to stop so Holly could call to me. "Suz?"

"Yes?"

"Maybe you two oughta meet at the diner sometime." Friendly concern knit her brows. "You know, to talk about old times."

If Holly knew what Seth and I had once meant to each other, she never would have suggested we spend one minute together alone. I searched Seth's face for some sign that he would entertain the idea, if only to bury old pains, and perhaps rekindle a friendship.

All that appeared on his face was a fresh frown and drooping eyelids, as if the thought of spending another minute with me made him want to shut his eyes and forget about it.

Holly waited for my answer, and I shrugged. "Maybe," I said, then turned toward the stairs and climbed them two at a time.

With Len in jail, I'd taken Jer and crawled like a dreaded pariah from my hometown. My back stiffened. Why did one grimace from Seth Russo wash that feeling over me again?

Ten minutes later, I stepped into the house and peeled my fingers from my journal and sketch pad. Quiet enveloped the house, giving me more opportunity to ruminate over yet another "chance" meeting with Seth. With little panache,

I poured water into a pan, added a splash of milk, tossed in a bag of chai tea, and heated it up. A note on the kitchen island caught my eye:

Suz, Callie and I took Jer out for a corn dog. Enjoy the solitude while it lasts. ~ G

When the mixture boiled, I poured myself a steaming cup of chai, adding a generous amount of honey, and plopped into a chair. A rodlike weight pressed into my spine. Not exactly the relaxing hour Gage had hoped to give me.

My purse lay open and I snatched the envelope that peeked out from one corner. My fingers ran across the words *Heinsburgh Valley Correctional Facility*, as if they could be rubbed away. I ripped open the envelope and yanked a folded page from within, harshly flattening its crease with my hand.

Dear Suz,
  How have you been, honey?

I looked up from the page. Blinked twice, feeling the burn each time, before continuing to read.

First, I hope this letter finds you and Jer happy. That's all I have ever wanted for my family—for you to be happy.
  Second, and maybe this should have come first, but I should be ashamed of all I have done to make your lives so miserable. I am a wretched man and do not deserve your forgiveness. I write this in the hope you will

*forgive me anyway, as Christ forgives. (Knowing you,
I believe that you will.)*

*I am a new man, Suz. A new man. The chap-
lain here says that my wineskins are new. (It's from
the Bible, but I have given up drinking for good!) The
peace of God rules my heart now and I've been set free.
Remember the woman I told you about? The one I was
going to marry? That is over, my dear Suzanna. A terrible, awful memory from the past. I was deceived when
I left you and promised myself to her. It was wrong, but
I'm trying to set things right with you and with my son.*

*I know legally our marriage is over, but spiritually,
it is not. I'm torn up inside over hurting you and our
son the way I did, and my prayer is that when the
parole board meets next week, they will set me free for
good. My parole officer believes this will happen. When
it does (not "if" because I'm believing it will happen!),
I will do everything in my power to prove to you that
I am a changed man.*

Forever, Len

I let the letter drop from my hand and flutter onto the
floor, unable to digest much of anything.

Chapter Five

"Tell me what's on your mind." Callie curled her legs beneath her athletic body on the couch and leaned back against its cushions.

I sat erect in the recliner, clutching my empty mug. *Where to start?*

When the party of three had returned from their evening of corn dogs and ice cream, I managed to set aside Len's shocking letter and paste on a smile. Jer climbed into my lap then, smelling of grease and mustard, and I knew a bath couldn't wait. Yet as I stood and lifted my son into my arms, my brother's firm hand squeezed my shoulder.

"I'd like to put Jer to bed tonight." He held out open arms. "May I?"

It didn't make sense. Gage and Callie could—finally—enjoy some quiet time in this house while I wrestled Jer clean, read him some of his favorite stories, then tucked him into bed.

I leaned my head to the side, searching my brother's face for halfheartedness in his offer but found nothing but the brotherly affection he'd spoiled me with for much of my life. I let my suspicions go when Jer leapt into his uncle's arms, gurgling secret messages to him, the kinds of things I supposed young boys might often share with their fathers. If that didn't tweak my heart every time.

Now, as Callie sat across from me waiting for an answer, memories from the day tumbled through my head. After Gage headed upstairs with Jer, it didn't take long for my future sister-in-law to realize that my usually hopeful self was less-than. I had received a harsh reality check from Seth today, and after that I'd come home to Len's letter. Two men from my past: one unwilling to give me a second chance, and the other begging me to do just that. It's a wonder Gage and Callie hadn't found me coiled into the fetal position and sucking my thumb on the living room rug.

After I relayed the letter's contents, Callie glanced often at the staircase, as if hoping Gage would show up soon and cast a level opinion on Len's announcement.

"Do *you* believe he's changed, Suz?"

I fingered the letter. "I want to believe Len's a new man. Not for my sake." The words tasted strange. "But for his own good . . . and for Jeremiah's. A boy deserves a father in his life, don't you think?"

Callie nodded. "Of course. I just meant . . ." She sighed. Callie had been burned by both a former boyfriend and several local businesspeople. She probably felt conflicted over what she had learned from Gage about my ex-husband and the heart behind what he had written in his letter. "Wow. So much to think about. This changes everything, doesn't it?"

I nodded. "Maybe . . ."

"What changes everything?" Gage appeared at the foot of the stairs, smiling in his buttondown shirt, soaked through in spots. He finished drying his hands on a towel and tossed it into an empty laundry basket near the bottom step.

I held the letter out to him and his smile faded. He took it from me and scanned it in silence. Callie and I exchanged a glance before he looked up. "He's lying." He handed it back to me.

"Did you even read it?"

"You saw me, and I don't believe a word of it."

"How can you say that? He says he's sorry, and that he's a new man. Did you read the part about the peace of God ruling his heart? How can I turn my back on something like that?"

Gage paced. "Don't care. The guy's a felon. For all we know he paid someone to write that love note for him since I doubt he's capable of such . . ."

"Heartfelt words?"

Gage wagged his head. "He's gotten to you. I can't believe it. The guy who cheated on you, committed robbery—*sold drugs, Suz*—has with just one postage stamp convinced you he's changed. It doesn't work that way."

I stuffed the page back into its envelope. I would rather crumple up that letter than have to deal with its contents. "Maybe it doesn't, but maybe it does. Who's to say whether or not God supernaturally heals a person anymore? Not me, that's for sure."

Gage squatted down next to the love seat. "Can we leave God out of this for a minute? Just suppose I'm right and Len has some ulterior motive."

I opened my mouth to protest, but he stopped me with a held-up palm. "Maybe the other woman dumped him. If he really is about to be paroled, he probably needs somewhere to live, so he's turned to you—the only person who always gives him another chance. Don't you see? He's trying to use us."

"Aha. So you're afraid I'm going to bring him here, to this house. Jer and I already test the limits of your generosity and you think I'd have the audacity to inconvenience you further. I see now."

Gage threw his hands up and looked to Callie for support. "This is crazy."

Callie rose and slid onto the couch next to me. "Take some time, Suz. You don't need to respond right away or make any decision of how you will eventually handle this. Think it out. Pray about it."

Gage rose, his knees cracking. "Don't encourage her, Callie. She needs to shut this guy down now, because if she doesn't, he'll take that as a sign she might actually consider taking the louse back."

Callie put a calming hand on his folded arm. "Gage."

He turned away from her. "I need you to support me here."

An argument brewed between them, and it pained me

to see that happening on my account. When I stood, Callie stepped back and I struggled to keep the shake out of my voice. "What happened to the compassionate man who took us in when we had nowhere else to go? What happened to him, Gage?"

My hands clenched again and again. "I'm not asking you to give Len a home or anything else. This letter, though, has given me much to think about and I cannot discard it as easily as you apparently can. I've been praying for Len for years to turn his life around and to know the truth of God in his life. Maybe this is a sign."

"Do you still love him?"

My gaze dropped to the wooden floors, scarred from years of living. I raised my eyes to his. "Does that matter?"

"You let him go once, and it broke your heart. I'll never forget finding you in that distraught state. It broke my heart too." He ran a hand through his hair. "Don't allow yourself— and Jer, for that matter—to go through something so tragic again."

My mind flashed back on agonizing moments from the not-too-distant past. Maybe my brother was right. Maybe the smartest move would be to tear up Len's startling letter and toss it in the garbage.

Then again, when my mother died and Len rushed in to offer everything I thought I needed, I ignored a God-sized niggling in my soul, the one that cautioned me to consider the cost of my decision. If I ignored Len's declaration of faith, if I did nothing to offer support for his newfound way of life, was

I in danger of doing the same thing? Could I be ignoring God's direction in this situation?

"I hear you, big brother. I really do. But if there's a lesson here somewhere, something God wants me to learn through all of this, I hope he makes that clear to me." I glanced at Callie. "Kind of like the way he taught you and Gage to put aside your differences so you could find happiness together."

The hard line of Gage's features softened. He caught a glimpse of Callie watching him and smiled at her, sadness tugging at the corners of his mouth. "I'm sorry," he whispered and pulled her toward him.

Some of my brother's resistance had worn away, but not all of it, not by the way his mouth continued to dip downward. "I'm sorry if it seems like I'm being rash, Suz. We don't even know if what he says is . . ." Heaviness weighed in his eyes. "Well, until the parole board acts, seeing Len anytime soon may not be an issue. Promise me you'll take some time before responding. Will you do that?"

Part of me wanted to tell him that something about this moment appeared bigger than life, as if it didn't matter what I thought or even what I did. What would be would be. When I broke it off with Seth and soon after married Len, I could never have dreamed that life would bring me here, scraping by and living under my brother's roof.

My life hadn't been without its blessings, though. During those years Gage and I had lived apart, except for the rare visit from him, I missed my big brother. After our parents died, Gage moved to the West Coast for work, satisfied that Len would take care of me. Jer barely knew his uncle when we arrived here, heartbroken and needing shelter from the hurricane that had torn apart my marriage.

In the past few months, I'd witnessed Gage's career turned upside down in a good way, and I'd watched him fall in love and become engaged to a woman who started out as his chief nemesis. That alone made my relocation more palatable. And now I had been given the opportunity to restore some of the greatest art pieces in the world. How could I allow regret to suffocate my soul?

Worse yet, how could I ever believe that a new soul turned to the Savior would not be showered with equal blessings?

To soothe my brother's worries, I nodded with deliberation. "Agreed." Even as I said the word, though, I could not help but think that the week until the next parole board hearing would fly right on by.

Chapter Six

Some things in life remain a mystery, while others stay as sure as the sun setting over the Pacific Ocean.

As a teenager, I learned it best not to attempt to slip into a pair of jeans after applying nail polish, and that to order spaghetti on a first date (while wearing white, no less) was asking for it. Later, as an adult, I became convinced that airing out the house after making egg-salad sandwiches was always a good idea.

So when Letty showed up at work this morning at the warehouse, smelling of nutmeg and lasering me with penetrating eyes, I didn't flinch. My new friend had a way of letting me know when she was about to pounce.

"You blew me off yesterday." She wore layers of crushed cotton in shades of pumpkin. Coupled with the scent of her perfume, her presence reminded me of Thanksgiving, although the holiday was months away.

I continued wiping down the long table that would serve as my workplace today. Fred said he had a surprise for me and to prep the work surface, so I scrubbed it beyond clean and avoided Letty's imploring expression in the meantime.

"Well?"

"Well . . . what?"

She plopped onto the stool across from me and dropped her faux-leather bag onto the concrete floor. "You may think I didn't notice how you skirted my question yesterday—the one about the envelope sticking out of your purse—but I only let you off the hook for twenty-four hours."

I raised my brows. "I don't know what you mean."

"You received mail from *prison*."

The technician behind her, a scruffy artist named Timo, dropped a metal scraper and it clattered to the floor. He reached for it, red faced and avoiding my eyes, which told me he heard Letty's question clear as the view of the castle after a rain.

I frowned, flashed my eyes at him, then turned back and found Letty watching me. "Like you never have." I managed to keep my voice level.

Timo snorted and made a *rawr* sound. I wadded up the rag in my hand and pitched it at his head, causing him to yelp.

Letty laughed, then slapped him on one side of his head. "You are a wicked boy. Acting like you have a front-row seat at a cat fight!"

He scowled and rubbed his skull.

I motioned for Letty to follow me outside. The crisp air awoke a plethora of thoughts from the night before. I didn't know what to make of the emotions ricocheting through my heart and mind like some old-time pinball machine at the penny arcade. One minute my mood felt light and ready for what life would bring, and the next? It felt like a cloud laden with the threat of a storm hovering over me.

I hadn't wanted to tell Letty anything about the envelope, but maybe a third party could help sort it all out. Gage and Callie lived too close to the situation to give unbiased opinions. And Seth knew all about my early relationship with Len, so he—

Seth! I shook my head. How I could allow myself to go there for even an instant?

"Looks like you're having a conversation with a ghost." Letty laughed, a surprising ripple in her voice. "What can you say to someone invisible that you won't tell me?"

"I could use some impartial advice." I let my gaze catch hers. "Are you up for it?"

She crossed her arms. "Try me."

We climbed a short way up the hill and found a weathered log on which to settle. I told her my story, how my ex-husband was about to be released from prison. I told her how I'd married Len and soon after become pregnant with Jeremiah. How it didn't take long for me to realize that Len, the man with great ideas, had zero plans to implement them. He had wooed me with diamonds and dinners out, with trips to the shore and shopping binges in New York City. After we married, I hadn't noticed, at least not at first, how often he changed jobs or shot off on some grand scheme, nor how he whipped out his Visa for purchases made on a whim.

Or maybe I just ignored the red flags.

The first time it happened, Jeremiah's warm body, swathed in a baby carrier, snuggled against my chest. I'd managed to fill my cart, place my groceries on the conveyor belt, and watch the order being rung up without a peep from my months-old son. Victory!

The cashier looked up from her register. "Do you have another card?"

I frowned.

She slid a look toward her growing line of customers. "The machine can't read this one. Do you have another you could try?"

My face grew hot. I dug through my wallet and pulled out a credit card, trying not to wake my sleeping baby. The first had been my debit card, and I remember thinking that I was going to have a serious talk with my bank. This was unacceptable.

I swiped the second card.

After a few seconds, the cashier turned to me, a gentle smile on her face. "I'm sorry. This won't do either."

My lungs seized, constricting my breathing. I cradled Jeremiah's head with one hand, while trying to keep my voice calm. "What do you mean? Is the machine broken? Because I don't have another card with me today."

"It's not the machine, honey." She leaned toward me, attempting

*to save me from imminent embarrassment, an elusive endeavor at best.
"Both cards were declined."*

*When I arrived home red faced and without even the barest bones
of a meal, Len exploded. "We won't be letting those losers manage our
money anymore. We'll change banks tomorrow!"*

He took us out to dinner that night—Jeremiah still groggy
in the carrier—and the next morning brought me cash. So
I chalked the whole mess up to an error.

Our debt mounted, but somehow, even with "in-between"
jobs, we managed to make the minimum payments. I should
have questioned that. Then he started working evenings and
later, the night shifts—at least that's what he told me. My
mother died just before Len and I married, and a year later
my father followed her. Between grieving and caring for
Jeremiah, maybe I didn't have time to think about Len's deeds.

Or maybe I just didn't care to know.

"So he's in prison now for credit-card debt?"

I glanced at Letty, shading my eyes from the sun's light.
"Stealing drugs and then selling them." I didn't mention that
there had been a concealed-weapon charge too.

She nodded. Her question had been her way of helping
me spit out the truth. "And he'll be out of prison this quickly
for that?"

"That's what his letter said—that he's up for parole."

"My, my. And what else did the letter say?"

Should I tell her more? Len's profession of faith should be
something shouted from every high hill in sight, right? His

accompanying plea, however, the one about setting things right with me and with Jer . . . I wasn't ready to share that yet. My own reactions were a mystery to me.

"Not much. He did say he was sorry for what he had done and that he wanted to see Jer."

"And that is what has got you all twisted up?"

I shrugged. "A boy should have a father, don't you think? Even one who's made some . . . mistakes?"

"I'm all for forgiveness, but not sure how much forgetting you should do. Can I be blunt?"

"Like I expected anything else from you."

She poked her open palm with her pointed fingernail. "You tell that no-good ex-husband of yours that he cannot send you some letter and expect you to fling open your skinny arms and welcome him home. He has got to earn that right."

"I didn't say I wanted to welcome him home. I'm just, um, concerned about Jer and—"

"Blah, blah, blah. I have told you before, you are soft. I can read you like a menu. The man was your husband and you are wondering if you ought to be giving him another chance."

Again with the second chances. Seems to be a valuable commodity these days. I shook my head, not wanting to hear Letty expose my thoughts to the wind. Gage alluded to the same thing yesterday when he asked if I still loved Len.

Sometimes I wondered if I ever did.

Letty leaned close enough for me to see the black of her eyes, her perfume igniting my nostrils. "Some people are evil through and through, and no amount of anything can fix them."

Her words landed like a slap.

"Now do not go getting all offended, Suzanna. You married the man so he must have had some redeeming quality. And who knows, it is possible that someone reached him while in the slammer. All I am saying is that knowing what you know, you cannot be too careful. Especially with that beautiful towheaded boy in your care."

Jeremiah. Blond, blue eyes, and lean, reminding me of one of the surfers hanging out at Moonstone Beach—and his father, who he resembled more than me. I bit back a roll of emotion. As my son grew, my choices would become more and more difficult. How could I tell him about his father's criminal past? And would he ever need to know that his father cheated on me?

Nearby a truck pulled up. I stretched to make out its occupants, shaking off the tangle of thoughts that threatened to consume me. Fred made his way out of the wide cabin, tossed us a brief wave, and began directing two men as they lifted a massive, narrow crate from the truck. One of the men was Seth.

Of course.

"Expecting a delivery?" Letty's cherry-painted lips curled into a smile. Gone was the finger-shaking mama from a moment ago, and in her place emerged the town matchmaker. "Seems like every time I turn around that fine window washer appears right there in front of you."

"Oh, really? Doesn't that mean he's in front of you as well?"

Her smile turned coy. "That reminds me. If you are not from around here, how is it that you know Seth again?"

I ignored her and stepped down the hill where the men lugged the heavy crate across uneven ground. She followed behind me. I knew by her scent.

"Is this the surprise, Fred?" I asked, more interested in what lay beyond the thick wrapping of plastic and thick cardboard.

My boss winked. "She's a beaut, a real treasure in wood that needs some TLC."

Even as the men lugged the crate toward the warehouse's double doors, I touched one side of the treasure through its plastic covering.

"Careful there," Seth muttered.

I stepped back. "Wouldn't it be better to use a dolly?"

He shot me a sharp look and sweat beaded across his forehead.

Fred cleared his throat. "I drafted Seth here and his new trainee to help me with her after the movers tried to charge me a premium for driving up the hill. I'm delighted they obliged. Offered them a cup of coffee first, but they didn't take me up on it."

Letty propped open the double doors and I followed the men in, noting that despite their added strength, they struggled to keep the piece aboveground. I tried to ignore other details, such as the way Seth called the shots even while holding up the back corner and how his arms had thickened over the years, as if from the hard work of molding him from a young adult to a man.

The guy up front stopped and Seth grunted while swinging to the left in an attempt to stay steady, which he may have done had I not been standing there analyzing him.

His left shoulder collided with my right arm, and the force of impact could have had disastrous results. Instead, on instinct, my arms swung open and encircled his waist, steadying him. I froze, unable to avoid breathing on him. He grunted again. Was this a natural reaction to events that annoyed him?

Then he righted himself without a word.

Fred continued to lead the way through the busy warehouse. "Bring her over here." He motioned to the specially designed table I had prepped earlier. "That's it." He guided them with his words rather than his might.

Seth's spiked hair stood saturated at his crown, and a drop of sweat followed a course along his cheek. Together he and his colleague lifted the piece onto the work surface and eased it down, their faces darkened by redness.

The prize lay beneath all those layers of wrapping. My hands fanned against the protective plastic, and my fingers searched for carvings in the wood. The faint scent of Letty's perfume reminded me that although I longed to be strolling through a museum or up at the castle, discovering priceless treasures for the first time, we were still in a plain warehouse somewhere on a hillside.

Seth still stood beside me, hands resting on his hips. "Are we going to open her up?"

Fred nodded his approval from the other side of the workbench.

Seth stepped closer, reaching out to help as I pulled away the plastic. His voice cut into the moment, low and nostalgic. "Your enthusiasm reminds me of the day your father brought home that oilcloth sketchbook."

I sucked in a breath and froze, plastic wrap in midair. He remembered? My father had taken it upon himself to find me a more suitable home for my sketches than the pile of scraps that had accumulated in my bedroom. Although I hadn't thought of that in years, the memory of it shone vivid in my mind. "The one with the rounded corners. I filled every page of it—there were at least a hundred."

He nodded. "At least." A hint of a reluctant smile tugged at his mouth and all else melted away: the other artists waiting in anticipation, the towering bare walls and half-clean windows, my knotted-up heart . . . It was as if we were standing on the front porch of my parents' home again, head to head over something that only the two of us could understand.

A cell phone rang and Seth patted his pocket. I looked away, the moment broken. Seth switched off the phone mid-ring and slid it back into his pocket. As Letty and several of the other artist apprentices joined in, Seth reached for a large section of wrapping and peeled it back.

"Let's do this thing."

Chapter Seven

What lay before us resembled a tall, narrow door made for monarchy. Much like the balcony ceiling outside of Doge's Suite in Hearst Castle that had been painstakingly restored several years ago, this deteriorated nineteenth-century treasure needed the same care.

"There's been damage by wood worms, paint's faded, and look here." Fred pointed to a bright blue area beneath a cornice. "Someone tried to touch up the paint, but you can tell they had a devil of a time. Just look at how the various materials faded differently."

The enormity of the task stilled my breath.

My boss winked. "Not to worry, Suzi-Q. We'll show you how it's done."

Seth caught Fred's attention. "Good seeing you. We'll be heading out now."

Fred nodded, his smile wide. "Thank you again for your assistance. Couldn't have done it without you."

For the brief time Seth was here, it felt like the yesterday from long ago when our friendship moved along as easy as a spring breeze. He walked away, his gait confident as he led his trainee out of the building and up along the ridge to the rising wall of windows outside. They found a ladder and propped it against the warehouse. Despite the damaged treasure lying on the table and awaiting surgery, today would not be distraction free.

Fred gestured to Timo. "I've assigned Timo here to help you and Letty begin the process of restoring this piece."

I shrunk back. "I'm afraid to touch it."

Letty's eyes quizzed me.

"I just mean—it's valuable, isn't it? Are you sure I'm ready for this?"

"Don't get too excited yet," Letty said. "There's not much glamour in this part of the process."

Fred glanced at her. "That's right, Letty. I'd forgotten how much experience you have in this area." He paused. "Well, then, it's always good to have a refresher. Be sure to have Timo here check your work."

Letty's eyes narrowed and her mouth begin to pucker, but the expression vanished. Maybe I had imagined it.

On the other hand, Timo looked less than thrilled. He kept scratching his ear inside and out, his mouth twisting in fascinating variations. "Guess we oughta assess the piece."

I hoped Letty would offer a more detailed explanation. She only scowled and huffed a sigh.

I approached Timo. "So should I get a pencil and paper to, uh, write things down?"

He continued to scratch his ear and shrugged. "Guess so."

Letty whipped around, grabbed her bag from the floor, and pulled out a couple of pens and notepads. She handed one to me.

"Okay," I said. "So what do we do first?"

Timo mumbled something about flaky paint and consolidation, his words separated by long pauses and drawn-out instances of the word "Hmm."

"Oh, for heaven's sake." Letty tossed her notebook and pen onto an open workstation. "Listen, we are going to have to remove all that flaking paint and then clean the areas until they are smooth again. Eventually we'll have to fill in those paint losses with the appropriate materials after the lab determines exactly what to use."

She continued, her graceful fingers lightly touching upon specific areas. "Looks like we'll have to create molds to fabricate some parts that have deteriorated."

Timo stood straighter and shifted his shoulders. "Of course. Replacing the missing parts is a no-brainer."

Letty twisted her gaze to meet Timo's, her open mouth and contracting eyes displaying her irritation with him.

He didn't react except to look at us and say, "Better get started."

We worked until afternoon, our lower backs aching from bending for hours. More than once I longed to straighten up, search for a discarded paintbrush, and let myself create something wild and free across the blank walls of our studio. A kaleidoscope of fanciful butterflies maybe? Or massive herons lofting above the artists? But each time, I fought the urge and made myself focus on the task in front of us.

Why were the walls kept so bare? All my painting classes had taken place in rooms that could be characterized as works of art themselves with splatters on the floor, favorite sketches, watercolors and oils tacked up or framed depending on the whim.

Fred's voice called me from my thoughts. "In need of a break, Suzi-Q?"

"Is it that obvious?"

He grinned. "There's a fresh pot of coffee by the door. Take your time."

Letty waved me off. So I followed Fred's advice, poured some brew into a mug, and headed outside. The sun shone but the air felt cool. In anticipation of my first day of "real" work, I had signed Jer up for aftercare at the preschool, so with that in mind, I wandered along a dirt path untethered to time. My walk took me away from the warehouse and toward a clearing that offered a clean view of the sea from high above Pacific Coast Highway.

"You don't give up, do you?" Seth's voice startled me. He sat on the ground, his knees pointed toward the sky, his arms relaxed on top of them.

"You remember me well."

He smirked. "Haven't seen you in, what, six years? Now all of a sudden you're everywhere I look."

I took a step toward him. "How do I know it's not you stalking me?"

As his eyes narrowed, they seemed to turn a deeper shade of green. He gestured for me to sit beside him.

We both stared out to sea. "So," I ventured. "*Are* you stalking me?"

He examined the dirt hill, then shook his head. "I read about Gage."

I tore my gaze from the placid ocean and stared at him. *Maybe he is following me.* "You knew my brother was here? In Otter Bay?"

"Kind of hard to miss, Suz. That development he headed up was in the news every other day. That SOS team gave him a tough time about it too."

"Oh." My pulse slowed. Callie headed up Save Our Shores, a group that had opposed Gage's work on the development— then she fell in love with him. "So you saw his name and thought maybe he could send some work your way."

He seemed to roll my comment around in his mind, taking his time to answer. "Couldn't hurt to ask."

"I see. And did you ask?" *Why didn't my brother mention this?*

He tossed a spring weed into the air. "Not yet. Turns out we have almost more work than we can handle." He swiveled his face toward me. "Don't tell him I said that."

I forced a laugh. "Okay. Well, I guess you're off the hook then."

"Off the hook?"

"You haven't been stalking me after all."

He nodded like he understood. "Why would I? You made your choice a long time ago." He dipped his chin. "And I made mine."

"And by all accounts you've done well for yourself."

He offered me a halfhearted shrug.

I jostled his arm with my elbow, like old times, a small laugh escaping. "What? Holly sounded so proud of you the other night, and I don't blame her. Pretty impressive being asked to handle the window maintenance of the Hearst Castle."

"It's a window-washing business, Suz. I'm not ashamed to admit that."

His use of my nickname warmed the parts of me exposed to the cool wind. "I never implied that you should be. All I'm saying is that not everyone is invited onto castle grounds. If it were me, I'd be doing cartwheels every morning when I turned out of bed."

He sat back and gave me an incredulous smile. "You can't be serious. It's a building. It doesn't deserve all the glory it gets."

"Oh, I don't know. When I'm up there, I feel like I can do anything, like I can see the whole world before me and it's one great, big opportunity."

He shook his head. "Really? So you don't think that mausoleum is overkill? Hearst tore out and rebuilt one of those pools up there twice. To me that's more like rinsing money down the drain."

I paused. "He was a perfectionist."

"Who changed his mind a lot."

I tried to read Seth's face. For a man who made it to California like he always said he would, he didn't seem satisfied. "Mr. Hearst was a dreamer and I respect that."

"Dreamer. *Shew*, the man was a narcissist."

I crossed my arms. "Wow. Pretty resentful toward someone you've never met."

A frown crossed his face. "Never been all that impressed with people who use their money to buy whatever they want, including people."

Ouch. Though it had been years, his statement sounded like a rehashing of the past, like he'd hung on to the notion that Len had used money and pretty things to win my devotion. His bitter words sounded like a swipe against Len, and for that matter—me.

I took in the sea again, trying to digest it like one would a cup of chamomile tea. After several calming breaths in the quiet, I determined to offer grace to us both, though our reasons for splitting up came back to me: We too often sat on opposing sides.

"Maybe we ought to agree to disagree on this. I really am happy to see you again, Seth. Glad to know you made it out to the coast like you always wanted and found success."

He let his arms fall to his sides, arose from the ground, and ran one hand across his backside to brush the dust from his jeans. "Surprised to find you here."

I took a sip of lukewarm coffee. "Yes, well, while some people make plans and follow them . . ." I motioned toward the distant castle. "Others of us stumble our way through life, hoping not to fall off the twists in the road."

He stood closer, both of us gazing at the sea. "Hard times, then, I guess."

I nodded. "Yeah, hard times." My cell buzzed, splitting the quiet. I flashed him a guarded look as I pulled the phone from my pocket and glanced at the screen. "Sorry. It's my son's preschool. " I answered it. "Hello?"

"Suzanna? This is Cynthia from Jeremiah's preschool. We received a call today that we thought best to let you know about right away."

I cast a quizzical look at Seth. "A call? What kind of call?" Concern knit Seth's brow and I turned away from him.

The preschool director paused. "She said she was affiliated with the Heinsburgh Valley Correctional Facility."

I tried to keep alarm from my voice. "What did she want?" And how did she know where to find my son?

"She seemed to already know Jeremiah was here. Her reason for calling had to do with your husband's—"

"My ex-husband."

Seth shifted next to me.

"Right, well she said your ex-husband was being considered for parole and she needed to verify Jeremiah's whereabouts.

She told Marilyn, our school secretary, that his release hinged on her being able to provide this information to the parole board."

"So you didn't talk to her but Marilyn did? May I speak with her . . . please?" I regretted how strangled the word please came out.

"Unfortunately, Marilyn left school today with a migraine."

"Did she get the woman's name? And what did she tell her?"

"Yes, her notes say the woman's name was Nina."

"And?"

"I'm sorry that policy wasn't followed, Suzanna. Marilyn verified Jeremiah's registration, then thought better of it. We had a long talk about this, and I'm afraid that's when the migraine set in."

"I see."

"I hope this isn't going to be a problem for you. Should we be concerned?"

It wasn't as if Len didn't know where we lived. Besides, I'd held on to his letter for a couple of days before reading it, so it made perfect sense that as the date for the hearing grew nearer, his parole officer would be doing everything she could to make sure all information was available to those who could set Len free.

At least I told myself that.

"Suzanna?" Cynthia asked. "Are you still on the line?"

"Yes, I am. Thank you for calling."

"I'm sorry if we've caused you concern."

I pressed the phone against my ear and drew circles in the dirt with the toe of my boot. "You know? I think maybe I'll pick up Jer a little early today."

"Certainly. We'll have him ready for you whenever you'd like to come."

We hung up and I slid the phone back into my pocket, swallowing against the building lump in my throat.

"Anything wrong?" Seth's voice jerked me from my thoughts.

My eyes focused on him. "No, no." I shook my head. "Not really. I just need to pick up my son early today, that's all."

He paused. "You sure you're going to be all right? Didn't mean to eavesdrop, but that call sounded like there's some trouble."

Hearing Seth say that snapped off some of the worry hanging over me. Some, but not all.

My shoulders tensed. Should I be concerned? Len's letter made it clear he was a new man. So why was I so slow to believe? After a tumultuous couple of years, no doubt it would take me a while to get used to Len's newfound faith. The suddenness of Len's declaration, I guessed, coupled with Gage's obsessive worry last night, had made me paranoid.

"It's fine. Really." My shoulders began to relax. "I should probably go."

Seth nodded toward the warehouse. "What about that treasure in there you were all excited about?"

Scrubby bushes and low-hanging trees may have shrouded the old warehouse, but he was right, a treasure waited for me

inside. The first of many. And yet nothing was more important than a mama checking on the well-being of her son. I also
didn't care to admit to him at the moment that the tedious-
ness of art restoration had already rubbed away some of my
initial enthusiasm.

Seth waited for my answer and I shrugged. "It'll wait."

Chapter Eight

My brother eyed me. "So why the impromptu dinner out?"

"Can't I show my appreciation for all you've done by buying you dinner?" Jer snuggled next to me, tired from his long day at preschool. Although I'd washed his hands and face, his baby-fine hair smelled of crayons and soft clay.

"Sure you can, but you already do the cooking for Jer and me nearly every night—"

Callie touched Gage's arm and smiled at me from across the table where she sat next to him. "Maybe Suz wants to relax and enjoy dinner being served to her for a change."

The day's worries had drained me and now all that spent energy felt silly. Rather than staying home tonight and dwelling on my overreaction to that surprise phone call, the one

I'd yet to mention to Callie and Gage, I decided on the spur to go out. "You know I love cooking, but I thought it would be fun to take us all out. The RAG's not fancy, but the food's creative."

Callie laughed. "The rum muffins are lethal, though."

"I've heard that."

Jer lifted his head and looked at me through half-closed eyes. "What's rum?"

I shushed him and patted his back until he lowered his head again.

Mimi, the regular nighttime waitress, appeared at our table, ready to take our orders. Holly worked most mornings and afternoons, so for obvious reasons, I hoped she wouldn't be here tonight.

Character lines crisscrossed Mimi's face, the kind earned by a mother of four young women. "Such a beautiful family you are." She pulled a packet of crackers from her apron and set them in front of Jer. "How're the wedding plans coming, Callie?"

Callie tilted her face up, and her makeup-free skin glowed. "They are going well. Thank you for asking! The gazebo's being erected on the Kitteridge land this week, so it should be finished in plenty of time. We're having a simple wedding, so it's not too overwhelming."

Mimi gave her a wide, understanding smile. "Not yet anyway. How about the job? You likin' being the new camp director up at Pine Ridge? Haven't seen you in here half as much lately."

"Oh, Mimi, I love it. Beyond my best expectations, really. I was overwhelmed when they offered me the position—"

"But she's the best director they've ever had." Gage rested his arm on Callie's shoulder. "The hottest one too."

Callie's face flushed and she reached over and pinched Gage's cheek. Mimi whacked him on the shoulder with the stack of menus.

Gage's continual gaga behavior over his fiancée made me smile and shake my head. Not that I didn't love it; I did. But it's a new phenomenon in his life and one that took a long time to come about. I'd waited many years for a sister-in-law. Callie was a miracle maker.

The banter between the lovebirds made me wonder what my life would have looked like today if I had made faith a headline—rather than a sidebar—in my decision to marry. How might things have been different if I hadn't ignored the inklings about Len's lack of faith in God? My parents had provided the perfect example of a Christ-centered marriage. Why hadn't I tried to live my life by their beautiful example?

Seth's face appeared in my mind, sending me back to a time so long ago.

"Why now? And why him?"

I hadn't seen Seth in two months, not since we'd broken up over his plans to run wild out to California, to live a meager life on a journey of finding himself. When he showed up on my porch, demanding to know why I'd accepted Len's proposal, I nearly slammed the door in his face.

"You made your choice, Seth."

He stood there, clean shaven, imploring me. "And I chose you."

I stepped onto the porch, leaving the front door of my father's home ajar, my hand still gripping the handle. "How can you say that? The only choice you gave me was to leave everything I know behind and chase some whim with you."

He stared at the ground and wagged his head back and forth, appearing to struggle to gather his thoughts. Almost from the start of our relationship, not knowing what Seth was thinking had been a problem for a girl who tended to wear her feelings on the outside. Seeing him struggle should have lighted compassion, but instead it made me angry. Seth had to have known what he felt and what he would say before coming over here and demanding that I explain my decision to marry Len. Surely he knew that Len, my neighbor and friend, could give me what I needed: his presence.

Minutes passed. Seth lifted his head and stared straight into my eyes. "Of all people, I thought you, the dreamer, would understand. God has gifted you—I've seen it for myself. Haven't you always wanted to paint your way across this world, Suz?" He lowered his voice. "I wanted us to do this thing together, to go out and grab the life neither one of us has ever had. I can't imagine doing this without you."

I could have said, "Then don't." Only I didn't. My mind, once open and carefree to what the future held, had been closed down by grief. I couldn't see all the effort and how much of Seth's heart this passionate plea had cost him. I could only think about what it would cost me.

"Go to California or Oregon or wherever you think you'll find happiness, Seth." I let go of the door and slid my hand over the marquise-shaped diamond on my ring finger. "My mother's gone now and Len has offered me a life here, where my roots are."

Seth didn't say anything, but his gaze fell to my hand and his eyes seemed to glower. He implored me again, his eyelids heavy, a tinge of gray in the skin beneath them. When I said nothing, he swiveled around and bounded down the stairs. He never looked back.

"Coffee?" Mimi held a hot pot over the table, her brows standing at attention, waiting for my response.

I blinked. "Sorry, I—"

She pulled the coffeepot away. "What was I thinking? You're a chai girl, aren't you? Can I bring you a cup?"

I nodded. "Yes. Sure. Please."

Gage pulled his arm from around Callie's shoulder and crossed his arms in front of him, leaning on the table. His temples shifted as he studied me, the way our father's used to before starting up one of his heart-to-heart talks. "We lost you there for a minute. Care to tell us what's on your mind?"

I hesitated. "Hunger."

Callie laughed. "If what you ordered isn't enough, I will gladly share half of mine. Otherwise, I might not fit into my gown for the wedding."

I shook my head. "Not possible with all that running around you do, chasing kids all over camp. Speaking of your gown, can I see it soon? You won't make me wait until the wedding, I hope."

He sat back, smiling. His buildup to intense questioning vanished, and instead he appeared pleased to be here with his family around him.

In the distance, bells jingled, signaling that more customers had entered the restaurant. Gage's facial expression moved from contentment to surprise to confusion. I looked over my shoulder, drew in a breath, and held it.

Holly and Seth just stepped inside.

The day's phone call wasn't the only news I had neglected to pass on to my big brother.

His eyes riveted on the couple. "That looks like . . ." He turned to me, compassion softening his features. "Suz? I hate to bring this up, but the guy who just came in with Holly looks a lot like . . . Seth."

I swallowed and allowed my gaze to drop to the tip-top of Jeremiah's head. My hands stroked his hair.

Gage reached across the table. "Suz?"

I let out a sigh and looked at my brother. "Didn't I mention that we'd run into each other?"

"You *forgot* to tell me? Wasn't he . . . ? I mean, you and he were pretty, um . . ."

Callie leaned forward. "Who is he?"

"Suz's ex-boyfriend from back home." Gage turned back to me. "What's he . . . ?"

Holly noticed us from across the diner and her face brightened even more. We all watched as she took hold of Seth's hand and dragged him toward our table, talking before reaching us. "The whole family's here! How's everybody doin'? Seth and I were going for a drive when I remembered my wallet was at the diner. Not that I needed it." She patted Seth's upper arm. "He's a gentleman and always pays, but I don't like bein' without it. Know what I mean?"

"Seth, you remember my brother, Gage, and this is his fiancée, Callie." I motioned her way and then looked at my son. "And this is Jeremiah."

Seth kept his gaze neutral, almost professional. "Hello, Gage. A pleasure to meet you, Callie." His eyes locked on Jeremiah. "Hi there."

Holly let go of Seth's hand and linked her arm through his. "Such a small world isn't it? I just couldn't believe it when we ran into Suz at the beach yesterday."

I watched as Gage's brows rose. His smile couldn't have been more forced. "What brings you to California, Seth?"

Seth politely answered his questions, as if we were all new acquaintances rather than old friends from back home. He told Gage things I never knew, such as how he managed to drive cross-country for free by delivering a car to Arizona, and how he bummed around in that state for months before realizing the heat and dry air weren't doing him any favors. "After Arizona, I found another job delivering a car, this one to Seattle, but all that rain made me tired all the time."

Holly cinched him closer. "So he started hitchhikin' south, through Oregon and northern California, and found himself along the coast highway with all our blue sky and pine trees."

Seth nodded. "I've never looked back."

He stared at me a beat longer than comfortable when saying that. After all this time, was he still trying to prove he had been better off without me? *I get it already. Move on.*

Holly looked up at him. "I'll just run and get my wallet so we can go." She dashed off toward the back office, but not before stopping and hugging Mimi on her way. Holly had a way of drawing people to her. People like Seth.

Standing there, he fidgeted with his fingers, his discomfort on display. He nodded as if saying good-bye, offering us both relief, then stopped. "By the way, Suz, did everything work out with that phone call you were concerned about today?"

My eyes darted to Gage, who looked downright irritated, and then flitted to Jer, who wriggled in the booth. "Yes, fine. It all worked out. I shouldn't have been worried."

He smiled and reached out to tousle Jer's white-blond hair. "Glad to hear it."

Holly scooted to Seth's side again and snuggled into him. "Ready?"

"I am." He wrapped an arm around her shoulder before raising a glance to us. "Nice to see you all."

Not until the happy couple had reached the diner doors and left the building did the fissures in Gage's demeanor widen. He waited to speak until Mimi, who arrived with our meals, finished serving us.

"Enjoy your dinner, folks. I'll be back around with the water pitcher." She scampered away.

My Cobb salad, though a work of art with colorful rows of chopped, fresh toppings, sat untouched. My appetite had waned. Gage didn't touch his soup either. Callie, bless her heart, offered Jer the ketchup for his fries and spoke in uplifting tones like a true peacemaker.

Gage leaned forward, the undersides of his wrists against the table edge. "I noticed a change in you but couldn't figure out exactly what was going on."

I went through the motion of picking up my fork and spearing crisp lettuce crusted with bacon bits.

"I could understand your reaction to Len's letter."

I whisked a look at him.

"I said I could understand it, not agree with you. But now this? Seth's in town and you didn't tell me?" He sat back. "I'm confused about how you could talk to him earlier today and not mention that. And what phone call was he talking about?"

Callie's hand slid to the crook in Gage's arm, and despite his growing annoyance with me, I couldn't help but note how he placed his hand atop of hers. Had Len ever treated me with such tenderness?

"I don't know why I didn't tell you about Seth. He owns some big window-washing business near SLO."

"So he lives down in San Luis Obispo?"

"I don't know where he lives, Gage. All I know is that his company cleans the massive windows at the art studio and he's about to acquire a contract for Hearst Castle."

"No kidding."

I rolled my shoulders and shook off this line of questioning. "Could we just forget about all this and get back to dinner now? My salad's getting, uh . . ."

Callie smiled. "Cold?"

I mouthed the words *I love you, girl* to her and she laughed some more.

"Just a second." Gage's eyes didn't let me go just yet. "What phone call were you worried about?"

"Oh, that." I glanced at his bowl. "Soup's getting frigid."

He stared at me.

"Fine." I glanced at Jer, hoping my brother would see the warning in my eyes.

Callie slid out of the booth. "I'm going to look for some mustard, Jeremiah. Would you like to join me?"

"Yeah!" He didn't wait for me to move and instead slipped off the seat and under the table. I cringed thinking of all the bacteria his pudgy hands just picked up.

Callie caught my eye. "I think we'll make a stop in the restroom to wash our hands."

When they were gone, I turned back to my big brother, who wore the intense look that reminded me of our father. "I was up on the bluff near the studio taking a break when Cynthia from the preschool called. Seth happened to be up there too."

Gage's eyebrow shot up.

"Anyway, someone from Heinsburgh had called the school and Cynthia was upset because the secretary messed up. She confirmed to the caller that Jeremiah attended there."

"Who called?"

I reached for my tea and held the lukewarm cup in my

hands. "I don't know. A woman named Nina. She said she needed the information for Len's upcoming hearing."

He groaned. "Suz."

"After I thought about it, the call made perfect sense. This shows me that Len must be serious about making amends. I can't deny him that, Gage."

He eyed me, the slight shake of his head telling me all he held back.

Chapter Nine

 "You'll be cursing my name tomorrow morning, Callie," I told her. "Trust me."

Jeremiah didn't care if it was Saturday—he woke up *every* morning with more energy than swells rising off the shores of Waikiki. I tried to warn Callie of this when she had invited my almost five-year-old for a sleepover last night. Due to all the building happening on the hill, the camp she directed at Pine Ridge was closed. Why she didn't take this opportunity to relax, well, I couldn't understand it.

She laughed and waved me away, making Jer promises of ice cream on his pancakes or something like that. *A true mother in the making.* More than ever, the pressure to allow Gage and Callie to have the space to raise a family of their own hung on my shoulders. I tossed around most of the night and dreamed of finding the little cabin in the woods Fred told me about.

At five o'clock, wearing my most worn-out sweats to keep me warm and careful not to slip on the dew, I padded down the front steps and found my beach cruiser leaned up against the side of the house. After righting it, I hopped on and headed north through winding streets lined with cottages that yawned and stirred as I passed.

My pulse increased along with early morning awareness that a new day had dawned. After returning home last night, Gage and I had continued to discuss his concerns about Len over cocoa and biscotti while the evening news played in the background.

Gage pursed his lips while swirling the remaining hot cocoa in his mug. "You don't have . . . What I mean to ask is whether you still have feelings for Len."

I grunted. "You, big brother, are entering into territory reserved for sistahs."

"Excuse me?"

"Girls. You're asking me to make girl talk with my brother. It's kind of weird." I double-dipped my biscotti.

"No, it's not." His hushed tone told me he knew this wasn't the kind of conversation a girl had with her brother. Yet I understood why he wanted to know.

I sighed. "All right. I guess we can go there, even though . . ."

"Yeah, yeah, it's none of my business."

"Right." I blew a breath into the air, like a deflating balloon.

"Okay, Len's letter meant a lot to me, but mainly because it means he's quite possibly not lost anymore. If making the mistakes he's made and walking away from his family led him to his knees, and ultimately to his Savior, then . . ." My voice lowered to a whisper. "It was worth it."

This time Gage looked me in the eye and offered me a liberal dose of compassion. "But do you love him?"

A million memories overflowed my mind, memories of when we met and how we laughed and how he treated me . . . at least in the beginning. "Do you remember how I learned to drive?"

He released a startled laugh. "What?"

"You heard me."

"Um, well, no I really don't."

I searched his face. "I was a late bloomer, as they say. I didn't learn until I had to, until Mom could no longer . . ."

Gage nodded, pain trailing across his face.

"Anyway, after Seth and I split up and Mom got sick, it became apparent that I needed to get my license so I could help out around the house more. I was nearly twenty! Dad was too grief stricken to help, so Len stepped in. He helped me study for the written test and took me out for dinner to celebrate when I passed. Then he risked his life and his fancy car by letting me sit behind the wheel while he braced in the passenger seat."

Gage chortled.

"Yeah, it was something. It felt like such a generous gift at the time because I really needed the help." I looked up. "And Len was there for me."

My brother drew in a deep breath through his nose and then sat back, his shoulders drooping. I knew he was remembering more than *how I learned to drive. He was remembering the sadness over losing our mother to heart disease and, not long after, our father to cancer.*

We sat awhile, draining our mugs of cocoa and listening to the wind and waves howl through an open window. After revealing the events of the week to Gage and hashing them out with him, I made the determination to appreciate all the Lord had done for me—providing me with a new home, a loving brother, a job—but I needed to move on, just the same.

My bike and I continued to travel from our neighborhood of sea-colored cottages, up past the Kitteridge property where Gage's handiwork had begun to appear, and along the inn-dotted lane that abutted Moonstone Beach. I vacillated between watching the road and staring out to sea in hopes of discovering a sea lion or two or maybe some otters or other marine life bobbing on the water. Maybe even a gray whale migrating south.

After following the length of the bluff boardwalk for two miles until reaching The Landing, I stopped at the lookout carved into the landscape. Straddling my beach cruiser, I scanned the sea. Waves crashed over rocky tongues leaving mini tide pools in their wake. If Jeremiah were home, I'd jump back on my bike and hurry to make breakfast. Who was I kidding? If my son waited at home, I would never have left.

I drew in a deep breath of sea air. My hands revved my cruiser's handlebars, as if it had a motor, and I hopped back on, only this time traveling east toward gently sloping mountains.

Halfway up the first hill, my body expressed its dissatisfaction with my choice. My legs burned above the knee and turned my thighs leaden. By the second hill, it was mutiny—against myself. *So much for pastoral slopes.*

My body wanted to give up, but with a full-time job and a child to raise, how many chances to wander about Otter Bay would I have? I searched for the end of the trail and found it, causing a second wind to inflate my lungs. Satisfied my strength would help me make it up the last incline toward the small house in the woods Fred had told me about, I tucked my chin down and pedaled harder.

The morning's faint sun rays disappeared above the tree-tops as I coasted beneath canopied branches at the plateau. The temperature dropped enough to cause goose bumps to rise on my arms and legs, but when the cabin appeared in a small clearing, turning around wasn't an option. I'd found Shangri-la.

"It's an antique redwood cabin, built in the 1920s," Fred had told me.

I'd laughed believing the word *antique* was his euphemistic way of saying "really old." I needn't have worried. Cradled in a grove of manzanita and Monterey pine, the red log cabin had been restored to picture perfection with fresh paint and new double-hung windows. It existed in the Hearst area, and like the famed castle, Fred told me that he and his wife had decorated it with works of art, including some of his own abstract originals. I rolled my bike closer, wishing to peek inside but thinking better of it when I heard the distinct patter of child-sized feet across wooden floors followed by the chatter of doggy paws.

I settled for examining the outside from a respectable distance. Stones trailed up one end, shaping the chimney. Sprays of willowing sunflowers stretched up from the earth, accenting the cabin like sunshine against a red sky. The side yard was another matter. Thick brush shaped into cavelike mounds bumped against the log siding. Someone had propped a wooden lean-to next to the brush, as if extending the children's play set out from the corner. I smiled. Like the child living in this cabin in the woods, Jeremiah would love to play hide-and-seek back there too.

Most of the other homes in the area were shrouded by ages-old pines and native plants, as if the residents preferred the rustic environment. The ocean appeared through partings in the branches, but the scents up here were different than at sea level. More earthy and floral.

The crunch of tires rolling through dried pine needles pricked my attention. Still straddling the cruiser, I rolled backward to see a familiar truck pulling up to the house. The driver side door creaked open and Fred eased out.

When he spotted me, he didn't look surprised. "Found her, did you?"

I nodded, then swung a look back at the house. "Stunning."

Fred rooted himself, stuck his hands into his pockets, and admired his own cabin. "When my wife and I bought her, she was in sore need." He shook his head. "Sore need, indeed. Barely enough room inside to move around when we were working on the place, but we did it. Made us closer too, I think."

I smiled. "That's sweet."

His cheeks grew rosier. "So you think you'd like to live in her?"

My heart fell a little, knowing it would be a while before I could save enough money to move. A sigh slipped from me. "I'd love to, Fred, but I don't think I'll have the funds in time. When will it be vacated?"

"Not for another month or so. I drove up here to drop off some extra moving boxes for when the family needs them. After they leave, the missus and I will want to go in and do some touch-up. I'm thinking of moving my paintings to the guest room at home."

"Oh, really?" I wanted to hide my disappointment, but the squeak in my voice betrayed me.

"After we give the whole place a clean coat of white paint, I was hoping to hire a freehand artist to give it a fresh look." He smiled at me. "Know anyone who might be interested?"

My heart, which only a moment ago had begun to sink in self-pity, pitched upward. "You know it." A knot lodged at the base of my throat. "I would be honored to leave my mark upon your walls."

His laughter rumbled from him, and I felt the joy in it as his wire rims bounced with the bridge of his nose. He nodded, those hands still stuck low in his pockets. "The job is yours. I'll let you know when we are ready for your handiwork."

I nodded, speechless. Until Fred suggested it, I hadn't realized just how much I missed the freedom of painting images from my mind onto the blank slate of a bare wall. Fred moved to his truck and opened the tailgate to pull out a stack of boxes piled up inside.

He stopped when he noticed me watching him and peered around the side of the truck. "You all right, Suzi-Q?"

I slid my bum onto the seat of my beach cruiser and rolled past him. "Absolutely. Thanks again, and I will see you Monday."

"Indeedy you will!"

I drifted down the first hill and then the next, braking only twice to avoid deer foraging for breakfast or excessive speed. The trip back home took me past scenic overlooks, the kind that made me glad to be alive and living in this tiny oasis with its small-town presence, quirky residents, and vast blue sea.

Already my mind whirred with possibilities for Fred's rental cabin. The chain of intricate rocky tide pools near Gage's home could provide plenty of inspiration, and I determined to find more time to spend there in study.

I may not ever be able to afford living in the antique cabin in the woods, but I could sure whip up some livable art to decorate its walls.

Chapter Ten

 I couldn't wait for the weekend to end.

With the romance of an antique cabin in my sights—or at least the cabin's bare *walls* in view—my enthusiasm for getting through the workweek grew long and unrestrained like the sunflowers growing all around the decades-old structure. Jeremiah must have sensed my budding excitement because getting him ready for preschool went smoother than most mornings. He didn't beg to lie around in his jammies in front of the television before preschool nor dawdle around, nor hide his shoes (again).

Right on time, I walked him into his classroom and kissed him on his sweet-smelling head. "Mama will pick you up after day care today. Love you."

He ran off, then stopped and launched himself back into my arms. "Love you too!"

I sailed into the art studio ten minutes later with an easy step, all while humming "This Little Light of Mine" in a less-than-lyrical voice. But I didn't care. Timo smirked at me as I zipped by, so I tossed him a wink before plunking my bag next to Letty's on an empty stool. The scent of coffee beans, resin, and old wood permeated the air.

At the worktable, the ancient door lay in disarray as the stripping of its defects had begun. Still, despite sections of thinly painted wood and divots in need of filling, the relic appeared brighter already, as if fully submitted to its restoration. I could see its potential.

Something slammed onto the table and I jerked my head up. Letty stood there, her hand resting on a toolbox. "You showed."

I glanced at the clock. "Am I late?" I knew that I wasn't.

"I've been here since seven."

"Wow. I was still in my slippers making Jeremiah's oatmeal."

Did Letty just roll her eyes?

I grabbed an apron from the vacant booth and slipped it over my head. "Since you got a head start on things, Letty, where are we with this project today? I'm itching to get going."

Timo butted in. "Looks like you'll have to dig out an entire section of wood."

Letty glared at him. "A lot you know. That would be a tragic way to restore this piece. Shame on you. We have already removed all that we should to keep this door's historical significance alive."

He turned both palms up and scowled at her. "Really."

"Yes, *really*. Now go on. I will be fitting the gaping holes with matching wood that is cut to fit. " She turned from him, grabbed a hair dryer from the box, and handed it to me. "Here. Plug this in and start softening that second layer of paint."

I stared at her. "Be nice to our Timo."

She pursed her lips, ignoring me. "You do know how to use a hair dryer, do you not?"

"Letty! What's got into you today?

She shook her head, causing the yellow scarf on her head to shift. "Nothing much other than I would like to see this door restored properly, not finished willy-nilly by young Timo here."

Both of Timo's fists found his stick-thin waist. "Hey."

"I do not want to see this project's character diminished on my watch. That is all." She nodded my way, her eyes less piercing than her tone. "The hair dryer?"

"Okay, yes." I offered Timo a shrug and smile before turning to find an outlet.

She moved closer. The spice of her cinnamon perfume reached my nostrils, not as pungent as in past days. "You are going to have to remove the top layer of paint from the carvings on the north end of the door. Aim the dryer nozzle into the cavities and when they are sufficiently softened, you can *carefully* scrape away the top surface. Can you do that?"

I didn't know what had caused Letty's surly attitude today, but I would not let it affect me. This job had taken on greater meaning in the past couple of days. It was more than a paycheck and more than a way to increase my knowledge and love of the field of art. I'd gone from my parents' home to Len's apartment to my brother's cottage, and it was time to find the strength and means to find a place on my own. This job meant independence.

I switched the dryer to low. "No problem."

An hour ambled by as I focused on the intricate carving at the north end of the door's surface, careful only to apply heat deep enough to soften the top layer of peeling paint. A familiar ache spread across my lower back, but I pushed through, stopping only to swipe my forehead and temple with the side of my hand. My mind swayed in and out of focus, sometimes fixated on the task before me, and other times remembering things I'd rather forget.

Like the way my heart spun the first time Len kissed me under a rainbow in Myers Field.

Or the way my throat tumbled when I watched Len hold newborn Jeremiah close to his chest.

My shoulders clenched as my mind turned to memories of another kind. I hadn't been able to shake the gnawing, empty sense of loss when I learned all that Len had done without my knowledge: the drugs, the filthy money he gave me to fill our pantry, the lies . . .

The criminal activity wreaked confusion in my mind, but

the infidelity attacked me in a more personal way—like a stab to the heart with an extra twist for surety.

Len's twisted face had glared at me. "What did you expect? That a guy like me could be with just one woman? C'mon, you didn't believe that, did you?"

"I took you at your word."

A laugh marred his face, a perverted, ugly laugh. "Big mistake."

How was it possible for a man to change from a decent human being to a criminal? From a solicitous boyfriend to an adulterous husband? I pushed away my memories and focused on the present.

I switched off the dryer for the umpteenth time and inhaled, steadying my pulse. My attention wandered to Letty, who just installed a short piece of board where the old wood had rotted. She set down her tools and placed both hands on her back, stretching.

"Tough on the bones, isn't it?"

"I will give you that." Letty stretched her arms in front of her and allowed a yawn to escape. "Julia Morgan was unappreciated."

I leaned my head to the side. "Random comment. How so?"

"She spent hours and hours up at that castle, assuring Mr. Hearst of all the details—even those he changed as often as his shorts. Then she would switch gears and throw herself into designing YWCA buildings and the like. Imagine. Going from the mission and classical styles represented in the castle to something, say, Chinese, like the YWCA in San Francisco."

Her words resembled gibberish. "She left a legacy, that's for sure."

Letty's forehead bunched, as if trying to reign in her thoughts. "It's more than that. It is true that William Randolph Hearst had the money, but he gets all the credit for that castle up there when it was designed by one very patient Julia Morgan. Can you imagine a man being told to redo so much of his work?" She scoffed. "He would have told Mr. Hearst where to put his drafting board and then stalked off that monstrous hill."

If he were Len, definitely.

I tried to focus on Letty's banter. All my library reading told me that Julia Morgan and William Hearst had an atypical working relationship. They could sit in desks across from each other and ping-pong ideas to each other for hours. But should I point this out to Letty when she's in no mood to release one of her time-held beliefs?

When I didn't respond, Letty took a step closer. Her forehead bunched beneath her scarf. "Don't you agree?"

I bit my lip. "I don't know, Letty."

"What do you mean, you don't know? Don't you have an opinion?"

"I didn't study architecture, so my knowledge of Miss Morgan is perhaps not as thorough as yours. I guess my take on her is different." My shoulders raised in a shrug. "I'm just grateful for the legacy of inspiration she left behind."

Letty stared at me, open mouthed, as if digesting my answer. She lowered her eyelashes and turned to look again at the prize laid out before us, still waiting for complete restoration. "That's a good way to put it, Suz." She surprised me with a smile. "That is why I like you so much, my friend."

I had been holding my breath, so I let it go and laughed.

We returned to our work, and with gusto. I fed off of Letty's intensity, reeling in the energy to work straight through the morning without a break. If it weren't for the growl in my stomach, I wouldn't have known that lunchtime had arrived. Before I had a chance to pursue food, though, Fred appeared for the first time all day and handed me a lab coat.

I gave him a questioning look while accepting it.

He motioned with a single nod "You'll need to put that on."

I slipped on the coat, eyeing the pristine white fabric and picturing how it would look after just one day with me and a paintbrush.

He gave the table a single tap with his pen. "You'll be joining a group of students at the castle, and this will make you look official."

"Official?"

His smile reached his eyes. "Yes, you will be joining some textile research interns from the university and viewing those rooms not being toured at the moment." He glanced through the studio's sky-high windows. "Should be a fine day for it, Suzi-Q."

I could not contain a squeal.

Letty's bewildered voice cut into our conversation. "Suz is going back to the castle?"

Fred nodded. "That's right. I would like her to tour the upper floor like a student." He turned to face me. "Take your time. Take notes. Bring your questions back to me, if you have any. Every artist should take the opportunity to admire another artist's work. I think you'll find that it adds toward the strengthening of one's own gifts."

My gaze swished back and forth between Fred and the door project before settling on Letty, who watched me from the far end of the table. "I promise to pick up where I left off right away tomorrow morning. Look." I pointed at the undulating carving I'd been cleaning for hours. "Nearly every bit of flaking paint has been removed. You could eat off it, it's so clean."

She offered only a limp shrug before turning back to the project.

I hesitated, then reached for my purse as Fred continued with instructions. "The university van will pick you up outside, and it will bring you back here to retrieve your car later."

I smiled. "Thank you, Fred. I can't wait."

As I walked past Letty, I paused, hoping to catch her eye. "Hope you don't mind me leaving you to work alone."

She didn't look up. "Enjoy the upper floors of Casa Grande." I nodded my thanks and moved to the exit, almost sure I heard her add, "I never have."

Chapter Eleven

Letty's whispered comment that she'd never toured the second story of the castle niggled at me. So when I stood in front of the studio, listening to giggles volleying through the university van as the driver hopped out and stepped over to the passenger side, I worked to rustle up a smile of my own.

I needn't have bothered. All laughing stopped when the van side door flung open. The students exchanged glances, but no one made eye contact with me. I felt like a field trip crasher.

The driver held out his arm. "Be sure to duck."

An open seat waited for me in between two students in the last row. *Oh, joy.* I stumbled to the back of the fifteen-passenger van, trying not to step on too many pedicured toes while offering apologies along the way.

The van started back down the hill to the ribbon of coastal highway that would take us north to the castle. Before entering the highway, though, a truck pulled up beside us and the van came to a stop. We all watched as the passenger door of the truck opened and a man in jeans and a denim shirt climbed out and approached the van.

It was Seth.

A wispy blonde in front of me cheered. The girl with curly dark hair next to her spoke in a hushed voice. "Maybe this won't be a snooze fest after all."

Seth took the empty passenger seat in our van, then shook hands with the driver. If only I could have transformed into a snake and slithered to the floorboards. He turned to acknowledge the students sitting behind him, but I could tell that his sight reached only to the first row. After that, he faced forward and settled into his seat.

The student next to me with bug eyes and blunt-cut hair leaned over me to talk to the girl on my other side. "He's hot."

The girl responded with a vigorous nod. "Wonder if he'll be our tour guide."

"I doubt it." The words blurted out before I thought them through.

The girl who had wondered aloud whipped her chin to face me. "Oh. Sorry." Her sudden giggle sounded nervous. "You must be our guide. Sorry I didn't realize."

I shook my head. "No, I'm not the guide. Just a student like all of you."

"Oh, so who do you think he is, then?" She craned her neck to get a better look. "He's got nice hair."

"I'll say." The student on my right concurred.

Heat filled my cheeks. Any time now Seth might turn around and spot me here among the teenagers, hiding like a coward. I've never found sitting in close quarters among strangers comfortable. Calling his name from the back of the bus wasn't an attractive option. Yet if I didn't say anything at all and he noticed me later, he'd probably think I was spying.

I glanced out the window, wishing for magic skills, particularly the one that could make me disappear. How could I have known that Seth would be joining a bunch of college students on a road trip to the Hearst Castle?

That's the thing. I didn't know. So no good reason to hide from him existed. Right? I pulled my gaze from the window and steeled myself, ready to swallow my embarrassment and offer my old friend a "Yoo-hoo."

Before I could, though, Seth already turned toward the back of the van, his attention held by a willowy redhead in an ice-blue lab coat. While the rest of the ladies fell into conversations peppered with surges of college-aged bravado, the redhead continued to chat with Seth. She leaned one hand on the passenger seat and her fingers nearly grazed his cheek. Her chin tilted toward him, and she spoke in tones low enough for only those two to hear. Our van driver began the five-mile journey up the winding hill that would take us to the castle and Pretty Redhead did not stop talking. Not once.

My gaze slid over the heads of several students as I watched him responding to her. Often, he nodded. Occasionally, he cracked a smile. I couldn't tell if the connection forming was something Holly needed to worry about, or if Seth had learned the art of staying still and listening.

Although Seth never talked much when we were younger, he expressed his enthusiasm for life with his ideas. Lots and lots of "let's do it now" ideas. When I think about those days now, I picture myself as a passenger of a race car on the speedway. I'm the one hanging on to the overhead bar and calling for Jesus's intervention. Seth was, of course, at the wheel.

Those ideas of his often carried an impulsive quality. Once after dropping off his cousin at the airport, he took my hand and dragged me over to the flight board.

"Pick a number."

"Why?"

"Just do it. C'mon, hurry."

"All right, um . . . six."

He stepped closer to the board and counted down the list until he hit the magic number six. "Athens, Georgia." He reached an arm around my shoulders and cinched me closer. "That'll do. Let's go."

"Where?"

He let his arm drop and faced me. "To the city that gave the world the B-52s. C'mon, Suz. Flight's leaving in forty-five minutes."

I laughed and gave him a teasing push. "You're crazy. I don't even have a hairbrush."

I recalled a wistful expression on his face when he smoothed my long hair with his fingers. "Aw, you look beautiful."

His spontaneity attracted me, a girl who had never stepped outside of her hometown except to visit Mother's sister in Virginia once a year. That is, until my mother's illness pulled me into the reality of death as a part of life. Since then, spontaneous trips to anywhere no longer held their appeal.

A hush quieted the students as our van creaked and whined to our destination. Through the windows I noted trees bursting with pomegranate, persimmons, and lemon. Must have been too heady with excitement last week to notice all that glorious color. Our driver pulled to a stop, hopped to the ground, and opened the door to allow the young women to spill out.

I waited for my turn to exit, hoping by the time I climbed out of the van, Seth would have disappeared into the maze of steps and passageways that characterized the castle. As I moved closer to the open doorway, a rush of orange blossoms in bloom filled my field of vision and permeated the air. Unfortunately, Seth's presence grew just as strong. He stood next to the van like a gentleman, offering a hand to students as they filed out. The pretty red-haired student in the cool lab coat stood by his side, her mouth still moving.

I sucked in a deep breath, ducked, then stepped out of the van into a clear blue day. I raised my gaze to meet his, and Seth's eyes took an instant to adjust. He held my hand longer than the other women and pulled me to him. Then he kissed my cheek. "How was it riding back there, hon?"

I had no air to answer.

Pretty Redhead's eyes fluttered, and a tinge of rose highlighted her cheekbones. Her focus pivoted from Seth to me to the comingling of our hands. She took a step back, mumbled a good-bye, and clattered up the stairs to join the others.

I held my breath, trying to avoid the happy memory of his scent a second time. The first time was purely accidental.

Seth dropped my hand. "Thanks for saving me."

I exhaled. *Of course.* He needed me to help him pry a pretty coed from his arm. I blushed as I grasped the meaning behind his sudden affection. Then I laughed. It sounded forced. "Yes, well, you know me: mom by night, superhero by day."

A faint spray of crow's-feet developed around Seth's eyes when he smiled. "Better watch yourself. That girl may try to fight you back with some of her own powers—evil ones."

I glanced up the stairway where the students had gathered for instructions near the Neptune Pool. The student Seth referred to cut her gaze in the opposite direction after catching eyes with me. I swung my gaze back to him. "I can take her."

Seth's expression grew mellow, and his voice took on that old familiar wistfulness. "I have no doubt that you can."

We trailed behind the group, walking side by side like comfortable friends. I had longed for this. The idealistic eighteen-year-old Suzanna may have conjured up other images with Seth once upon a time, but the older and wiser me simply cared to repair the tattered ends of a friendship.

Seth slid a glance at me from the corner of his eye. "Good to see you with a sketchbook in your hands. That's how I always picture you."

"You picture me?"

"You know what I mean."

The bitterness I had witnessed in him the other day seemed gone "Ha. Yeah. And I usually picture *you* with wings on your feet."

He slowed his step and feigned surprise. "Really? Like a Greek god?"

"You wish! Not exactly, Seth. What I meant is, you were always so . . . so *busy* back in the day. You had more plans than, well, Donald Trump." I turned to him. "I often wondered if you ever slowed down."

His expression turned serious, then he looked off to a fog bank that drifted over the ocean. "Those dreams took me all over the place: Breckinridge, Seattle, San Francisco . . . Worked every place that would hire me." Seth swiveled his gaze in my direction. "Especially those that didn't require a contract."

"Hmm. And now?"

His brow furrowed and he didn't answer. This was somewhat familiar territory. The old Seth often needed time to process his thoughts before speaking, but this time, something in his expression bothered me. He clenched his jaw. Had my question made him angry?

A moment passed before the look on his face softened by the smallest degree. "Took my time figuring out what I wanted to do and realized that I'd been most content climbing tall buildings and washing windows, where I could stay outside all day and listen to the air move. I worked for the former owner of my company until he retired, and then he sold the business to me."

I nodded, surprised. Not at the window-washing part, but at the notion that moving around had brought Seth to a place where he could find peace and settle down. Buying a business was a sure enough sign of that.

We continued to meander along behind the students, first through the botanical gardens where I noted the precise placement of statues. Some looked sober, cold as though they wore the title of sentry, while others lounged about as if basking in sunlight, much like I imagined yesteryear's celebrity guests to have done.

We reached the vast red-tiled courtyard but trailed so far behind the group that the door to Casa Grande closed before we reached the side entrance that would take us to the second floor. Seth picked up his pace and found the door unlocked. He held it open for me.

I tucked a strand of hair behind my ear as he followed me into the house. "So I haven't asked this yet but . . . do you regularly join coeds on field trips?"

"Guess I could ask you the same."

I wrinkled my nose. "My attendance doesn't conjure up the same thoughts as yours does."

He laughed. "Oh, really."

I shrugged, glad that his pensive moment had passed. "Just sayin'."

He nodded. "Fair enough. If you must know, our bid was accepted and my crew started work yesterday. I'm here to check on them."

"Check on them? What . . . while going incognito as a college student and *spying* on your employees?"

"No, of course not. I'm also here to view areas that have been recently added to the project. I need to assess the amount of time and crew the added work will take." He glanced at me as if reading my mind. "I know, I know. I could have waited a day or two for someone from park services to let me in, but Fred told me about this tour and I figured *why not?*"

"Wait. *Fred* told you about this field trip?"

He tucked in his bottom lip, a sheepish grin stretching across his face. "Yes, he . . ."

I jabbed an accusing finger at him. "You *knew* all the time that I was in the back of that van."

He stood still, his lips pressed together, his eyebrows pulled upward like Stan Laurel's.

I locked one hand on my waist. "And you didn't say a thing, didn't say hello, or anything."

He quirked his head to the side. "And neither did you."

"Pssh. Like I knew you'd be joining us. I didn't even know if *you* knew I'd be in that van."

"Awkward?"

"I'll say." Both of my hands flailed into the air, and my sketchbook went flying.

Seth stepped around me and retrieved it. "Guess I should've said something then. Might have saved me from an unwanted advance." He flicked his chin toward the group of students winding their way up the Gothic stairway.

I followed his gaze. "Didn't look all that unwanted to me." I flinched after saying it. Now he knew I'd been watching him. *Rats.*

A tinge of smugness overtook him, and Seth lowered his voice. "I maintain that the interest given me was neither wanted nor encouraged. Maybe the question I should be asking is why you felt it necessary to hide while analyzing me from that strategic seat in the back." He paused. "Planning to tattle to Holly?"

My skin grew warm. Holly. Did I forget they were seeing each other? Or just tuck that knowledge away somewhere? I had put myself in the position of discussing Seth's love life with one of the sweetest women in town—like there was trouble brewing or something. I tightened my grip on my sketch pad. No way would I condone or even expect Seth to be anything but respectful of their relationship.

Rather ornery of him to suggest I had an ulterior motive, though, even in jest.

"Are you saying you don't trust me, Seth?" Maybe I shouldn't have smiled as I allowed those words to roll out of my mouth. We had fallen into a familiar cadence, one of old friendship. I didn't want to lose that. In some untidy corner of my mind, the thought remained that we might have some kind of relationship again. Until Seth answered my question, that is.

"That's exactly what I'm saying." His tone had deepened and he sounded serious.

I swiveled a look at him. "Seriously?"

"I stopped trusting you ever since that day on your parents' front porch." He said the words as casually as if ordering a hamburger. Then he shrugged, as if this news didn't matter much anyway.

He was wrong.

Chapter Twelve

 The studio door creaked open, the sound of it like an echo from my heart.

Everyone but Timo, who remained hunched over his desk, had gone home. I would have too if Gage hadn't called offering to pick up Jer from preschool. I considered refusing his generous offer, but he claimed he wanted to practice his parenting skills. After I heard Callie twittering in the background, I figured this wasn't a pity mission but an honest desire to play with his young nephew. So I agreed.

With the memory of Letty's morning consternation in my head, I decided to spend the evening working on the door. Maybe my taking the time to work alone in the quiet building would ease her concern over the project's completion.

And maybe, too, I would discover a way to digest Seth's earlier declaration that he would never trust me again.

After Seth dumped those words on me, I found it difficult to gather a full breath, as if his unwillingness to forgive me for the past wound around my lungs like the thin, sharp tendrils of a morning glory vine. Everyone knew those things grew like weeds, strangling everything in their path.

We drifted apart on the tour after that. Mercy reigned and I became mesmerized by the restored sixteenth-century ceiling of the Doge Suite and, soon after, the guest library blanketed by one of Mr. Hearst's Persian rugs and filled with art influences from Spain, France, and Italy. Our tour guide even allowed us to stop and admire the gold-adorned bedroom often requested by gossip columnist Hedda Hopper and the nearby suite where Clark Gable and Carole Lombard stayed.

Seth found his ticket out of there when he spotted a ladder up against a building opposite from the one we toured. I saw him only once after that. He must have found his own ride off the hill.

Timo glanced up from his work and stood. "Good. You're here." He tossed me a set of keys. "I was about to lock up, but now the honor is yours. You know the combination to the lockbox outside, right?"

"Yes, of course. I'll lock up the keys. No problem."

His muffled footsteps stopped at my workstation and he turned back around. "Unless you want me to stay?"

"No, not at all. You go. I'm just planning to finish up what I started this morning."

He raised his eyebrows, a weird smile growing on his face. "I was thinking the same thing."

"Excuse me?"

He stepped closer to me, that strange little grin still hanging on his face as if it had been drawn on with a Sharpie. "You were awfully into me this morning."

Shocked laughter flew out of me. "What?"

He leaned one scrawny arm on my worktable and dipped his head to the side, his eyes bobbing at me through his spectacles. Except his hand slipped and caught the bottom edge of a glass dish of shavings, sending it crashing to the concrete floor. Shards of glass mixed with dried paint shavings scattered like pollen.

"Oops." Timo continued to lean against the table, his sickly grin unnerving.

I tied the bow at the back of my apron. "Are you planning to clean that up?"

"Maybe later."

"I know there's a whisk broom around here somewhere . . ." I muttered. As I pushed past him, he grabbed my arm with bony fingers. I twisted back to face him and yanked myself from his grasp. I rubbed the skin on my forearm. "What do you think you're doing? Are you out of your mind?"

He jerked straight up and jammed his hands into his pockets. That disturbing smile melted until his face resembled a poorly carved jack-o-lantern. "I–I thought you were, you know, sending me signals." He hung his head like a naughty child.

I crossed my arms and looked into the studio's rafters. *Lord, why do I continue to have bad encounters with men?* I glanced at Timo. *And boys?*

With no answer forthcoming, I mustered up a deep breath and pushed it back out, determined to turn this kid around. "Timo, let me give you some advice. Number one: Engaging in passing conversations with a girl does not mean she's into you; she's just being polite. Number two: Unless you want to have to call your mother from prison, *never* grab a girl unless she requests that you do so. And number three: When a girl asks how she looks, the word *fine* is never an appropriate response." I uncrossed my arms and brushed a stray hair from my face with the back of my hand. "Consider that last one a freebie."

"Yes, ma'am."

"And number four: Never, ever call a woman in her twenties—even one who is slightly older than you—*ma'am*. In fact, why not drop that word from your vocabulary altogether, hmm?"

He nodded, eyes wide like a skittish puppy during a thunderstorm. He turned tail and jogged to the exit, stumbling over his exceedingly long pant legs.

After he left, I swept up every sign of him, then filled a kettle with water, set it on the small stove against the wall, and switched on the burner. Strange day. Was it just this morning that I bounded in here like a kindergartner on her first day at school? *Mercy*, things had gone awry.

I grabbed a chai tea bag and plopped it into my mug, tapping an impatient foot as I waited. How dare Seth say he still didn't trust me? We were *kids*. Couldn't he see how much I'd grown since our teenage years? The concept of telling him the dirty details of Len's past—which incidentally was *my* past too—made me ill. Maybe I *should* have spilled some details so he might better understand the tough decisions I've had to make.

The kettle whistled and I switched off the fire. I filled my mug with scalding liquid, then added two squirts of honey and some fake creamer. After giving the tea a quick stir, I sipped it, my mind still a hundred paces away.

Seth may not be aware of the reason behind my singleness, but couldn't he see how hard I worked to make a decent life for Jer and myself?

Maybe not. Gingerly, I blew on my chai tea and took a slow sip, its spicy flavor heating me from the inside. I stared into the expanse of emptiness before me, the creak of the studio door registering as an afterthought.

"Suz?"

I blinked and turned to see Seth peeking through the gap. "Hi."

He stepped inside, closing the door behind him. As he approached, he glanced around the airy space, looking for what I didn't know. The walls stretched wide and blank, empty as a street after the sweeper had gone by. "Saw your car here and thought you might have decided to work late."

"Hmm. Yes, I'm planning to get back to it after my tea." I took another sip, wishing he hadn't decided to come here, bringing judgment along with him, and yet wondering what he wanted.

He cleared his throat. "Well. Since I was here, I figured I'd check on you. You know, since you're all alone up here."

Check on me? This from the man who so blithely stated he'd never trust me again? There would always be some things I would never understand. I remembered the teakettle on the stove. "Can I offer you a cup?"

He shook his head. "Thanks. No. I'm good."

I watched him over my mug, waiting. Was it always up to me to herd along the conversation?

"So . . ." he said.

I tilted my head to the side. "Yes?"

"You enjoyed the tour then?"

My nod included a noncommittal shrug. "It's always helpful to get a feel for the life behind the art."

He nodded the way some people do—as if they understand—then he paused and shook his head. "Okay, I tried." A single laugh escaped him. "But I'm not sure what you mean."

I set down my mug. "Sometime after you left, I started painting art on people's walls. As a hobby. Sometimes they knew what they wanted, like my friend Renee who asked for a daisy on her ceiling. Most of the time, though, it helped to spend some time walking around their homes. I usually could figure out what they wanted even before they knew."

He moved closer. "So you're going to suggest adding a mural to Hearst's place?"

I allowed myself a smile at this, but just a small one. "Not a chance." My eyes found his. I waited a beat and then blurted, "Was there something you wanted?"

He blinked several times, his gaze falling to the ground before he raised his chin and looked me straight in the eyes. "I've got some questions for you, Suz."

"Really." I sat back against the wall, keeping my eyes level with his. "Ask away."

"It's about the elephant in the, uh, art studio." He glanced around. "So to speak."

"You're going to have to tell me what you're asking."

"It's hard."

I swallowed, sympathy whittling away at my pride. Still, I waited.

He released a harsh sigh. "What happened between you and . . . that guy?"

Here it comes. "Len?"

His shoulders drooped. "You're saying I shouldn't have asked."

"Don't put words into my mouth." My forehead bunched. "I never said that."

He looked almost forlorn, waiting for my answer. "So?" His expression took me back to that day on the porch when I refused to join him on his crazy adventure. Surely he was long over that.

"We divorced last year." I raised the tepid mug of tea to my lips in an effort to buy some time. How much did I want Seth to know about what happened with Len? Did I want him to know that I'd chosen a man to give me stability in life, only to have him pull my very foundation from under me?

"Jeremiah and I came out here to live with Gage. Of course, you probably already guessed that."

He rocked forward and back, eyes down, as if thinking of his next line. Would it be sympathetic? Or an attack?

He raised his head. "You've had it rough, then."

For the first time in months, pressure built behind my eyes. I blinked it away. I had already been through the shock and pain of Len's betrayal. I had already climbed out of the pit of depression followed by the wallowing that comes from being rejected by a man I trusted with every part of me. Somehow, though, seeing my old friend—my first love, really—standing before me, offering pity, threatened to rupture the dam I'd worked hard to erect.

"I guess Gage is a father figure to your son now."

I swallowed hard to erase all trace of tears. "He really is."

Seth relaxed his shoulders and walked toward me. He slid onto the stool next to me. "Can you tell me what caused you to run?"

You mean 'this time'? I could see it in his eyes. Seth had made up his own mind about who made the decision to end our marriage. And why shouldn't I have? Not only had Len broken my trust by committing his crimes, but he cheated on me. Over and over again. Even the most devout Christian could support that decision. At least I hoped so.

If I had actually been the one to make the decision.

Len said he loved someone else and wanted to marry *her* behind prison gates. Although our marriage had ended long before the papers had been signed. Remembering the sting of his letter all those months ago never failed to inflict another gash to the wound.

I pulled myself out of my trance to find Seth staring at me. "I don't need to defend myself to you, but if you really want to know, Len wanted the divorce. Not me." *At least, not at first.*

He winced and I didn't know if he did that on my behalf, or because he realized how much I had loved my husband. The expression of hurt on his face lingered for a long while. And then he reached over and laid his hand on mine. His skin felt warm and strong, like comfort wrapped up in his touch, and I gave in to it, allowing my eyes to close. I didn't feel any need to fill the quiet with words and, as usual, neither did Seth.

I opened my eyes, hoping to see again a glimmer of our old friendship in his. "Thanks for caring, Seth. I appreciate that."

He dragged his hand away, leaving my skin to cool. "I've been there."

I tipped my head to the side. "Really?"

He shrugged and looked away. "Don't talk about it much, but I know what it's like to make mistakes you can never take back." He glanced back at me. "Just didn't want you to be overcome with guilt."

I shrunk back. "Why would I be?"

"I'm trying to offer some support here."

"But why do you think I should be the one overcome with guilt? Len left me."

"I heard that. But people in love don't just up and leave. Not unless they've got a reason."

Sarcasm rose like bile. "You're one of those people then who thinks if a man leaves his wife, it's probably all her fault? What is it you think happened, Seth? You think I gained weight? Served up some lousy dinners? Maybe I lost one too many of his tube socks in the laundry?"

Seth pressed in, something in his eyes unshaken by my outburst. "Take it from a guy who knows."

"I think you'd better go." I slid off of my stool. "Work awaits."

Chapter Thirteen

Any fantasy about resurrecting something resembling friendship with Seth had been dashed during that moment last night when he took the position that I had *anything* to do with the dissolution of my marriage to Len. If believing someone at their word constituted fault then, *whatever*, call me guilty.

I plunged a wooden spoon into the morning's oatmeal, stirring it away from the pan's edges as it began to thicken and bubble. Callie appeared on the other side of the kitchen window with her pup, a beagle mix she found and named Moondoggy, in tow. They bounded up the outside steps, and the screen door creaked open.

A few seconds later, she peeked through the kitchen doorway. "What's for breakfast, Sis?"

"Head on a platter." I pivoted, smiling sweetly. "Care to join me?"

"Sounds delish." She pulled out a chair, and Moondoggy danced around her, nails clacking against the floor. She sat and he curled up under her chair. "It's a delicacy, I hear."

I switched off the burner. "You bet."

"Anyone's head in particular? Or just your garden-variety noggin?"

"I picked this one out myself. Like lobster."

She laughed as I served up four bowls of creamy oatmeal and left two on the stove to stay warm for Jer and Gage. I slid one bowl in front of Callie, set the other at my place, and took a seat.

"Something on your mind?" Callie topped her breakfast with a pad of butter and watched it slip down an oatmeal mountain.

I huffed out a breath. "Do you trust my brother?"

"Of course." She poured cream on her oatmeal.

"What if he started staying out late or suddenly began working nights and weekends? If he drastically changed his schedule and ran around with a silly grin on his face, telling you how great his work was, well, would you still trust him?"

Callie stopped sprinkling brown sugar on her oatmeal, her spoon hovering over her bowl. "What are you saying exactly?"

I reached over, removed the spoon from her hand, and finished dusting her oatmeal with sugar. "It was a hypothetical question. Don't worry about Gage. He's golden, you know."

She smiled. "I know."

I batted the air with one hand. "Ah, pssh. Forget it."

Gage showed up with Jer on his back. "Forget what?" His eyes lighted at the sight of breakfast. "Ooh, oatmeal. You girls save us any?"

I pushed my chair away from the table, wincing as it scraped against the floor. "Yes, yes. Come sit." Jer climbed on my chair and grabbed me around the neck, preventing me from reaching the stove.

Gage brushed past me. "I've got it."

I kissed Jer's head, his hair smelling of baby shampoo—although he didn't like me to call it that since he's not a baby anymore. Still, he wriggled on my lap like one, teetering left and right. "I'm hungry!"

Gage plunked a bowl in front of him. "You've come to the right place, kiddo. Camp chow in honor of Auntie Callie being with us for breakfast."

Callie snorted. She sometimes did that when laughter caught her off guard. She covered her mouth with one hand. "I had nothing to do with the grub. That was all your sister's doing. I just showed up here—like she really needed another mouth to feed."

"It's not camp grub," I cut in. "It's comfort food. And you're always welcome, Callie. If anyone's on her way out of this charming coastal cottage that would be me."

Gage shook his head. "Not this again. Is that what you were talking about when I came in?" He slathered a less-than-healthy amount of butter on his oatmeal.

Callie and I exchanged a glance. I hadn't had a chance to explain my cryptic remarks, but surely she had guessed they involved a man.

"Sort of." I tossed my spoon in the bowl and sat back, lacing my fingers around Jer's waist. "Well, not really. Although I did find a darling place to rent once I save enough."

Gage's brows rose. "Where?"

I motioned toward the hills with a nod of my head. "My boss, Fred, owns a log cabin up there. It's darling."

"The red one?"

I nodded, grateful to avoid talking about what really gnawed at me this morning. "Cute, huh?"

Gage whistled. "It's a beautiful place. Fred owns it? That's a property I wouldn't mind owning myself one day."

I slapped his arm. "No way. This one's mine. If you took that sweet cottage over, you'd put solar panels on the roof and tear down all those logs in favor of some kind of *green* insulation."

Gage jerked upright. "I beg your pardon."

Callie watched us with an amused expression. "Careful there. Don't mess with my boyfriend's sense of stewardship." She winked.

"All I'm saying is that it's a Hearst-era cottage and I'd hate to see a lawn on the roof or something strange like that."

Gage tossed his napkin at me. "Sheesh. You sound like some of my clients. You obviously have no idea what I do." He raised his voice above Callie's laughter. "On another note . . ."

"Yes?" I prompted, trying not to laugh.

"You never told us about your impromptu trip to the castle yesterday. How'd that go?"

"Ah, well, that. Climbed a mountain, saw some art, went back to work. The usual."

This time Callie and Gage exchanged a curious glance followed by something peculiar and familiar at the same time, something that often passed between our parents. With a simple wink of an eye and nod of her head, Callie seemed to telegraph a message to her beloved, one that said, "Let me try."

Did they not know how obvious they were?

Callie perked. "Did you get to see the Neptune Pool up close?"

I nodded. "Last time, I did. This time, I only got a glimpse." Laughter bubbled up from me. "Fred swears that in the good ol' days, after the state took over the castle, some of the neighbors were invited to big soirees up there. He has a picture of himself lying on a longboard in that pool."

Callie snorted. "No way. Really?"

"There's a bigger question at stake here." Gage pointed at me with his spoon. "You saw Fred in swim trunks. What was that like?"

I waved both of my hands in protest, then covered Jer's ears. "Stop. Please. We have an impressionable young man in our midst."

Callie cleared her throat. "Speaking of impressionable young men . . ."

Jer wriggled from my grasp and rolled off my lap. "I'm gonna go get my shoes on."

"You do that," I encouraged.

Callie sat poised to continue speaking, but over his bowl of oatmeal Gage made a teepee with his fingers and eyed me with intensity.

"You want to know what happened yesterday? I ran into Seth. Again. And you know, I'm a little tired of these coincidental meetings with someone I once knew. Someone who used to . . ." I stared at my less-than-appetizing oatmeal. "Anyway, I thought I knew him."

"So he's changed a lot, then." Gage's expression never wavered.

"Yes, he's different now." I shrugged, leaning my forearms onto the table, fatigue setting in. "Or maybe he's really just the same old Seth."

"Funny that you should mention him. I saw Holly and Seth taking a walk along the Kitteridge property the other day, and well, he didn't seem that into her. Not very attentive, in my opinion."

I shook off her comment. "Seth's life isn't any of my business. I remember him being full of life, always coming up with wild ideas and taking them on. Now he seems bitter almost. Then again, maybe I allowed myself to forget the things I didn't like."

Gage nodded. "And the more you get to know him again, the more you remember."

I nodded, as if to agree, then gave my head a sad, slow shake. "No. I don't know." I pushed myself away from the table. "Sorry, guys. Kind of distracted today, but I'd better clean up and get to work."

Callie reached across the table and squeezed my hand. "You never know how the past six years have shaped a person."

I cleared my plate. Six long years. Callie was right: I had no idea what had transpired for him along the way. Nor did he realize the extent of *my* personal trials.

Gage and Callie insisted on cleaning up the kitchen, and considering the way they flirted nonstop in the process, was I doing them a favor by hanging around, ducking in and out of their way? Nothing, it seemed, could tear those two apart. When it was time to leave, Jer and I had to nearly shout our good-byes to get their attention.

I dropped off munchkin at preschool, reminding him that Uncle Gage would pick him up after work, and then made the arduous drive to work. In the past twenty-four hours, my enthusiasm for the future had dimmed, and that annoyed me. Why were my emotions swayed by the attitudes of others? Even this morning I found myself hoping Letty's mood would improve once she saw the pristine condition of my end of the project.

About a mile out from the studio, I noticed a figure walking beside the highway. I slowed my car when I recognized the woman's long, gauzy wrap. Pulling up next to her, I rolled down my window. "Letty?"

She jerked backward and whipped a look my way. She crouched next to my car. "Why not run me over? Would do the job quicker than you driving so close and giving me a heart attack!"

I offered her an apologetic smile. "Just trying to save you from wild zebras. Get in, would you?"

She yanked open the door and plopped onto the passenger seat, and as she did the inside of my car began to smell like a floral garden. I waited for her to tell me why she had been walking along the side of a busy coastal highway.

She turned her chin. "You know how to drive this thing?"

"What are you doing here, Letty?"

She exhaled a dramatic sigh. "My car wouldn't start. No biggie. I will have it looked at tomorrow."

"Why didn't you just call me for a ride?"

Her expression hardened for a moment, then she gave me a guilty smile. "It is a beautiful walk, but you are a sweet girl. Thank you for the offer."

"Beautiful, but dangerous. Promise me you'll never do something so risky again."

She glanced at the sky. "Fine. I promise." Then she gestured toward the road with a flick of her chin. "Now are we going to go to work, or are you waiting for Prince Charming to gallop by on his white steed?"

I drove the car off the gravel path and back onto the highway. Several minutes later, after pulling into the small parking lot near the studio, we hurried inside. I wished I'd brought my coat instead of this drafty sweater missing a button. Timo sat crouched over his work desk. He didn't look up, but his neck turned the color of beets as I passed.

Letty reached our workstation first. "Well, Fred." She turned to our boss who stood beside her. "Either Suz decided to burn a candle until late into the night or you truly do have elves working for you."

I held back a laugh at her Santa Claus reference. *He did know that he looked like the jolly old man, right?*

If he did, Fred didn't acknowledge the fact. "It would seem that our Suz became inspired by her trip to the castle yesterday." He crossed his arms in front of his belly, grinning to himself. "As I had hoped."

I acknowledged him with a smile while forcing away unwanted memories from my visit to Casa Grande yesterday. *Focus on the art, Suz. Focus on all that creativity bound up in one beautiful house.*

Letty continued to inspect the door, her fingertips trailing over the smooth and bare sections of decorative carvings. She nodded, her face a mixture of quiet appreciation and questions. She looked up. "Beautifully done."

"Thank you."

She turned to Fred, her voice subdued. "Are the paint samples back from the lab yet?"

He scratched his chin. "Not yet. I suppose you could use today to apply an isolation layer to the untouched areas."

Letty bobbed her head. "We could, but they are few." She caught my attention with her eyes. "Fred's referring to a thin coat of varnish we will put over what is left of the door's original surfaces."

"Perhaps Suzi-Q would like to try her hand at the isolation layer. We could move you to other projects today, Letty."

Her eyes narrowed, an expression I was beginning to become accustomed to. *Didn't she trust me? Did I trust myself?* I glanced at Fred. "If you don't mind, I would love for Letty to watch over me, you know, to make sure I'm doing it right." I watched for his reaction. "Okay by you?"

Fred nodded once. "Certainly. In the meantime, I will check with the lab to make sure those color mixes are on schedule for delivery by tomorrow."

As he stepped away, I plucked my apron from a nearby hook and pulled it over my head. By the time I'd tied my bow and smoothed my hair, Letty had already moved to the end of the table where we'd be working. For the first time in days, she looked content.

Why did it feel like I had just dodged one fast-moving bullet?

Chapter Fourteen

No matter how I tried to will it away, Letty's breath pulsated on my neck. I twisted a look up at her. "All that heavy breathing will get you nowhere."

Letty's black eyes flashed. "Please. You need Leticia to help you. Isn't that obvious?"

I laughed and jostled my elbows into the air. "Give me some space, will ya, Leticia?"

She spiked the air with her fingers. "You are timid as a mouse when it comes to stripping and preparing surfaces, but with a paintbrush in your hand, such a *diva* you are!"

I straightened. "A diva. I like that."

She grimaced. "You would. Keep working, girl. I am going to go and drink some caffeine. I would offer some to you, but you don't need it."

A guffaw slipped out of me as she wandered away. Laughter of any kind felt good for the soul these days. As I bent over to inspect the new layer of applied finish, I made the decision to stop at the video store to pick up a romantic comedy. Scratch that. A plain, old comedy would do.

A sudden pungent odor surrounded me and I sneezed into the crook of my arm, careful not to let loose all over the door project. *Had Letty just doused herself with perfume?* A sharp tickle shinnied up my nose, causing me to draw back into an all-out fight against the approach of another sneeze. I was not up to the fight. I sucked in air in snatches—once, twice, three times—and sneezed so hard that the impact of my inner arm to the chin probably caused some bruising.

"God bless you." Letty stood at my side with the most monstrous floral display I had ever seen outside of a funeral. "These are for you."

"No way."

"So now I am a liar?" She handed me a napkin from the pocket of her apron.

"Thanks." I turned away and blew into it. *Who would send me flowers?*

"Somebody is in love with you. Either that or just terribly indecisive. Look at this thing. Rosemary, sage, lavender, eucalyptus, not to mention all the color: roses, plumeria, *and* stargazers too."

I sniffed and searched for the card, plucking it from a plastic fork stuck somewhere in the middle. *"Thank you for being a great mom to our son. I will be in Otter Bay next week to see you* both. *Affectionately, Len."* I glanced at Letty with itchy eyes. "My ex-husband."

"Well, then . . . surprise?"

I groaned. "Just put them down anywhere, but make sure it's far . . . far . . . *achoo!"* I blew my nose again into the wadded napkin in my hand. "Far from me."

"Yes, madam."

I sunk into my stool, fatigue with a tinge of worry rolling through me like gray clouds. "I'm not sure how to feel about this," I said to Letty when she returned.

She set her cup of coffee down next to me. "Looks to me like the man is trying to pave a path over his sins."

I pursed my lips, pressure building behind my eyes. "I should stop him from coming here right now, shouldn't I? I'm not ready for this . . . to see him again. Not after all the lies and the pain . . ."

"Maybe this is how he shows you that what he tells you is true. He says he is reformed, and so he sends you flowers as an offering to prove it to you."

"You sound like you're on his side."

"Are we taking sides here?"

I shook my head. "Sorry. No." I paused, thinking. "I don't want to give Len the wrong impression, though. About me."

"Tell me this. Is a jailbird so enticing that he would think you would fall in love with him again so easily?"

Her words tore at something inside me. Len, a jailbird. The idea still shocked me like a flash of a photographer's camera on a starless night. At first, I had become obsessed with picturing his day-to-day living in a bare cell with concrete floors and an indiscreet toilet. *Could he sleep at night? What did his meals smell like? Had he been brutalized in any way?*

In the days of revelation after Len's arrest, I still clung to the lie that despite his drug conviction, he had never strayed in our marriage. His desire and passion for me had always been so convincing, even till the end. I wanted to believe this one last thing about him—even though neighbor after neighbor told me otherwise.

I glanced at Letty. "I hope he knows that will never happen." Something curdled in my stomach and I doubled forward.

Letty touched my back. "What's wrong?"

I pressed my forearm to my belly, but the nausea continued to come. "I–I think I'm going to be—" I lurched forward toward the waste can, as did my breakfast. A groan escaped me.

Letty rubbed my back as I began to wretch, the onslaught of sickness too sudden for me to become embarrassed. "Our Father, who art in heaven, hallowed be thy name . . ." Through the fog engulfing my mind, I felt Letty's touch and heard her prayer over me.

Again the rumbling took over, my body unable to wrest itself from its control.

". . . give us this day, our daily bread . . ."

The skin of my forehead felt hot against my hand, and I wretched and coughed until fatigue replaced illness. I rolled from my knees onto my haunches, confused. Letty's heels had clicked away then returned.

"Does your ex-husband always make a splash like that?"

My head hung forward, a headache gripping my temples. "What?"

"The flowers. I think they made you sick. My hunch tells me it was the eucalyptus mixed with sage and those sweet-smelling roses. Odd concoction."

"Oh." My eyes refused to open.

"If you trust me to drive your car, I can take you home."

Anyone willing to pray over me as I vomited deserved my trust. I nodded with care, wanting to ask how she would get around after today but too tired to force out the words.

Shortly thereafter Letty craned her neck around the steering wheel to look through the windshield. "Is this your home?"

I peeked through two fingers at Gage's cozy beach cottage. "It is."

"You are a blessed girl." She pulled my car into the drive. "Your home is beautiful."

"Thanks, but it's my brother's place." I unlocked my door, then stopped. "Wait. How will you get home? Why don't you just take my car and pick me up in the morning?"

She brushed me off. "Oh, I couldn't do that."

"Why not?"

She thought a moment. "Because I have plans to walk to church. Today is a warm afternoon and I would enjoy taking advantage of that. You're not planning to tell Fred that I played hooky, correct?"

"Correct."

She assessed me with a glance. "Are you feeling better now? You do not look so hot."

I opened up my car door, my laugh weak. "Thanks. I can always count on you for honesty."

"I cannot deny it. You bring out my nurturing side."

We walked together up the steps and Letty followed me inside. "I'm starting to feel much better, Letty. I have no idea what happened back there—"

"You want me to fill you in?"

"No, ha ha. That's okay. Why don't I just make us some tea?" I headed for the kitchen to wash up and set the kettle to boil.

"And toast for you," Letty called out. "I promise you there is nothing left in your stomach."

I leaned my head through the doorway. "You think I'm not aware?"

She crossed her arms in front of her multicolored vest. "The bigger question is, what are you going to do about a man who sent an arrangement that made you so ill? Wouldn't your ex-husband know the type of flowers you could not tolerate?"

While waiting for the teakettle's whistle, I leaned on the doorjamb and pondered Letty's question. "I hadn't thought of that, but then I usually bought the same kinds of flowers over and over again. My favorite flower color has always been yellow."

"Really? Hmm."

I cocked my head. "What?"

"Did not see a daisy in the bunch."

I shrugged and turned back toward the stove. "Maybe he forgot. It doesn't matter anyway." My laughter sounded harsh. "It's not like there could ever be anything romantic between us again."

"And you are sure about this?"

The question hung in the room until I carried in cream, honey, and two mugs of tea on a tray and set it on the coffee table. "Positive."

Letty reached for a mug and added cream. "Well, then. Good to know." She settled into the couch and took a long sip. Her warm-toned skin glowed in the afternoon sun, highlighting her striking features. Letty had pushed her way into my life, linking arms with me at the art studio even before I learned where the staff kept the bathroom key. She had assessed me, but I still knew little about her.

I wrapped both hands around my mug. "You must be tired of hearing about me. Why don't you tell me more about you?"

"We have been friends for nearly a month. What else do you need to know?"

"Well, okay. For starters, when and how did you get into the art-restoration business?"

Something akin to disappointment flickered in her eyes, and she gazed out the window in silence for several seconds. *Did she think I was prying?* She turned away from the window and held me with a steady gaze. "I have my degree, but truly, my husband taught me everything I know."

"I didn't know you were married."

"I am a widow."

Her words sucked away the little bit of energy the tea had brought back to my body. "Letty, I'm sorry. You're so young . . . I had no idea."

"Of course you didn't because I never told you. I keep him with me every day, right here." She touched a hand to her heart. "Then I don't need to talk."

"So he was an artist, then?"

"Yes. A painter. I could watch him work for hours—he had the most creative mind. He taught me patience and he taught me the right way to hold a brush and mix colors." Her eyes seemed to bore into me. "He often displayed a free spirit who painted whatever came to mind, and yet, he came to understand that restoration was his forté."

"He sounds like someone I would have liked to have known."

She nodded, her face cracking with a glimmer of emotion. "Yes, I'm sure you would have been great friends."

Quiet fell across the room as we sipped our tea in contemplation. I released a long, relaxed sigh. "I appreciate you bringing me home, Letty. Phew, I've no idea what made me so sick. Thank you so much."

"Stress. Stress made you sick." She seemed to have recovered from a trip to melancholy lane. "That and a mix of scents that God never intended." She drained her cup. "You're very welcome, of course, but it is time for me to go."

"I'm feeling better. Let me drive you."

"Stop trying to save the world, Suz. I am perfectly fine to

walk to my church from here. It is only a short distance up the hill behind the town." She checked the time on her phone. "If I leave now, I will arrive in time to say the rosary with the others. And if you will allow me to leave without pouting, I will include you in my prayers too."

Her promise to pray brought unexpected comfort. Somehow I knew I was going to need them.

Chapter Fifteen

They say that nights are for lovers, but by
the number of beachcombers gliding hand in
hand this morning as the mist burned off the
rocks, I'd say the poet got it wrong.

I wasn't proud that my envy reared itself. Or was that even
what I felt? If I had taken the witness stand and sworn an oath,
I couldn't say that what I wanted out of life right now was a
man. I'd had two, and look how that turned out?

What I did long for, however, was the contentment that
these lovebirds along my path displayed with abandon. The
serenity in their expressions, the relaxed way they meandered
along the boardwalk, all spoke to the way they had rolled out
of bed with great expectations for the day.

Could I say the same thing?

The air had turned cold overnight, chilly enough that as
I puffed my way north along the coast, I could see each breath

Fade to Blue

leading the way. At the northernmost tip of the pathway, before the bike lane turned to highway, I coasted into a small park, hoping for a spot to think. The lookout at the far end provided an arc of unobstructed views of the bay and waters beyond. It was one of my favorite places to listen to the cry of gulls and to watch for otters floating on their backs among the rocks.

Too late. Two teenagers intertwined themselves at the center of the lookout rail, as if hoping to star in the show that visitors would come to see. I skidded to a stop, startling them both, then made a U-turn.

In the end, I had their public display of affection to thank because if their presence had not deterred me from reaching my contemplation point, I might not have yanked my bike down the stairs and onto the sandy beach. And I might not have encountered the most heaven-sent display of open sea anemones living just inches beneath clear sea water.

I swallowed the emotion that rose within me. *Did you put those people in my path this morning, Lord, so I could find all this evidence of you?*

After ditching my bike in the sand, I moved closer to the tide pool splash zone teeming with a multitude of sea creatures, an impressive display of emerald green sea anemones, far and wide. Tucked between them other varieties in pink and purple clutched the rocks. I hauled in a cleansing breath. Together they resembled a vast, undersea mosaic.

If only I had my sketchbook with me.

I slipped off my shoes and tiptoed through icy water to

reach a dry, flat rock to sit on. Without paper and pencil, I would have to rely on mental snapshots. Nearly microscopic fish swam in and around the free-flowing tentacles of the anemones. With a pushed-up sleeve, I dipped my finger into a pool and tickled the ends of one of them, laughing at the slight suction to my skin. The anemone reacted by curling its petal-like tentacles inward.

Is that how I am sometimes, Lord? Do I reach out for you, then withdraw when you offer me your hand?

No answer came, but I sensed God listening, prodding me toward answers of questions I had yet to ask. My mind ricocheted from my responsibilities at the art studio, to Letty's revelation yesterday, to Len's about-face when it came to matters of faith. The thought of my ex-husband used to cause my heart to plummet, to leave me grasping for the strength to take another breath. This morning his name elicited no physical pain, nor frantic reaction. At the moment it garnered no reaction at all.

Instead of dwelling on the painful things that had long passed, I sat curled into a ball on that rock, my arms wrapped around my legs. I admired the tapestry of tides for as long as I dared and then, reluctantly, returned home.

Jeremiah's voice carried into the street as I pulled up on my bike, tired but contented after my morning excursion. I leaned the bike against an outer wall, headed up the stairs and into the cottage, the sound of my son's voice growing louder.

"Vroom!" Jer dragged his knees across the wood floors, one hand bracing himself and the other pushing a pint-sized, painted-metal tractor trailer. One sock dangled from one foot, and the other was AWOL.

"Mama!" He craned his head around, veering the truck nearly into my feet.

"Red light, red light!" I pushed my palms forward and he careened to a stop with an accompanying high-pitched screech.

I plunked myself on the floor in front of him, and he gave me an impish grin. "What're you up to—?"

Too late. He grabbed hold of his metal tractor trailer and drove it up my shins, my knees the pinnacle he had to achieve, and at the top, he let the truck tumble sideways onto the floor. I winced at the cringe-worthy crash. *Another ding in the floor I'm going to owe Gage for!*

"Oh, Mama, you moved."

"*I* moved?"

"Yeah, but I forgive you anyways."

"Gee, thanks. Go finish getting dressed for school, okey-dokey? Make sure to look for your other sock."

"'Sthat 'cuz you don't like my toes to be naked?" He thrust his chin in the air, displaying a row of shiny white baby teeth.

I tousled his hair and bent down to nuzzle our noses. "I love your naked toes but don't think you should be showing them off at preschool. Now git!"

He scampered to his room.

Gage padded into the living room, his bed head untouched. He yawned and moved straight for the kitchen, and as he paused, I tugged on the cuff of his sweats. He dropped his gaze downward.

"Hey. Guess Jer's been pretty busy this morning. Sorry about that."

"What?" He rubbed his unshaven face. "No, he's fine. I'm fine."

I pointed to the hair smashed against one side of his head.

He ran a hand over his disheveled head and smiled, rueful. "Slow morning, but it's not because of Jer. Lot on my mind." He pointed to the kitchen. "Coffee?"

"Not yet. Let me get it going for you." I dragged myself off the floor and followed Gage into the kitchen.

He waved me away. "I wasn't asking you to make it, just if you wanted any. Go ahead and worry about Jer. I've got this."

I glanced at the hall. "Could I talk to you first? I've got some news I think we should discuss."

Between loading spoonfuls of ground coffee into the filter, Gage's eyes attempted to focus on me. "Oh, yeah? Can I handle this before my morning coffee?" He shoved the plastic filter holder into the slot and switched on the pot.

"Maybe not, but I wanted to tell you before Jer comes down." I shifted. "I received a card from Len yesterday at work, and he says—"

"Wait . . . what?" He leaned his arms, bent at the elbows, on the tile sink behind him, looking ready to pounce. "He contacted you at work? That's quite the clandestine operation going on up there. How did he know how to find you?"

"Oh, I don't remember, Gage. You know that I had some correspondence with him during the divorce proceedings. I probably mentioned something about applying there. Besides, I can't imagine it being too difficult for the government to figure out where I work."

Gage grabbed a wet sponge from the counter and threw it into the sink. He tried to hide his face from me by turning away, but I could see his mouth curling.

He's not making this very easy. I pressed a palm to my cheek, massaging my temple with several fingers. "Well, anyway, I thought you should know."

"What are his plans?"

I shrugged. "He said he wants to see Jeremiah." *And me.*

"Okay. Where will he stay and for how long? Is he going to challenge custody? Will he find work here—if anyone would even hire him, that is?"

My brother deserved answers to these questions and more. But I had nothing to offer. Although Len had made contact with me in various ways, I hadn't reciprocated. Instead, I'd been turning the news of his release from prison over in my mind for days, waiting with a catch in my breath for him to show up. Beyond that? I hadn't planned out a thing.

"I don't know, Gage." I sighed and glanced around the kitchen, anything to avoid meeting his eyes. "One thing I need to do is prepare Jeremiah. He used to ask about Len all the time, but you're more of a father to him now." I turned to face him. "Well, anyway, I need to work on that."

The harsh edge to my brother's eyes relaxed, and he

replaced the scowl with a sad smile. "I want to be there when that reunion happens, all right?"

I nodded.

"After that, we'll take this one step at a time."

The slower the better.

"WHERE'S FRED?"

Letty, her hands covered in swaths of various pale shades, shook her head. "He has not shown that cherub face of his all morning long. The lab sent over some colors to try, and I have experimented with all of them. Want to come look?"

I shed my jacket and laid it on the stool next to my purse. "Sure."

Letty's heels clacked along as she spoke, tossing comments over her shoulder as I tried to keep up. "The lab did an excellent job analyzing the colors. Once we determine the parameters of each shade, we can start in-painting right away. Fred should have been here by now—he always wants to approve our plans at this point." She slowed at a palate of hand-marked shades. "Look at how fabulously perfect these matches are."

I crossed my arms and peered over the colors: drab, more drab, and most drab. I squeezed my eyes shut, annoyed by my own sarcasm, and took a fresh breath and another look. Letty was right. The colors were perfection.

All around us artists worked on various projects, many I had yet to see up close. Most liked to keep to themselves, lost in contemplation as they worked. I understood that.

Something about the silence pulled my most creative work out of me.

In the background, the shrill ring of the phone split the silence. Letty didn't flinch but wagged her head side to side, over and over. "I am always amazed at the work our lab does. I just wish Fred were here so we could get started."

I nodded, wondering too why he hadn't yet arrived.

"Suz?" I turned to see Timo, breathless, at my side.

"Yes?"

He held out the cordless phone. "It's about Fred. He's had a heart attack!"

Chapter Sixteen

Letty lunged for the phone, but Timo yanked it back. "He's asking for Suz."

If taking the phone from Timo's hand and turning it over to Letty would have erased the sudden, deep creases that crisscrossed her forehead and the sad droop to her eyes, I would have, without question, done so. Hindsight was not my strong point. Just look at my marriage to Len.

I brushed the thought away as I drove as fast as legally possible to Twin Towns Medical Center. Fred's wife, Sherry, had called to tell me the news, and asked me to please come over and bring a sketch pad. I thought about Letty's expression again. Had it perhaps been worry?

After parking I hurried into the hospital, my sketchbook under my arm. My mother had died from a heart attack, and the words alone made my lungs contract, squeezing the air right out of me. But Sherry, who I had yet to meet in person, sounded calm on the phone.

I exited the elevator, my heart beginning to pound, the ominous and pulsating sound filling my ears. The hospital reeked of spilled alcohol and I held my breath.

A stout woman with graying curls and a white shawl draped around her shoulders greeted me at the door. "You are Suz." She smiled and reached for my hand. "I recognized you right away."

I forced a smile. "I am." Her resemblance to Mrs. Claus didn't surprise me in the least. "Sherry?"

She nodded and wrapped one arm around my waist, ushering me into the room. Fred sat propped up in the bed, a tray of unidentifiable foods in front of him, his skin paler than usual. "Oh, good. You've brought your sketch pad."

If Sherry wasn't behind me, shoving me toward him, I might have stopped in the doorway. Instead, I approached my boss, trying not to react to seeing him in a hospital gown. "How are you feeling, Fred? You had us all very worried about you."

"Tell everyone not to waste a minute worrying over me. I'm doing fine—strong as a fat ox." He pushed away his tray and spoke to Sherry. "Would you ask the nurse for something more substantial, dumpling?"

Dumpling? My eyes flitted to the window before settling back on Fred. "So the prognosis is good?"

"Nothing to worry about. Now sit down. I want to talk to you about the cabin."

"That pretty little log cabin in the woods? Is that what you mean?"

He smiled and looked at his wife. "See, Sherry? She has already taken to it."

Sherry beamed.

He laced his fingers together and propped his folded hands onto his belly. "Now. Tell me your ideas for the cabin's walls. Do you have something in there to show me?" He gestured toward my sketch pad with his chin.

I held it up. "In here? I'm so sorry Fred, but no I don't think I do." I swiveled a gaze at Sherry. "Although a stunning idea came to me this morning. I just haven't had time—"

"Now's as good a time as any." Fred cut in. "Go ahead and get comfortable in that chair, well, as comfortable as you can get in a hospital chair, and sketch away. We'll wait."

Sherry hurried over and pushed the chair closer to the wall, then motioned for me to sit. "The lighting's better over here, dear. You just go ahead and do your work, and we won't bother you one bit."

Bewildered by this sudden attention on me—after all, I'm not the one who had the heart attack—I shuffled over to the vinyl padded chair and sat. I plucked a pencil from my bag and flipped open my sketch pad.

Fred's eyes seemed to bore into me. I glanced up, my smile self-conscious.

Sherry bent over him then and fluffed his pillow. "Let the girl draw, Fred. I think you could use another pillow. Could you use another one, dear? Yes, I think you certainly could."

She continued fussing over him, and I glanced away, hoping to recapture the morning's inspiration on the page in front of me. I shut my eyes, allowing a picture to form. I tried to recapture the vast, colorful tide pool, but something in my mind focused on a spark of fluorescent green. My eyelids shut tighter as my mind, like a camera lens, worked to pull the image into sharper view.

And all of a sudden, it appeared. My eyes snapped open, and like a racehorse out of the gate, my pencil took off. Strokes flew across the page like dirt clods behind a horse. Inspiration rounded the corner, fast and furious, my fingers moving at breakneck speed. Something like endorphins charged through me, giving me both the gumption and the wild spirit to bring to life on the page what I'd witnessed in living color earlier this morning. My pulse throbbed in my chest, but unlike it had this morning out of fear, this time the effect was caused by all-out adrenaline.

I'd missed my art.

Though I thanked God every day for the opportunity to work at the studio, I'd missed the freedom in transforming a blank page, an empty wall—a bare ceiling!—into something wild and inspiring. A project that didn't require restoration to its original luster, but instead was set free to be transformed into something brand new.

With a breath to expand my lungs, I continued fiddling

with my sketch of a giant green sea anemone. Of course it was still in black and white, but in my mind its translucent green coat glowed.

Sherry peeked over my shoulder. "Ooh, Fred told me all about your talent. That's the liveliest sea anemone I think I have ever seen. They are usually such sedentary creatures, but oh, it is lovely."

"Now, dadgummit, don't you two leave me hanging over here. Let's have a look."

Sherry pivoted toward Fred. "Now, you, shush. She's working as fast as she can." She gazed down at me. "Don't worry about that man. He can be impatient at times, but only when it's something he's excited about."

I shielded the sketch. "It's really not much yet, Fred. I'd prefer to fill it in better, maybe even take my book down to the water and observe for a while longer." I flipped shut the sketchbook's cover. "We should be talking about *you* and how you're faring right now."

He sighed and frowned at Sherry, who patted his hand like a baby. "Help her understand, dumpling, that I will heal faster if we talk about something other than that blasted ride over here in the ambulance."

"Please, Suz? Won't you please show Freddy your sketches?"

With her smile so sweet, I didn't know whether to laugh or cry. I stepped over to the side of the bed, flipped open the cover of my sketchbook, and placed it in Fred's pudgy hands.

He shot out an arm, wiggling his hand toward the nightstand. "My glasses, please."

Sherry placed them on his nose, and he smiled and settled back against the starched whiteness of firm pillows. He traced the outline of the anemone's free-floating tentacles with his fingertip. He murmured to himself while studying my hastily drawn sketch, then he glanced up at me, his eyes kind, a bit of warm color returning to his cheeks.

"For someone who has not seen the inside of the cabin, you've chosen just the right subject to paint on the wall." He eyed his wife. "I imagine this on the eastern wall of the living room, so that as the sun sets, the colors will glow. Is that what you were thinking, lovey?"

Lovey? Dumpling? I stepped back and watched them interact. Witnessing the tenderness they had for each other made me miss my parents more than ever.

Fred snapped a glance in my direction and held out my sketchbook. "The job is yours. The tenants moved out early, and as soon as I'm released from this prison"—he turned to Sherry—"which had better be soon, then we will do some cleanup and paint and patch those walls. After that, we would be honored for you to decorate the interior with, hmm, let's just say a tide-pool theme."

Sherry nudged his shoulder. "Tell her about the pay."

I winced, still very much aware of Fred's recent heart attack.

He glanced at her, his brow furrowed. "Would she think I'm asking for a handout? She knows there is pay involved." He nodded in my direction. "You will be paid handsomely. Of course."

I accepted the sketchbook and stuck it under my arm, feeling much like the proverbial hardscrabble businesswoman who would move her meeting into a hospital room if it meant she'd score the deal. Only I would never want to be that woman. Instead, give me a paintbrush and a Saturday afternoon, and I'm your girl. Fred and Sherry's appreciation for my work, cursory as it seemed, touched me.

By the time I returned to the studio, Letty had disappeared. A tarp covered the project, and our workstation showed no sign of a work-in-progress. When I asked Timo where she went, he shrugged and wriggled his eyes at me in an inappropriate way. No way could I work on the project without her, not at this stage, so I decided to use my excess energy to sweep and scrub down every lackluster surface inside the massive building.

"You could just leave," Timo said.

"I'm being paid to be here, and dadgummit," I said with a laugh, "I'm staying until the afternoon whistle blows."

Timo wrinkled his nose and glanced at the requisite inventory paperwork on his desk. "Yeah, this blows all right."

I finished up, put away the broom, then zoomed away from the studio to pick up Jer from preschool. The sun still blazed as we pulled out of the school parking lot, so I made a U-turn without much thought.

"Hey! Where we goin', Mama?"

I tossed a look over one shoulder to my son who sat in a booster seat behind me. "I want to show you something."

He paused, his little face staring out the window. After a minute or so, he spoke up. "Will there be ice cream?"

I laughed. "Not where we're going, but maybe afterward we can stop for some. If you're a good boy, that is."

He thrust a fist into the air. "All right! I'll be really, really good!"

We turned away from the ocean and up the steep incline that led away from sunny paths and into the canopied peak where Fred and Sherry's log cabin sat beneath a forest of pines. I rolled down our windows and slowed the car, allowing the minty fragrance to waft into the car and the crackle of dried pine needles to fill our ears.

"I never been here before." In the rearview mirror I saw him dust his gaze back and forth between the side window and the windshield. When we reached the top, he pulled himself forward in his booster seat, craning his neck and pointing out the windshield. "Hey! We can see the ocean from way up here."

"Yup, we sure can." His enthusiasm made my heart leap a little. Knowing the cabin was empty, I pulled into the grassy driveway and turned off the ignition.

"We coming here? It looks like Lincoln Logs!" Jer's forehead wrinkled when he was unsure of what I might say.

I pulled the key out of the ignition and swiveled around to him. "We sure are. Want to go investigate?"

"Yeah."

"'Kay," I whispered. "Come on."

I unlatched his booster seat and he dropped into scattered

pine needles and bounded away from me. If I hadn't jogged over and scooped him up, he might have scaled the tiny cabin built from logs smooth enough to resemble toy pieces. We pressed our noses against a wavy glass pane, squinting and straining to see through the gauzy curtain that hung over the window.

"Are we like spies or something? I seen this on TV, Mama, and you're supposed to be wearing black clothes."

I giggled. "So are you."

He wiggled from my grasp. "Let's go see what's 'round here."

I chased after my son, noting that the speed he'd gained over the last few months corresponded with the lengthening of his young legs. The air felt crisp and clean up here, and I gulped breaths in an effort to keep up with him.

"Look, Mama! A jungle gym!"

As I had hoped, the former tenants left the play area intact. I'd wanted to ask Fred if the play set belonged to him, but living up here was dream enough. Why push it? I kicked my toes through dried leaves and needles, and then settled against the squeaky fence to watch Jer scramble up the slide. He threw a guilty look over his shoulder, knowing this was not allowed in preschool, but I laughed and waved him on.

Lord, will I be able to pull this off?

Arms crossed, I glanced around the property, imagining us living here, Jer and me. I pictured smoke curling from the stone chimney, golden light showing through the windows, maybe a puppy romping around the rustic backyard.

Something about that fantasy felt all too familiar. I'd had this dream before when married to Len. Oh, I would never have done anything about it. I'd promised myself to him for life, believing in the sanctity of marriage.

But every once in awhile, when Len was away and before I learned the truth about his criminal activity—and worse, his ongoing, remorse-free affair—I'd wonder what life would be like without him. I'd picture Jer and me living somewhere not unlike this quaint cabin. I'd grow a garden of vegetables and he'd chase our dog in the yard until the sun dropped beyond the horizon and I called him in for dinner. Len never appeared in that picture.

The memory made me feel ashamed. *I'm not worthy of your sacrifice for me, Lord.*

Jer tumbled off the steps and landed with a thud, breaking me out of my self-imposed misery. I rushed to him, hoping not to see this moment end with his tears. Instead, his laughter broke through the clouds forming in my heart.

"That was fun! I'm going again!"

He scrambled up the stairs then, taking the same old chances, not worrying whether he'd keep his footing this time—or come tumbling down again.

Had I ever been that carefree? Could I ever be? As I stood there, my heart sank a little. Unlike my son, I was afraid of falling.

Chapter Seventeen

I hadn't meant to be so lax in attendance. Gage had invited me to church with him for weeks, but I'd put him off.

Ever since Wednesday when Fred called for me from his hospital bed, inciting the curiosity and downright suspicion of others at work, I'd begun to feel like a pariah. Between Letty's near silence while restoring the door project the rest of the week, Timo's raised eyebrows, and a few snarky stares from the others, it appeared that I had been tagged the brownnoser of the day. Scratch that—make that the month.

If that weren't enough, I had my own conscience to deal with. Sure it was clear when it came to Fred and Sherry. They had hired me to decorate the cabin, and I jumped into the task with eagerness, hoping that the miraculous would occur, and

I would somehow earn enough to live in it too. Nobody needed to know about that.

Deeper issues, though, kept cropping up, reminding me of my unworthiness and need for something other than a long walk at the beach. Any day now, Len would show up here, and how would I handle that? What if he wanted partial custody of Jer? Or, to patch up our failed relationship?

And what about Seth and his belief that somehow I'd been the one to walk away from my commitment to marriage? True, Len was responsible for the ultimate sever, but shouldn't I share in the responsibility, remembering how I had fantasized about singleness?

I needed God to show me what to do.

Gage stopped at the entrance to a long hall. "Do you want me to walk with you to Jer's Sunday school class?"

I waved him off. "No, go ahead and sit. I'll come find you in a minute."

"Let's go, Mama!" Jer pulled me by the hand down the hall and into a sea of preschool-aged children. A couple of women blocked the entrance but parted rather than let Jer plow right through them.

"Hello again." A middle-aged woman with straight silver hair and round wooden beads in primary colors hanging around her neck greeted me. "Good to see you. Please sign in." She tapped a clipboard, then took off toward two young boys sparring with a couple of plastic chairs.

"Divorce is so easy to come by these days, but look at what it does to the children."

I jerked my head around. The women blocking the door-way now stood to the side of it, chattering on as if in a bubble.

"If people realized the long-term effect of divorce on children," the other one said, "they wouldn't agree to one so quickly, would they?"

The first one bobbed her head. "Mm-mm, no ma'am. I don't think they would."

My pen hovered over a blank line on the sign-in sheet, but my mind spaced out on my own son's name. *Maybe if people had a little compassion and realized the reasons behind a person's divorce, they wouldn't be so quick to judge!*

"Did you have a question?" The Sunday school teacher reappeared at the clipboard with a smile and a questioning gaze.

I stared at her. "Sorry?"

She pointed at the clipboard.

I blinked. "Of course. Sorry. Lost in thought for a moment."

She patted my shoulder. "Happens to me all the time. Not to worry. He'll be safe and sound with us." After I filled out the line with Jeremiah's name and my signature, she handed the pen to a parent waiting behind me. "Enjoy the service."

With a vague nod, I spun around and hurried past the two women who continued to share their opinions about my life.

Callie met us after church in the late afternoon for a stroll in downtown Otter Bay. Okay, *downtown* was a stretch. More like Main Street USA, with a candy shop, knickknack boutiques, and a corner bank. Kind of like Stars Hollow from an old *Gilmore Girls* episode, only with two thrift stores, and that whole beachy West Coast vibe going for it. The entire town, it seemed, stepped out of their homes on Sunday afternoons wearing their flip-flops and frolicking about the streets on sunny days like this one.

"Wish I could've joined you at church. How was the sermon today?" Callie bit into a caprese sandwich she picked up at the deli before meeting us.

"Oh, fine." *Yeah, that's good, Suz. Don't give it away that you weren't listening all that much.*

Gage picked up the conversation. "It was all about the woman at the well. Erik talked about how surprised the woman was that Jesus would actually talk to her."

"Oh, right." Callie licked one finger, then pointed it in the air. "Because not only was she a Samaritan, but everybody knew she lived with a man." She turned to Gage. "I always thought that was a twentieth-century-and-beyond thing, but whatever. Anyway, it would have been a no-no for a respectable Jewish man to speak to her, especially in public."

I nodded as Jer clung to my hand, swinging my arm front and back like a seesaw. "Yes, uh-huh, the woman at the well."

We stopped in front of the town thrift store, just a rock skip from the Dairy Cone, and waited for Callie to finish her sandwich. A movement through the thrift-store window caught my attention, and I pressed my nose against the glass, shading my eyes with one hand.

Gage continued. "Anyway, she got over her surprise and—"

I turned to him, my hand still shading my eyes. "Who did?"

"The Samaritan woman."

"Ah, that's right." I went back to peeking through the window.

"So when Jesus offered her water, she was all for it. But she was thinking he meant *real* water, not spiritual water. She didn't want to have to keep making the journey to the well and thought if she drank the water he talked about, maybe she'd never be thirsty again."

Was that Letty? I pushed my nose against the glass again, then pulled back. I'd just left a skin smudge against it. *Gross.* When I leaned forward to take another peek, the woman I'd seen through the thrift-store window had vanished.

Callie finished her last bite of sandwich. "Then there's that part where Jesus starts telling her things about herself, things he could only know if he was, well, God."

Gage nodded. "At first she thought he was a prophet, but then he revealed to her that he was the Messiah. Up until that point, she had kept mostly to herself. But when she realized that she'd met Jesus, she became so excited, she ran off to tell everyone about him."

I'm not sure who resembled fish more—me pressed up against the glass or the myriad customers swimming through the thrift store's clearance rack. When no sign of Letty resurfaced, I backed away from the window.

Callie's eyes searched Gage's face, one hand propped on her hip. "I love that story." Her voice was breathless when she said it, and somehow, I couldn't imagine her using the same tone when complimenting the pastor.

Gage smiled at her and tweaked her nose.

She knocked his hand away and laughed. "I'm serious! I love God's heart in that story. How though we may have things from our past we're ashamed of, God changes us by his grace and uses us to win others to him."

I watched as my brother grinned and pulled his fiancée in close to nuzzle her cheeks, the words splashing over me afresh. *God changes us by his grace.* Is it possible that Len had experienced God's life-changing grace in a prison cell? Could I believe it to be true?

Gage broke my reverie when he squatted down until face-to-face with Jer. "Ready for some ice cream?"

You would think my brother had invited Jer to Disneyland. My son threw both arms around my waist, squeezed tight, and looked up at me with that toothy grin of his. "Let's go eat lotsa ice cream, Mama."

I wrapped my arms around his shoulders. "Before your dinner?"

Jer wiggled his head up and down, and I shot Gage a mock withering look. "Okay, buddy. Just this once!" I paused. "And you know what? I'm having something with mocha in it."

Jer pulled away and began to skip. "I want something purple!"

Gage screwed up his nose and mouth, but Callie pushed him along, laughing all the way. "Purple's all the rage, my love. Get with it."

I followed them all to Dairy Cone, stopping short of the entrance when something familiar caught my eye. I swiveled toward the thrift store, and there stood Letty on the sidewalk rummaging through a bag. Back inside the ice cream store, Gage was holding Jer up to the freezer case. Callie stood next to them, reading off the names of the different flavors. *They won't miss me.* I slipped away and walked up to Letty.

She jerked her head up. "Oh. It's you."

"I thought I saw you in there." I flicked my head toward the thrift store. "Beautiful day, isn't it?" The words sounded hollow, but what could I do? She'd been ignoring me for days, and I wanted to break the ice somehow. I hoped to fix whatever had turned her cold toward me.

"So what? Now we're going to talk about weather?"

I smiled. This was the Letty I knew and loved. "So what'd you buy me?"

She frowned. "Oh, this? Just some old rags to use around my house. Nothing important."

"My family's in the Dairy Cone. Will you join us?" She didn't answer right away. "I'm buying!"

Letty scowled. "You make me sound cheap. Okay, I'll have an ice cream, but if I gain even a single ounce, you will hear from me."

I looped an arm through hers and laughed, pulling her along. "Come on, my friend. Let's go get fat together."

With our old camaraderie held together with tape and twine, we entered the ice cream shop. Callie and Jer huddled around a chipped metal table while Gage caught sight of us and dragged over two more chairs. We hurried and ordered our cones—raspberry swirl for her, mocha chip for me—and joined the rest of the clan.

And that's when I noticed Seth and Holly quibbling at the corner table. *How could I have missed them?* I didn't mean to stare, but never before had Holly looked so . . . animated. Her curly hair bobbed each time she jabbed her forefinger at his face. Seth stared back at her, his expression as frozen as the ice cream in my cone. Silence permeated the air.

Callie spoke first. "Looks like trouble in Paradise. I've seen Holly perturbed before, but she's giving him what for like nobody's business."

One of Gage's eyebrows rose. "Perturbed?"

Callie grimaced and swatted his arm. "Stop it. What would you call it, then?"

He turned his head only to have every woman around the table lunge for him. He swiveled back to us. "What did *I* do?"

"You can't look at them," I barked. "It's rude."

He laughed under his breath. "Oh, really. And what are all you ladies doing, then?"

Letty watched him, stone faced. "Observing."

He pressed his lips together, clearly unable to read Letty and know how much she enjoyed messing with him. *I loved how easy it was to play my sweet brother.* He rested one elbow on the table and eased his gaze over to Holly and Seth's table. "Why didn't you tell me we were *observing*? If I'd known, I'd have gotten into proper position."

Okay, so he wasn't all that easily played. *Touché, big brother.*

A spoon clattered to the floor. Holly stood, kicked her

chair under the table, tossed a wadded napkin onto the table, and fled the Dairy Cone. To his credit, Seth attempted to charge after her, but before stomping out, Holly told him in no uncertain terms to leave her alone. With no shame for guidance, all four of us—Jeremiah excluded—gawked as Seth slunk into his metal chair, an embarrassed frown on his face. Not to mention the added insult of a melting sundae.

Callie flicked her chin in Seth's direction. "You should go over there, Suz. He needs a friend."

"Can't. We're not friends anymore."

Letty let out a sigh. "What did you do to make him mad?"

My fingers clenched. Letty had done the same thing as Seth: cast blame on me. "He said some pointed things about me . . ." I glanced at Jeremiah who noshed on the final bites of his waffle cone. "Things both untrue and unfair. He has this twisted philosophy that he understands how I got to this particular spot in life. And that I carry the bulk of the blame."

"So stop acting like a wounded animal and set the record straight. And if he still won't accept you as you are, then as the Bible says, shake the dust from your feet and move on. It will be his loss." She shrugged in a dramatic, *que sera, sera* kind of way.

Gage drummed his fingers on the table, but when I glanced at him, he threw both hands up. "Don't look at me. I've been here before and know when I'm outnumbered."

I scowled. Seth's opinion of me still hurt. *"People in love don't just up and leave. Not unless they've got a reason."*

Callie nudged me out of my pity party. "You could offer him a little grace today. It's Sunday, after all." Her love of God's ways, coupled with her nurturing spirit, made Callie a gifted camp director. I admired her and didn't take her advice lightly.

Seth did look miserable over there, sitting alone and slurping his soupy ice cream. Maybe I could follow Callie's advice and offer him an olive branch. He looked like he could use a friend, and, as Letty pointed out, I needed to set some things straight with him. My gaze swung back to my artist friend, who with ice cream finished, had begun playing "Itsy-Bitsy Spider" with Jeremiah.

With a resigned sigh, I pushed away from the table. Maybe this would be my twofer—a time to patch up two relationships in one day. Purse and heart in hand, I approached Seth.

Chapter Eighteen

I don't know why a simple walk across to an ice cream shop required this kind of effort, like I was about to interview for some competitive job with the cranky head honcho of the corporation. Seth hadn't noticed me yet, so would it matter if I kept on walking out the door and up Main Street? I took another breath, another step. Seeing Seth slumped in that chair, looking much like a little boy whose water pistol had just been taken away from him, made me continue to put one foot in front of the other.

He didn't glance up when I reached his table. Instead, he offered a slight nod. A tiny smile attempted to form on his lips, one that seemed to say, "It figures." I think he may have even stifled a groan.

He wasn't going to invite me to sit; I could tell. So I pulled out my own chair and plunked myself into it. "Wanna tell me about it?"

He kept his head down but raised his eyes, surprising me. I thought they'd be filled with loathing, but instead I saw pain. Seth's downcast eyes made him look as if he wanted to cry. It shook me. *Had Holly broken his heart?*

"You don't have to say anything, Seth, but if you want to talk about what just happened, then I'm here."

He pressed his eyes shut. "Why?" Then he raked his head side to side, reopened those steely eyes of his, and let them settle on mine. "Why are you here?"

His directness unnerved me. Could he be wondering about my presence here so late on a Sunday afternoon? Or, more likely, was he questioning my reason for sitting across from him moments after a rather public argument with the town sweetheart?

A tiny ball formed at the base of my throat, and the cloak of stupidity enveloped me until I, too, began to ask myself the same question. *Why, Suz, did you think you had the right to come over here and offer a shoulder to a man who can no longer stand the sight of you?*

"You do know we were arguing about you."

My hand flew to my chest and I sat back. "There is no way I could have known that. Want to tell me why?"

He smiled again, even less convincingly than the last time. "Holly thinks I've been unfair to you somehow. She called me, oh let's see—judgmental, ornery, and oh yeah, cruel." His fist dropped to the table. "All because I offered you some advice."

Emotion tugged at the corners of my mouth as I

remembered the night Seth crashed my quiet work party at the studio. "Unwanted advice."

"You made that clear."

I looked again at him, seeing a curious mixture of anger and sadness vying for top billing on his face. The Seth I once knew had been carefree, almost to a fault. It's what drew me to him, and in the end, what tore us apart. And yet, part of me realized that his carefree spirit was the one aspect I had tucked into my heart and carried with me on this move out west. After all the pain and mistakes of my past, I wanted to believe that dreams existed—and that I could follow mine.

I searched Seth's face. Something had changed. *When had he become so complex . . . so hard to figure out?*

He hunkered forward. "You had something to say to me?"

I inhaled. "I didn't want or need your advice the other night. You crossed into my territory that night at work and offered your judgment of me, without knowing the truth—"

He sat straighter, his gaze still unwavering. "I'm listening."

I waved my hands and shook my head. "Never mind. I didn't come over here to take over the conversation and make it all about me. I did want to offer you friendship, which appears to have been a mistake." I pushed my chair back against the linoleum tiles and stood, noting from the corner of my eye how my family scurried out of the shop.

Callie gestured to the door and mouthed *Meet you at home.*

With only fleeting eye contact, I turned back to Seth. "I hope you and Holly work things out, but believe me, I'll stay out of it."

He reached out, wrapping his hand around my wrist. "Wait. Not two angry women in less than fifteen minutes." He loosened his grasp but didn't attempt to remove his hand. "How would that look?"

This time the grin that spread across his face appeared to be genuine. I couldn't face him but glanced around the shop instead, noticing more than one pair of eyes set on me. With his hand still holding my wrist, the sensation more comforting than should have been, well, *comfortable*, I lowered myself back into my chair.

Silence settled between us.

His gaze had softened and for an instant, I saw the boy from my past. "Can I ask you a question?"

"Sure."

"Come with me to the castle. There's a great lookout I bet you haven't had a chance to find yet."

I smiled at him. "That's not a question." This sudden whim of an idea reminded me of the old Seth I knew and . . . loved. How I wished I could pick up and go with him. Instead I sighed. "I have my son to get home to, and I've already spoiled his dinner by allowing him to eat dessert first. Don't want to have my parenting license revoked."

That familiar pained expression replaced his grin.

I shook my head. "Only kidding, you know. About the parenting license, I mean. I still can't go to the castle today, but . . . maybe another time?"

He answered me with a mustered-up smile and a brief nod. I stood, as the ringer on my cell phone indicated I'd received a text message. "Take care of yourself, Seth." I read my message while walking away, then pivoted back around. Seth still sat at the table, staring into space.

His eyes moved into focus as I held my phone out to him. He glanced at the screen, reading the message I had received, then back at me, an upturn at each corner of his mouth. "So Callie's taking Jeremiah to the movies, then?"

I nodded. "I suppose I can take you up on your offer, after all."

Chapter Nineteen

 It felt like playing with fire. In my head I justified this ride with Seth in his pickup truck. Just two friends, he and I, taking an impromptu excursion—like old times. I reminded myself that we still had issues to discuss, like my dissatisfaction over his judgment of me and how it came about that he and his girlfriend had fought over that same topic.

Queasiness rolled through my belly and settled on this fact. Seth had a girlfriend, so did I have any excuse for being alone with him, friend or not, as we turned up this drive toward a quiet lookout beyond Hearst Castle?

We reached that part of the driveway where tour buses parked, but Seth kept driving. "Suz, why don't you reach around to the back and grab a couple of sodas from the cooler."

I unlatched my seat belt, turned, and knelt on the seat,

spotting the cooler in the back. After flipping it open, I grabbed the top two bottles, shut the lid again, and sat back down. Laughter bubbled out of me.

Seth watched me. "What?"

I shook my head. "Wow. You're still drinking orange and cream soda. Who knew?"

"Hey, don't knock it. That stuff's the best, although not the easiest to come by. Some people just don't know a good thing when they see it."

He stared straight ahead, but something about the way he said that, as if goading me, made me wonder what else he might have meant.

"Yeah, well, I'm not knocking it, just surprised. I doubt I've had one since . . ." My gaze took off toward the distant meadow stretched across the hills. "Since we were practically kids."

"Seems like forever."

"The years have been a blur—so much has happened, you know?" Actually, he didn't know. My hands began to freeze up against the cold glass bottles. "Anyway, sometimes I shut my eyes and try to remember the former me."

"And then what?"

I shrugged. "A few memories come tumbling back, as if little time has passed at all."

Seth didn't reply. He pulled the truck to a stop in a service area beyond the castle entrance, unbuckled his seat belt, and grabbed both bottles in one hand. "We have to hike it from here."

I hopped out and joined him around the other side of his truck, noting the nip in the breeze. Seth's gaze brushed over me, and he reopened the driver-side door and reached inside. He handed me his sage-colored windbreaker and waited while I slipped my arms into it and pulled it closed around me.

"Better?" he asked.

"Much. Thanks."

"Follow me, then. And watch your step. It gets trickier up at the top."

I allowed my curiosity to replace the guilt that had formed on the ride up here. We moved along without words, my mind absorbed with the wooded incline. Wisps of fog glided away from the hill, revealing soft sunshine hovering over an ocean that sashayed and glimmered below. The climb continued and I began to breathe heavily, but I didn't mind. Soon enough we might be able to watch the sun sink below us and drop into the deep-blue sea.

The path narrowed and gave way to rocks and loose pebbles. Seth turned and offered me a hand, which I took and clung to during the final moments of our climb through a stand of manzanita and pine trees. Guilt tried again to enter my consciousness, but I willed it away with the simple explanation that although our fingers intertwined with one another, once we had safely reached the lookout point, all nonessential touching would stop.

We hiked to a plateau in the clearing. Seth let go of my hand and gave me a bottle of soda. "Turn around and feast your eyes."

While making the trek up here, I had taken in sips of the water, admiring the view as often as possible. But seeing it from this precipice, as the sun began to show off with rays streaking like lightning bolts across the sea, brought certain breathlessness to my soul.

"It's beyond words," I told him.

He guzzled a long drink, never taking his eyes off the view. "Something Hearst and I could agree on." He waved a hand in the direction of the castle. "*This* is what inspired him. It's where he played as a kid, probably scrambling up some of those very trees with nothing but a slingshot and some of these dusty rocks." Seth took another sip and glanced at me. "He often called this place The Ranch. It fits."

I lowered myself to the ground and sat cross-legged in the dirt. "And he only developed a small portion of it. Look around. It's empty for acres and acres."

He dropped onto the earth next to me, his knees bent toward the unending sky above. "Next you'll be telling me he gave all his money away to orphans and provided shelter for the homeless."

"You make me sound brainless."

He laughed. "I do not."

"I don't know much about Mr. Hearst, but I do know that it takes more than money to build a place as grand as all this. It takes vision and persistence. Why shouldn't I admire someone with those qualities?"

"Can't argue with that. It is strange, though, how revered this mere mortal was." He downed the last sip. "And still is."

"Revered is a strong word. I like to think of him as a quirky character from the past, like Walt Disney or something."

A smile worked across his face, and he winked. "Only he created this *Happiest Place on Earth* all for himself and his celebrity friends."

"Well, I read that he housed workers up here for fifteen years and that he paid 'San Francisco' wages at the time. That's saying something."

Seth glanced at me from the corner of his eye. "You would make a fine castle tour guide, you know that?" He grimaced. "Getting back to what you said earlier, lots of people have vision and persistence, Suz, but most of them don't build museums to live in. That's all *I* was saying."

"Oh, but the castle isn't a museum to hold art." My shoulders settled. "It's more like a giant tapestry, every detail in place and having its own purpose."

He coughed out a laugh. "Okay now, be honest. Where'd you find that? A brochure?"

I turned and watched him. "So you brought me up here to this beautiful site to make fun of me. You used to be such an adventurer, Seth. But this is what you do now for kicks? How disappointing."

"If I remember correctly, you used to be able to dish up a mean humble pie and shove it right into *my* mouth."

Memories of our gentle sparring matches surfaced, buoying the moment. "Remember when the girls and I beat you and your macho buddies in a game of bowling? Ha! We didn't even know how to bowl!" I cupped my knee. "We beat your proud booties, all right. So what can I say? You inspired my pie recipe on a regular basis."

He snorted and shook his head.

With playfulness, I bumped his arm with my fingers. Our laughter drifted away on the breeze and the sky began its change into evening. If we stayed here on this spot for a short while more, we would end up shoulder to shoulder under a blanket of stars.

"What inspires me most about Hearst, I think, is that he was brave enough to follow his heart." My gaze traveled toward the horizon, its edges glowing in pinks and yellows, before turning to take in his chiseled face. "You did that too, my old friend."

He gave a conciliatory nod. "Still working on that one. Sometimes . . . sometimes I wonder if that's always such a good thing."

"Why wouldn't it be?"

"Oh, I don't know. Sometimes following one's heart or dream or whatever you want to call it also requires a high level of selfishness."

"Hmm. So maybe that's why Hearst also once said, 'Dreams are meant to be shared.'"

Seth whooped and flopped back against the mossy hill. He smiled, his eyes open to the sky. "Oh, okay. Who's been reading her share of romance novels?"

I leaned back on my arms. "Stop it. He said it—not me!"

"Yet it rolled off your tongue without much thought."

I sighed. "Just focusing on the positive. Every life has its share of darkness, but it's the light that shines far brighter."

He twisted his lips, his face reflecting faint highlights from the setting sun, his smile more rueful now. "You're really starting to sound like Holly, you know." He let out a groan. "Like I said earlier when I told her about the spat you and I had, she defended you, Suz."

Considering the way we sat up here before twilight, just the two of us, I wasn't sure what to say in my defense.

"Didn't mean to draw such fire from you ladies." He sat up, his tone less jovial than before. "It's just that I loved someone once and made horrible mistakes. Big ones." He drew a deep breath and let it go. "Was just trying to save you the heartache."

He didn't offer any more insight into his statement, and though I wanted to ask, I couldn't bring myself to do it. When I'd first run into Seth, after so many years apart, I'd found him cold, indifferent. And I'd been selfish enough to think it had something to do with how I had hurt him years ago.

Tonight, however, it sounded like he struggled with another demon.

I took a breath. "My mother always told me that was impossible."

"What was?"

"She said it was useless to try to make me learn from her mistakes because in the end, I'd learn better when I made my own. Dad was always right there beside her, smiling and nodding. Sometimes he'd hide behind her saying 'yup, yup' while shaking his head 'no, no.'" The sudden memory caused me to laugh until a teardrop slid down my cheek. "They were such a pair."

Seth's voice took a heavy turn. "I don't understand how you do that."

My smile faded and I wiped my temple with the back of one hand. "What do you mean?"

His eyes searched mine, doubt creasing the space between his brows. "How can you talk about your parents without even a trace of bitterness?"

I blinked and thought for a moment. "Don't think for a second that I don't miss my parents terribly." I snapped a dandelion from the earth and twirled it between two fingers. "Maybe the reason you don't hear bitterness is because of what they left me with—the ability to see beyond my problems. Not that I have perfected this, of course. I struggle with doubt like anyone does. But my parents trusted God and stayed committed to each other, and that gives me hope. So much hope."

He nodded but didn't respond.

"Do you understand me better now?"

He kept focused on the horizon, and his eyes began to glisten. "I think so. Maybe. Time has passed. It's easier to take now." He hung his head. "It's one thing to accept such a tragedy as fact, though, and something far different to embrace it . . . as you seem to have done."

"Then you don't understand."

"No, *you* don't. Listen, you and I, we were both dreamers in our own way. I was the adventurer. What I lacked in education, I made up for in endless quests to experience all the thrills that life offered and to figure out my purpose. You, on the other hand, might not have wanted to travel like I did, but you've always had your head in the clouds."

"Hey."

"Admit it—you would scale a wall if it meant you'd find a silver lining at the top of it."

"It's because I have hope. I believe in God's promises."

Seth touched the fleshy part of my shoulder. Even through his jacket, I felt a ripple down my arm. "Talking about your parents as if they're away on a cruise is not reality."

I flinched. "Excuse me? What happened to make you so bitter?"

"Plenty."

"Well." Heat rose up my neck. "You're not the one whose *boyfriend* wanted her to fly off to la-la land while her mother was *dying.*"

Seth drew back. "Is that what you think? That I wanted you to abandon your mother? I was just trying to help you feel better. You were so sad, and—"

"And you wouldn't stick it out with me and help me grieve!" I flicked away a tear and breathed in and out, listening to the sound of my own breathing.

"Suz . . . I'm sorry."

I steadied my voice, ignoring the stricken look on Seth's face. "After my parents died, I clung to God, and to my husband."

The line of Seth's jaw hardened.

"And Len betrayed me."

Seth's scowl dissipated.

"But you know what? God never did. When I had nothing left, I clung to him alone, and he met every need—all the way down to sending me clear across the country so I would have a safe place to raise my son."

Seth reached for my hand. I shoved it away. His bitterness had bruised, and it had brought to the surface a watery memory I didn't care to revisit. I'd needed Seth to stay and comfort me, to walk me through the dark underside of grief. Instead, his constant pressure to run from my heartache warped my thought process and sent me careening into the arms of another man.

Len's arms.

Seth reached for me again, and though I attempted to resist, the familiarity of his caress, the warmth of his skin, lulled me. Two factions warred for my heart: despair over the past and the desire to feel his touch again. He moved so close his steady breathing grazed my cheek.

"Holly defended you . . ."

I pulled my hand away, my skin scraping against his. *Had I learned nothing from Len's betrayal?* I stood and dusted the earth from my jeans. "I have no right to be alone and holding hands with another woman's boyfriend."

"Wait. Let's talk. This has gotten out of hand."

The nip in the air had turned downright chilly. "You're right about that. I don't know what I was thinking . . . coming up here." *With you.* I looked away and gathered my thoughts, before swinging my gaze back to the man who sat at my feet.

His earlier assessment made me want to lash out. If I could dash off as Holly had done, I would have. Yet considering how far we were up on this mountain that roamed with wild animals, the idea held little appeal.

"I have betrayed Holly, and therefore, I've betrayed myself." I held back the tears. "Please. Just take me home."

Chapter Twenty

Worm holers.

The phrase intrigued me. Anything, I guess, to keep my mind off yesterday and my lapse in judgment in agreeing to hike up the peak behind The Enchanted Hill with Seth. The only thing enchanting about the evening was the view and even that paled on the way down.

Letty and I spent all morning on the door project, prepping the back side of the wood for finishing, and it was from her that I heard about the worm holers.

"They were hired in Hearst's day to make restored areas of wood look as ancient as the rest of the subject. There is an arched room in the castle Julia Morgan had to lengthen to fit—they used real ceilings shipped over from Europe throughout the place, you know. Anyway, Ms. Morgan had to insert sections of new wood into the arch, but the surface appeared too perfect, so she hired professionals to drill holes in it to match the authentic damage done elsewhere."

"Huh. So people lived up on that hill with the job title Worm Holer. Wonder how that looked on a résumé."

Letty stopped, her painted brows stretched upward. "They were set for life. You do not work for William Randolph Hearst or Julia Morgan and find yourself without a job."

Oh.

"How is our boss? Have you seen him?" Letty switched subjects faster than a game of *Jeopardy.*

"I stopped in on him this morning after dropping off Jeremiah, but Fred was asleep. Sherry told me he'll be going home today, though, so that's good news."

"Sherry is a good woman."

"She's very sweet and patient. The way she set up that room with handmade blankets and an iPod dock playing ocean sounds, I'm not sure he'll want to leave." I laughed. "She even managed to blow the alcohol scent out of there with some fragrant oils. I could learn from her."

Letty's head jerked up as if she'd heard a gunshot.

I tilted my chin. "What? Did I say something weird?"

"No." She shook her head, but the bunch to her forehead concerned me. "I think we are ready to paint, but not sure how much Fred will want us to do until he comes back. I'll check with him, and perhaps we can get started after lunch."

I stepped back to examine my portion of the door. Letty was right. The exposed wood begged for something to cover its nakedness while the protected areas wore a fresh, dry layer of clear finish.

"Suz?" Letty implored me with her dark eyes. "I believe you have a visitor."

Something about the way her gaze held me made me hesitate before I turned around.

Len stood several steps behind me, bearing a full blooming bouquet of tulips in his hands. The contrast between the colorful flowers and the man with ashen skin attempted to suck the breath right out of me.

"Len?"

He held the flowers out to me, his expression tentative. "Suzanna. Wasn't sure if you'd accept me."

If I were to reach out and take those flowers from his waiting hands, would that mean I accepted him?

Before I could decide, Letty swept in from the side. "I will take those and find a vase for them." Letty plucked the bouquet from his hands and shuffled off, as Len's eyes widened like a puppy's before dinner.

"You look amazing. Wow. You were always beautiful, but this place . . ." He took in the walls and rafters before settling back on me. "It must make you happy because you are a stunning woman. Your life here . . . it suits you."

I opened my mouth to speak but stumbled over the words, like Hugh Grant in, well, just about every movie the man has ever made. After taking my time—and a few deep breaths—my wits returned. "I'm sure you'll want to see Jeremiah soon,

but you'll have to give me some time to talk to him first, Len.
I haven't prepared him yet."

Confusion, or something like it, flickered in his eyes. "You
did get my letter?"

"I did."

"But you didn't know if you could believe in me again."

I couldn't meet his gaze, not because he made my heart
flutter the way he once had, but because his assumption was
dead on. I didn't trust him and wasn't sure if I ever could again.
Guilt poured over me at the realization, so I forced myself to
return his gaze. He had traveled all this way and stood here
now with sad eyes, repentant as ever. Wasn't I called to forgive
and forget?

And yet how could I forget what he had done to me? To
Jer? To . . . us?

Letty reappeared and cleared her throat. "I am going to
lunch. Feel free to do the same."

At her assuring nod, gratitude welled within me.

Len took a step toward me. "Maybe we should go somewhere and talk."

"Sure, okay." I hugged myself with my arms. "How'd you
get here?"

He stuck a thumb into the air.

"I see. No problem, then. Let's take my car." I glanced at
Timo who watched us with curiosity. "Be back in about an
hour."

He shrugged as if he couldn't care less. "Yeah."

Outside, the sun's light did little to warm me. I unlocked both car doors and got in, wishing I'd remembered my sweater.

"You seem nervous."

"Buckle up." I flicked my chin his direction and waited. He watched me with brown eyes that used to mesmerize me to the point of complete absorption. We made it to the edge of the drive, listening to the engine rumble, while I contemplated entering the highway. I studied him. "This is weird, Len, and I don't know what to do about it."

He reached over and placed a hand on my arm as I held on to the steering wheel. "We can go anywhere you choose. You pick."

I wrenched my arm from him, then regretted it. "Not that. I'm not even hungry." I switched off the engine, sat back against the driver's seat, and took him in. "What are you doing here? You do remember the things you said, right? How our marriage was one big headache? How you took up criminal activity because of all *my* needs?"

Len also sat back, and a frown tugged at his mouth. He lifted his chin and stared at the ceiling of my car, his blond hair grazing the seat rest. "Remember after you learned to drive, after I taught you by letting you take my car up and down the parking lot of that old drive-in movie theater?"

"Yes, of course."

He touched my arm once more, and this time I kept from flinching. "I want to see your face like that again. Your mom had died and your dad was getting sick, and even though we got you your permit, you were too scared to get out on the road and practice. So I took you to the lot early in the morning and late at night, and you parallel parked and made three-point turns until you almost puked."

A guffaw scraped out of me.

His smile returned. "Yeah, you know it's true. And that's why I came back here. To make amends and see you happy like that again. And also because I want to see my boy. I *need* to see him, Suzanna." He dropped his chin forward. "I regret what has happened."

"I know you do." A million reasons to push him out of my car and onto the busy highway volleyed in my mind, but I tossed them all into a net, wrapped them up, and shoved them from view. I'd been given a chance to start again here in Otter Bay, so who was I to deny Len his own second chance? Despite a slight lurch of my insides, I stuck my key in the ignition to start the car back up when Len's phone rang.

He scowled at the screen and gave me a sympathetic look. "Sorry. Mind if I take it?" He paused and held up the phone so I could see. "Parole officer."

I sat back. "Of course, no problem."

He slipped out and shut the door while I waited, trying not to eavesdrop. I turned my attention west to where the sea had turned inky blue, waves lapping against a distant rickety pier that reached a spiny finger into the deep.

Mr. Hearst's famous guests often arrived by boat and disembarked on that very pier before loading into a fancy car that would take them up the narrow road to the castle. I imagined them dressed in their finery, excited as they crested the hill-top, leaving their private worlds behind.

Sometimes, I envied them more than I cared to admit. *What would it be like to be whisked away on a yacht to the lavish castle in the sky?*

Len opened the car door and slid into his seat. "Sorry about that, Suz. He was all over me about staying in touch, but I couldn't get a signal before."

"Oh, I know. Cell service is spotty here. Sometimes I have to drive over to the public doggy run to pick up a signal. Even the Golden State can't quite get service everywhere."

He shrugged. "No big. He's good. I'm good." He laughed, showing off his signature white teeth, which made his skin tone all the more sallow. "We're all good."

I turned my key in the ignition. "I thought your parole officer was a woman."

"What?"

"I know she called the preschool, Len." I pointed the car south. "Scared the daylights out of the staff. You know, she didn't need to do that. It's not like I would keep Jeremiah from seeing his father."

He relaxed against the seat. "Oh, that. She's my parole officer's secretary, and she was only verifying what I'd told her. They have this thing in the prisons about not trusting the word of inmates."

"Hmm. I can't imagine."

He smiled. "You've changed, Suz. Really. Stronger than I've ever seen you." He paused. "Good to see it."

Taking responsibility for that? I shook off the ornery thought and glanced in the rearview mirror at the pier, watching it shrink as our car took us south. A flock of pelicans flew over it in a V-shaped formation. I really needed to spend more time over there . . .

"So, where are we headed?"

"Little Mexican hole in the wall. Nice views, plus they've got the hottest salsa around. *Not to mention, the place is outside of Otter Bay.*

In the quiet, I turned to see him staring. "You remembered." He shook his head. Was that remorse on his face? "The salsa they give you in jail tastes like ketchup with some chili powder thrown in. It's disgusting. Thanks for thinking of me."

I swallowed and accelerated down the highway, as confused now as on the day when the truth came out about all of Len's illegal activities. Truthfully, I had suspected him— maybe not of selling drugs but doing *something* he should not have been doing. We had too much money beyond his wages. And then at other times, it seemed, we had none at all.

I pulled into the restaurant parking lot, about to have lunch with my ex-husband. Could a person truly be reformed? And what should my response be?

Chapter Twenty-One

"When are you planning to talk to him?" Gage hadn't looked at his menu since Mimi handed it to him.

I gave my brother a hard stare, warning him, and then glanced at Jeremiah who smeared more butter on a cracker than it could hold. "Soon. Before bed, I think."

Gage pursed his lips and dropped his gaze to the menu, although I doubted he read it. It occurred to me that another word for *protective* was *worrywart*. My brother's reaction to everything Len made me rethink myself over and over.

I sighed. Second meal out today. For a girl who liked to cook, I'd spent a lot of time at the mercy of someone else's kitchen lately. If Gage hadn't suggested we meet up at the Red Abalone Grill tonight, I would have been satisfied with a tall glass of milk and a peanut butter-and-jelly sandwich at home. Tired did not begin to describe my feelings at the end of this long day.

"So what are you going to say?" My brother raised his head again to pepper me with questions.

My eyes widened in response.

Gage took in Jer, who played with a pile of crumbs on the Formica table. He shook his head and waved a hand. "Never mind. I know you've got it under control. Just wish . . ."

"What do you wish?"

"I wish the guy would just go away."

Although that would make life less complicated, I held out hope for Len. He said he'd spent hours and hours alone, giving him much time to rethink all he had done to mess up our lives. He said he wanted to prove to me that he had faced down his demons—well, not in those exact words—but he did say he asked God for a clean slate, and one had been granted him. So what if a niggle of doubt crawled through me like an elusive itch? Did I really want to miss being a witness to a God-directed change in Len's life?

A gust of wind brought Mimi to our table. "How we all doin' tonight? I see you brought your hungry fella in here again. How are you, Mister Jeremiah?"

"I'm. Good!" He nodded his head once with each word.

"Great!" She turned to me. "So what'll you have tonight?"

I handed her my menu. "Just a salad and a roll for me."

"And for your growing boy here?"

I nudged Jer, encouraging him to answer for himself. He stuck his forefinger up his nose, as if it helped him think, and I dragged his hand away. "I will have the . . . the chicken fingers!"

Gage gave Mimi a teasing wink and looked at his nephew. "I don't think chickens have fingers, do they Jer?" He glanced at Mimi. "He'll have the chicken feathers instead."

Jer giggled and held up one pudgy hand like a stop sign. "No! Wait! I want the chicken head. Yeah, that's right!" Again with the dramatic head nodding. "Chicken." *Nod.* "Head." *Nod.*

Gage plopped Jer on his flyaway hair with the menu before handing it to Mimi. "I'll have my usual turkey burger with green chili, and Callie will be here soon. She'll have the turkey club."

With a giddy grin on her face, Mimi stuffed the menus under her arm, saluted, and padded away to place our order with the cook.

I flopped against the booth and laughed. "Oh, it's always so much fun to go out with two four-year-olds. Seriously, I think I just got my second wind."

Jer kicked the bottom of the booth with the back of his solid rubber heels more than once, making my shoulders cringe each time. "Nu-uh. Uncle Gage isn't four, he's *old*!"

"Is that right?" Gage acted incensed, crossing his arms on the table and giving my son a what-for look. I relaxed, glad to talk about something—anything—other than how I'd be handling my bedtime chat with Jeremiah about his father.

Callie slid in next to Gage, threw an arm around him, and kissed his cheek. As usual, she looked fresh from a run or some other exhilarating activity. "Hi, all. What'd I miss?"

Gage and I exchanged a glance, and then I shook my head. "Your boyfriend ordered a chicken head for my son, so I guess you really didn't miss all that much."

Callie rolled her eyes toward Gage, as if searching for confirmation.

"Yeah, he did order me a chicken head. Bawk-bawk." Jer jogged his head up and down, and I made the decision right then to request that he not be given so much fruit punch at school.

Callie reached across the table and squeezed Jeremiah's hand. "If you don't like it, you are welcome to have some of Uncle Gage's burger. I'll even sneak some of his fries for you, 'kay?"

Jer wrinkled his nose and gave a shout. "'Kay!"

I winced, but Callie winked in my direction and leaned forward. "Maybe some protein and warm milk will do the trick."

"Hope so," I whispered.

Gage stared off into nowhere, like he'd fallen back onto his earlier worries. If Callie noticed, she didn't make it a big deal. Instead, she continued to engage Jer in conversation. "So how about you coming over soon to play with Moondoggy? He misses you, buddy. We could give him a walk out on the Kitteridge property, you and I. Wanna?"

Jer gasped, eyes wide, mouth open, and dug his little hands into mine. "Can I, Mama? Moondoggy wants to see me."

I nodded and rubbed the side of his head, reveling in the downy comfort of his flyaway hair. "Of course. We'll set it up soon. Maybe even tomorrow, if I end up leaving work early."

Callie tore open a packet of crackers. "Short day?"

"Yes. Fred's still not able to make it in, so Letty thinks we should wait for him before proceeding too far on our *ultra-secret* project."

Callie shrunk back, her voice teasing. "Oh, my, yes, you wouldn't want to divulge anything highly classified to me, a *commoner.*" She chuckled. "Okay, then. When will you know your schedule?"

My light heart faded. I had forgotten—or pushed out of my mind—Len's presence a mere few miles from here. Maybe making plans for tomorrow should start with him.

"Suz?" Callie held a cracker up to her mouth but waited for my answer.

"Here we are!" Mimi swooped in carrying three dishes. "So sorry, young Jeremiah, but the cook was all sold out of those chicken heads. He hopes you won't mind these chicken toes instead."

Jeremiah let out a dramatic sigh and rubbed his cheek, but a small smile emerged. "O-kay."

She slid two more plates onto the table. "Salad and roll for you, Suz. And turkey club for Callie." Mimi cackled at Gage. "Had to go out and grow some more green chilies. Be back in a sec."

I caught Mimi's eyes. "And could we have some warm milk too?"

She smiled, her mother's heart showing. "Already ordered. I'll bring it my next time around."

For the next twenty minutes, our attention turned to food, and except for an occasional camp story from Callie or slurp from Jer, sound from our table stayed at a minimum. Mimi returned with Gage's meal, waters for all, warm milk for Jer, and without being asked, a sweet and cinnamon-infused chai tea for me. Until a few sips in, I hadn't realized how much I'd needed the sustenance. True, I had lunch out with Len, but even truer, I'd hardly touched a bite.

In the midst of our quiet dinner, a contrast to some dizzying days and choices to be made, we watched the diner's owner, Peg, march in with a scowl. Funny how the rest of the staff seemed to scatter at her presence, like water receded after a penny thrown into a pond. After heading to the register and collecting the day's receipts, Peg left with a bulging vinyl money bag and a lift in her step that made her appear taller than usual.

Gage pointed at Jer's half-eaten dinner with the tines of his fork. "Aren't you going to finish your chicken toes?"

Jer shook his head, then showed off a yawn that forced his eyes closed. *Thank you, Lord, for the relaxing properties in warm milk!* His eyes fluttered a few times before he pulled his little legs up and laid his head on my lap, burrowing into the flounce of my cotton blouse until sleepiness overtook him. My hand fell across his rump.

Is he out? Callie mouthed the words, her forehead arched. I nodded.

"Good." She kept her voice at a whisper. "Tell us about your meeting with, um, his father."

I hauled in a breath and filled them in, how Len showed up unannounced, this time with a bouquet of flowers that wouldn't kill me, and about his parole officer's call, and our long lunch over quesadillas, spicy salsa, and a tureen of guacamole.

Gage watched me, listening.

Callie quirked her head to one side. "Where's he staying now?"

"Over at the Drift's Motel, outside of town. He says he's got a line on some work with a construction crew remodeling that old hotel next to where he's staying." I darted a glance at Gage. "Don't worry. I checked."

He sat back, his arms still crossed. "Checked how?"

"I drove through and asked a guy with a hard hat if they were hiring. He basically said, bring 'em on."

Gage look pained. "I don't know about this, Suz. He's not really planning on settling here, I hope."

I shrugged. "We didn't talk about that. I didn't . . . I didn't want to give him any wrong impressions or encourage him in any way." I stroked my fingers through Jer's blond hair. Several of the tendrils lay moist against his precious head. "The thing is, he badly wants to spend some time with Jer, and it appears that he has changed—he said faith has given him a new purpose in life and that is to be a better father. Anyway,

I promised him I would call him just as soon as my little guy here and I had some time to talk."

Callie studied Jer. "Looks like that won't be happening tonight. Poor tired guy. He must sense all this going on."

"You think?"

"Kids are smart. They know when something's up." She cupped her face in her hands, leaning on the table. "If it helps any, I think you're doing the right thing."

"What? How can you say that?" Gage frowned at Callie and she shrunk back. Then he angled his gaze to me. "And what about Seth? I had hoped you two might have rekindled something yesterday. What does he say about this?"

A knot formed in my throat. I shushed him and looked around, hoping none of Holly's friends or coworkers heard that. "Did you have to ask? He and I may have a history, but maybe that's the problem. We always start out well, but his bitterness gets to me and I snap."

"*You* snap?" Callie asked, her cheeks still reddened by Gage's outburst. "I can't picture it."

"Maybe *snap* isn't exactly the right word." My laugh had an acerbic bite to it. "I've never known anyone who could make my mood swing from one end of the spectrum to the other so easily and quickly. I had hoped we could be friends again, but . . ." I shrugged. "You might as well accept that the idea is far, far off now."

Gage tossed his napkin onto his plate. "He's a business owner now with a lot of guys on his payroll. That would make anyone intense."

"Intense? Didn't you hear me, Gage? He's *bitter.* Over what, I've no idea."

He shrugged and looked away. "I'd take bitter over someone like your ex any day."

"Oh, really? Then you go ahead and take him—I'm not interested. And from what I saw and heard yesterday, neither is Holly." I wagged my head, tightness in my shoulders. "Please don't put me on the defensive when it comes to Len either. I'm well aware of how much he hurt us, but time brings perspective, and the man I had lunch with today . . . I don't know what happened exactly to him, Gage, but he is different. That I know."

"The guy's a charmer."

I dropped my head into my hands, moaning, the telltale sign of a tension headache pulsating up my neck.

Callie's soothing voice reentered the conversation. "Maybe she should give him a chance to show how he's changed, Gage. I'm not saying she should welcome him back into her life as anything more than Jeremiah's father." She addressed me. "You know I'm not saying that, right?"

I lifted my head. "Of course not."

She reached out for my hand while taking Gage's with her other. Classic camp director, helping campers hug and make up. "Through the camp experience, I have seen the Lord work in miraculous ways with people, and what could it hurt for her to allow him to prove that he, too, has been touched by God?"

He brought Callie's hand to his mouth, kissing it. "I love you for your faithfulness, Callie. You know that. But . . . you've been burned before."

I winced and glanced away, not wanting to see a head-on train wreck. My dear brother had just made reference to the way the two of them had met—over a fight to save vacant, seaside land in Otter Bay. He had been the architect and she, his nemesis. Only it turned out that she'd been deceived in more ways than one. Come to think of it, Gage had missed several signs on that one as well.

Had he recalled that? I waited for the crash but heard nothing. When I turned my eyes back to Callie and Gage, she was slipping out of the booth and taking a crestfallen expression with her.

He held out his arm to her, but she continued to walk away, slowly, without turning back. "Callie, wait." He turned to me. "Now I've done it."

Chapter Twenty-Two

 I shouldn't have bothered to expend even one breath in defense of either Seth or Len. I'd never seen Gage like this, and by her reaction, neither had Callie. It crippled me to think I might have anything to do with tearing these two lovebirds apart. *Not* an option!

I thought about this while puttering around the art studio. Letty swept while I dusted tools and racks of jars, our door project lying alone and forlorn at our workstation. Sometime around ten o'clock, Sherry arrived with a fresh batch of carrot muffins and a carafe of coffee.

"Fred asked me to hold a meeting with all you dear people," she said, her apron stretched over wide hips.

Letty sat on a nearby stool. "How is our boss?"

"He's doing wonderfully. Thank you for asking, Letty. He

wanted me to tell you all that he will be here first thing in the morning to check on projects." She fished around in her pocket and dug out several cards. "But I am here to tell you that I do not want my Freddie working too hard or too late, and I need you all to promise me that you will send him home early, whether he looks like he needs the break or not. My mobile phone number is on these cards. Please take one won't you? And be sure to call me if he won't listen to you."

I pressed my lips together, stifling a laugh, and looked down at the plain concrete floor. *If that just isn't the cutest thing ever.*

Letty, however, was all business. She took the cards and began passing them out to the few staff members that had shown up today. "You have our word, Sherry."

"Goodness, thank you all very much. I hope you enjoy the muffins." She turned to leave but stopped. "Oh, and Suzi-Q?"

I smiled at her use of Fred's nickname for me.

"Freddie would love to talk to you more about working on the cabin. Do you think you might have time to stop by our home soon? Maybe even tonight?"

I hesitated. How would I fit a visit in between my talk with Jeremiah and his reunion with his father?

"You could bring your little boy with you."

Still smiling, I let out a breath. "Sure. I have an . . . appointment later today, so if you don't mind, I'll call you to confirm."

"Thank you, deary. We will look forward to seeing you later."

After Sherry left, Letty's voice accused, but her eyes teased. "Oh, so you made an appointment, hoping our boss would not make it in today?"

"So not true." I let out a loud sigh. "It's just that something has come up and, well, if I happened to have some time off today, then I was going to use it to figure out my life."

"Maybe I could help you 'figure out your life.'" She tapped a nearby stool. "Sit down and talk to Dr. Letty."

I smirked. "Oh, brother."

"Is this about the ex-husband? You have been quiet today, and yesterday as well. Unusual." She observed me, one finger tapping her chin.

I examined the ceiling. "I've been all over this with Callie and Gage and it's a mess really. In a nutshell, Len's staying nearby and wants to see Jeremiah, only I haven't had a good chance to prepare him."

"And what about you? The man has given you flowers two times. He is trying to win you back, Suz."

My eyes flashed, realization dawning over me. A mental snapshot of Fred and Sherry's log cabin appeared before me, close enough in my mind to touch. I saw Jer and me in the picture—and no one else. "I don't want him back. I don't want *any* man in my life, Letty." I peeked at my friend. "Do you think I'm selfish?"

"Selfish? No. I think you are scared to make the same mistake twice. You have been hurt and it will take a wise man to woo you into his life." She slid from the stool, picked up my purse, and handed it to me. "Go now, my friend, and enjoy your half day of rest. I think I will stop in at church and light a candle for you and say some prayers. Call me if you want to talk."

I pulled my bag over one shoulder. "Thank you, Letty. I will."

With each step closer to walking out of this building came the understanding that Jer and I needed to talk. At nearly five years old, the poor child had witnessed too much already. I pushed open the massive studio door and stepped into glowing rays of the overhanging sun, never having dreaded a day off quite this much.

"WHAT'RE YOU DOING HERE, Mama?"

After checking in at the registration desk, I found Jeremiah in the play area, sifting sand through a plastic strainer shaped like a boat. I knelt beside him. "My boss said I could go home early today and I thought you might want to come with me."

He dropped the sand toy and ran off, shouting behind him. "Okay, I'll get my shoes."

I watched as he pulled rumpled socks onto sandy feet, and then yanked on his sneakers. The Velcro straps were so clogged with sand and dirt that they barely held his shoes closed. *You're going to have to teach your son to tie laces, Suz.*

He stood and took my hand. "There. I'm ready."

I squeezed his hand in mine and we made our way to the front desk where I signed him out before heading to the parking lot for my car.

"I was thinking you could make me a grilled-cheese sand-wich for lunch."

"You were, huh?"

He swung my arm forward and back with the strength of a teenager. "Yeah. You haven't cooked anything for a long time!"

I forced the sound of laughter from me, fighting a pout. Didn't every kid in America *want* to eat out every day at every meal? Or was that a lie we had all been fed? Kind of like the one about "thinking good thoughts makes them happen" or worse, "zits disappear with adulthood."

I opened the door to my car and watched him scramble to his booster seat. "That sounds great. I'll make myself one too—with lots of butter."

He latched it himself. "Yeah, with lots and *lots* of butter!"

His enthusiasm for my grilled cheese-making ability chased away my burgeoning pout. We made the short drive home, past the Kitteridge property that overlooked the bay, the one Callie's camp had acquired. Construction had begun on the cabins Gage had designed for the new high school wing of the camp, as well as a gazebo overlooking the sea. Callie could hardly contain her thrill at knowing she and Gage would be married on that spot. I tucked away the memory of last night's dinner fiasco, hoping Gage and Callie had taken the time to make up.

"What'cha thinkin' about, Mama?"

I glanced in my rearview mirror to see Jer staring at me, his little mouth a straight line, the look in his eyes pensive. *It's true what they say: they grow up before you know it.* "Adult stuff. Things that mommies worry about."

"Like what?"

"Well . . . I was thinking about Uncle Gage and Aunt Callie and how they will be married soon."

"Why you worried 'bout that?"

I shook my head. "Oh, I'm not. They will make a beautiful couple. It's just that earlier today I was thinking about where you and I will live once they get married. I might have to work a little bit more to make enough money for us to move." We pulled into the driveway; I put the car in park and looked over my shoulder. "How do you feel about that?"

He stared out the window, fingers in his mouth, his face bathed in afternoon shade and a touch of breeze tickling the top of his head. I watched him thinking, his eyes growing wide, until he pulled wet fingers from his mouth and splayed them on the partially rolled-up window.

"Daddy!"

Chapter Twenty-Three

My insides jolted and I shot a look out the window. *Len!* He approached Jeremiah's window before I could reach for my door handle and leap out of the car.

"Jeremiah." He reached his hand into the window so Jer could grab hold of it.

"What are you doing here?" I jogged up next to my ex-husband, my voice reaching Minnie Mouse level. "You were supposed to wait for my call!"

He twisted toward me. Some color had returned to his cheeks, and with wisps of white-blond hair blown from the breeze, there was no mistaking his relationship to Jeremiah. "I only wanted to make it easier for you, Suz."

Jeremiah squealed from inside the car. "Open the door!"

I ignored him but kept my voice as low and even as

possible. "Easier for me? How? I told you I needed to talk to Jeremiah first. You should not have come here."

His hand still stuck through the open window, Len looked from Jeremiah, who still clung to his fingers, then to me and back to our son. "I knew it would be tough on you, explaining how much I'd changed and all. Isn't it better that we let the little guy see for himself?"

Hands folded together, I pressed them against my mouth, my breathing harsh. *Gage is going to disown me.*

"Mama!"

"I'm coming, honey." I pushed myself between them until their hands separated.

Jeremiah scrambled from his booster seat, out the open door, and into his father's arms. Len scooped up his son, giving him a bear hug and grinning wide. Shame washed over me. *Why had I kept Jeremiah from this reunion?*

Len continued to hold Jer in his arms, rotating side to side to side. "How ya doin', buddy? You've grown. It's so good to see you!"

Jeremiah's little hands held Len's cheeks, grizzled from a day without a razor. "You too. Mama and I were just going to have grilled cheese. You want some too?"

"Tell you what, Jer. Let's save the sandwiches for later. Why don't we show your father our beach instead? Doesn't that sound like fun?"

No way would I invite Len into Gage's house without him approving that first.

If Len noticed my quick save, he didn't let on. He set

Jeremiah on the ground, then pointed toward the west. "Is this the way?"

Jeremiah hopped with all the energy of a preschooler. "Yeah! Yeah!" He took Len's hand and began dragging him down the street toward the water. "Come on. Maybe we'll see some otters down there!"

I hit the lock button on my car key and scurried up next to them, my heart and mind spinning. Jeremiah continued to skip and hop along, chattering with his father, as if no time at all had passed. Maybe I had been overthinking this. I'd planned to prepare Jeremiah for seeing his father for the first time in many months, but they'd fallen into step with each other from the get-go. Jeremiah swung his father's arm back and forth like he'd done with mine. He talked nonstop and laughed easily as they made their way to our beloved beach.

I slowed my step, taking in their closeness, watching Len laugh while Jeremiah pointed at who-knew-what to the north. It occurred to me that the one I really wanted to prepare for this moment was me.

My cell buzzed in my pocket. I pulled it out and focused on the screen before answering. "Hi, Callie."

"Hey, Suz. Were you able to cut out of work early today?"

I rubbed my lips together, watching from the landing as Jeremiah and his father descended the steps to the rocky beach. Halfway down, Len reached into his own pocket, glanced around, and answered his phone.

"Suz?

My mind snapped back to Callie. "Uh, yes. Yes, I did."

"Great, then. Would you and Jeremiah like to come by and see Moondoggy? Or I could bring him by there, if you'd like."

"Actually? If you could bring him here, I think that would be best."

"Is everything okay?"

I nodded, not feeling it. "Sure, it's just that we've only now arrived at the beach by our house, and I think it would be neat to play with Moondoggy here. If you don't mind?"

"Not at all. Be right there. By the steps?"

I told her yes and jogged down the steps two at a time, joining Jeremiah and Len. My son spun around and grabbed one of my legs, making it even harder to trudge through the sand. "You're gonna knock me over, my love."

He clung to my leg, his head hanging backward. "Just pretend you're an octopus on the beach."

"An octopus? In the sand?"

He giggled. "Yeah. Then you could just walk on one of your other legs!"

"Or maybe I should shake my leg like a tree branch in the wind!" I stopped and pumped my leg until it hurt, Jeremiah's high-pitched squeal rising above the sound of curling and crashing waves.

"I'll save you!" Len swooped down and hoisted Jeremiah into the air, giving him a quick toss before catching him again. Our son's squealing gave way to uncontrollable giggles, and I took in the sight of them, drinking in the scene, my mind regretful over what might have been.

A handful of surfers in shiny black wetsuits bobbed in the

cove to our left, waiting for that elusive wave, the one that would make all that they endured worth the cold, long wait. I knew from watching them before that sometimes the perfect wave never came and that life would go on. They'd be back on their boards again, sacrificing their comfort, waiting and hopeful that their time would come.

It took weeks to accept Len's betrayal and incarceration, and several more to pick myself and Jeremiah up and allow us to land on Gage's doorstep. I couldn't have asked for a more loving brother or a better place for us to restart our lives.

But when I received that letter from Len last year, the one telling me he'd filed for divorce so he could remarry, another wound peeled itself open, exposing me to fresh, raw pain. Or maybe the old wound had reopened.

Now, though, the pain of Len's rejection of our marriage had lessened and the love I'd once had for him vanished—it was Jeremiah's affection for his father that changed the game. For Jeremiah's sake, I might have to jump back on my board and wait out the wave. I just hoped the sacrifice would be worth the wait.

I slowed the pace, hoping Len would follow suit, not wanting my heart to lose one more drop of blood over this. Besides, Callie would be here soon.

"You coming?" Len called.

I leveled my eyes with his. "Let's stay here and watch the surfers awhile more."

He shrugged. "If that's what you want."

Jeremiah's frown at having to slow down dissolved.

"Callie! Moondoggy!" He let go of Len's hand and sprinted past me, back toward the steps.

Len craned a look. "Who's that?"

Callie handed over Moondoggy's leash to Jer and I waited until they caught up to us. "Callie, I'd like you to meet Jeremiah's father, Len."

She shook his hand, and I turned to Len while linking her arm with mine. "Callie's going to marry Gage soon, and I can't wait to have her for a sister."

Although he did manage to nod and utter, "Congratulations," his eyes could not seem to find their focus.

Jeremiah tore past us, Moondoggy pulling him down the beach with that big, ol' pink tongue of his licking the side of Jer's face. The remnants of a wave dribbled up shore, lapping over them, and I cringed. *Mama's going to have to buy him a new pair of shoes.*

Len furrowed his brow. "Where they going?"

Thanks to Callie, a sharp whistle trilled through the air. Len's frown faded when both the dog and Jeremiah halted, paws and feet sinking into wet pebbly sand. With Moondoggy turned around toward his mistress and yanking on his leash, Jer bent down, unhooked him, and called out, "Go!"

Moondoggy pitched forward at full speed, but instead of skidding to a halt at Callie's feet, his eyes homed in on Len. In the distance I heard a growl build, one that morphed into a harsh spate of deep-toned barking.

Callie pulled her arm from mine and lurched forward, placing herself in front of Len. "Stop!"

Moondoggy did as told, whinnying his displeasure. Callie kept her hand steady in front of him, reminding him to "wait."

Jeremiah jogged up behind him, then dug his chubby hand into the scruff of the doggy's neck. "It's okay, boy. He's my daddy!"

If only I would have realized the sequence of events about to occur, I might have grabbed the leash from my son's hand and latched it to the collar around Moondoggy's neck. But it all happened too fast.

Jeremiah leapt into his father's arms, and Moondoggy, the animal that normally would not hurt a kitty, charged ahead and placed a quiver-worthy bite on Len's calf.

Chapter Twenty-Four

 "That mutt should be kept away from Jeremiah. *Ouch!*" Len tensed against the hard back of the Adirondack chair on Gage's deck, his mouth and nose contorted as I dabbed antibiotic cream on his wound.

"It's just a scratch." I dabbed away while nursing a scowl of my own.

"Yeah, sure. You say that while wiping away my blood."

I glanced up at him. Did he realize how silly he sounded? "Spare me. You of all people have been through much worse than this little nibble." I stuck a wide bandage across his abrasion and gathered up the rest of my first-aid supplies. The vicious dog attack was not part of my plan for the afternoon, then again, seeing Len today—or ever—wasn't either.

Len unrolled the cuff of his pant leg and brushed it smooth

again. "What did you mean about me being through worse? Can't remember ever being bit by a dog before."

The glower on his face made me want to laugh. I used to call that his man-pout because it never worked on me. On those rare occasions when we'd argue and he didn't get his way, that expression would claim his face and stay there all night. Such a grudge holder.

I shook my head, not wanting to answer his question. How levelheaded would that be to mention jail at this moment? Especially with Jeremiah within earshot?

He reached over, rubbed his hand down my arm, and held my wrist, imploring me to answer his question. "I'm serious about what I asked you, Suz. What were you thinking about?"

I stilled, glancing first at his fingers massaging my wrist and then into his face. He looked as harmless as one of those surfers sitting on their boards out on the water right now. In fact, with his sun-bleached hair and skin that warmed to the sun, he'd fit right in with those who spent every available moment looking for the perfect wave. *Why did that unnerve me so?*

I freed my arm from his hold. "Forget it. I'm sorry about the dog bite. Really I am. Moondoggy's never reacted like that to anyone in my presence." A wry laugh escaped. "He's so congenial we always joke that if a burglar were to break in to Callie's place, Moondoggy would probably give him the grand tour and show him where she kept the silver."

Len's eyes narrowed. Apparently, this was not the kind of thing to tell an ex-con.

I stuck the first-aid kit under my arm and stood. "Okay, awkward. Let's change the subject—"

"Heard there's been some trouble." Gage climbed the steps toward us, an unwavering gaze focused on Len. He set a cardboard tube onto an empty deck chair and leaned back against a pillar, his arms folded at his chest.

"Gage." Len stayed seated but nodded his head in that way that cowboys in old movies did when they acknowledged a person. Just one brief, sober-faced nod. I half expected to hear cowboy showdown music blowing in from the west.

My brother turned to me. "Callie said the wound wasn't too bad." Was that regret laced through his voice?

"Might want to rethink bringing that animal home to live with you." Len's hands were folded across his flat stomach. "If it were *my* fiancée, I'd find her a nice poodle or Chihuahua to keep her company."

Gage set his jaw, pulled away from the pillar, and took a step forward. "Is that right?"

I slid in between the two of them, my back to Len, my eyes pleading with Gage. "I think that under the circumstances, I should make us all some dinner. Okay by you?"

A muscle in my brother's cheek flexed twice before he spoke. "Jeremiah's going to need a bath soon and to get to bed early. Don't forget that his sleep schedule was interrupted last evening."

I nodded and guided him with a nudge toward the front door. "I know, so this will be a quick, no-frills meal. Baked macaroni and cheese, and then it'll be off to bed for all of us."

Gage hollered for Jeremiah, and waited until he bounded up the stairs and into the cottage, his mouth run amok. My brother followed him in while I held open the screen door and raised my eyes at Len. He climbed out of the chair and hobbled in, milking his injury, no doubt aware of Gage's disdain at having him here.

While Gage hustled Jer into the bathroom to wash up, Len followed me into the kitchen. I motioned for him to have a seat at the table by the window. A fry pan sat on the stove, so I switched on the burner beneath it. While I removed milk, butter, a hunk of cheese, and a bowl of precooked elbow macaroni from the fridge, Len glanced around the room, his fingers tapping on the tabletop.

An idea lighted his face. "So I was thinking that maybe I could borrow a board from someone and try surfing this weekend. Jer would like that."

I plopped a pad of butter into the pan and watched it sizzle. *He thinks we're going to be one happy family? Just like that?* "I don't know, Len. Depends on what else I have to do this weekend."

"Like what?"

"Well, for starters, my boss asked me to do some freelance painting for him."

"Really. Your *boss*, huh?"

I threw a look his way, noticing something hard in his eyes. "It's not like that. He and his wife own an old cabin in the hills, and they've asked me give it some, um, panache." I added the milk to the pan, then chunked up the cheese and threw

Julie Carobini

that in too. "Poor Fred had a heart attack last week, but all he seems to think about is getting the cabin finished. I may have to go up there this weekend and at least figure out what to do."

"Where is it?"

I swallowed and gave the cheese sauce a stir, watching the solid chunks melt into silky cream. The log cabin had taken on a life of its own in my mind, sort of my personal crusade. The closer Callie and Gage's wedding date came and the more I felt pressed by yesterday's mistakes, the more I longed to find a way for Jer and me to start over in the antique cabin nestled among the pines.

Did I want to share that dream with anyone—especially Len?

I shrugged and puttered around the kitchen, removing dishes and silverware. "It's a drive from here. Anyway, I'll have to check on that before making other plans."

"I'll have to wait for you to decide then."

My cell rang and I answered it before checking the number on the screen. "Hello?"

"It's me. Seth."

My heart pounded, and I turned my back on Len. "Oh, uh-huh?"

"You barely said a word coming down the hill the other night."

"Yes."

"And you're still upset."

Small bubbles began to form at the edges of the pan. I glanced over my shoulder to see Len staring at me.

"Still with me?"

225

I swallowed back a response and peered again toward Len only to find Callie on the porch. I could see her through the large front window, Moondoggy in her arms.

Len whipped around, caught sight of her too, and shook his head, "What the . . ."

I wrapped my hand tighter around my cell phone, conscious of Seth waiting on the other end of the line. "Um, yes—no. It's not a good time."

Callie leaned her face against the window and peered inside. She gave me a smile and a cute wave but pulled back when she noticed Len glaring at her.

Seth's voice cut in. "We need to talk. There's more to say."

Len kicked the chair next to him and stood.

"Seth, I have to go. Sorry." I let the phone clatter against the kitchen island, then wove through the living room to get the door.

"You're not going to let her and that mutt come in here." Len stood in the doorway now, arms folded, showing no signs of injury. He reminded me of a belligerent toddler.

I gave him a withering look and yanked open the door.

Callie cringed. "So sorry," she whispered. "Didn't know he'd still be . . ."

I reached for Moondoggy's leash. "Come on in, Sis."

She stepped inside. "You sure?"

Moondoggy traipsed in behind her and jumped onto my hip for a pet. His long arms reached to my belly and I nuzzled his head with my knuckles. He dropped to the floor, his nails landing with a clack.

Len stayed put.

Gage arrived from down the hall and pulled Callie into his arms. How would that be to have a spat and long to make up quickly like they had done? Her mouth grazed his ear with a whispered *I'm sorry* and I turned away from their private moment.

"Moondoggy!" Jeremiah clomped into the living room and threw his body over the dog, who responded with a *womp, womp, womp* of his tail onto the hardwood.

"Son, don't do that." Len's order silenced the room. "You come on over here now, where it's safe with Daddy."

Gage glanced up. "Jer's fine. He and Moondoggy are pals."

"That right?" Len pursed his lips and shoved away from the wall. "Well, I don't think it's a good idea, not when he up and bites a perfect stranger."

Callie rubbed her cheek. "Again, I am so sorry for that, Len. I—I really don't know why he did that, but it had to be a fluke. To my knowledge, he's never exhibited that kind of behavior before." She paused. "Are you feeling okay?"

His man-pout began to appear and he stepped into the room. Unfortunately, I didn't have a great grip on the leash, and Moondoggy let loose a growl and then tugged out of my grasp, dashing right for Len.

"No!" Callie hurled toward the kitchen and tackled Moondoggy before he could reach Len, who leapt onto a kitchen chair and kicked one leg at the dog to prevent another bite.

"I told you that mutt was dangerous!" Len called out to Jeremiah. "You are not to go near that dog again, hear me?"

Jeremiah dissolved into a mess of tears and buried his face in my lap, his little arms wrapped around my legs. I shook my head at Len, while caressing our son's head.

Gage rushed over, grabbed Moondoggy's leash, and hauled the dog away from the kitchen. He wore a frown before grabbing a jacket from the coatrack and marching out to the front porch, shutting the door behind him with enough effort to shudder the wall.

A faint curl of burnt-toast smell wafted under my nose. I turned to see Callie's nurturing side emerging again as she coaxed Len down from the chair, apologizing profusely. Jer continued to cling to my legs, dousing my jeans with slobbery tears. I stroked his head, and lifted his chin, taking in the distinct smell of . . . smoke?

Dinner!

I wriggled out of Jeremiah's grasp and sprinted to the kitchen, just in time to watch my cheese sauce burning and bubbling over on the stove, the black and yellow substance as appetizing as melted candle wax. I switched off the fire and grabbed the fry pan without thinking.

"Yeow!" The handle scorched my palm and I dropped the overladen pan onto the floor, splashes of hot cheese sauce splattering across the fabric of my semiwhite sneakers.

With the leash still wrapped around her arm, Callie lunged for the freezer and pulled open the door, filling her hands with ice. "Here." She shoved several cubes into my hand. "I'll fill up a bag with the rest."

I held the ice on my hands, the burned area throbbing against the cold, as I took in the mess around me.

Callie took the dripping ice from my hands and replaced it with a clear plastic bag of ice. "Keep this on it." Sympathetic eyes flashed close to mine. "Listen, I'll take care of Jeremiah for you tonight. Why don't you and Len go over to the RAG and get some dinner?" She threw a look over her shoulder at him as Moondoggy whined at our feet. "My guess is you two still have a lot to discuss."

I swallowed and opened my mouth to protest but she shushed me, tears filling her eyes. "It's the least I can do."

Len gave Jeremiah a pat to the head and stood by the doorway. "She's right. We still have a lot of talking to do, Suzanna. There're things that need to be said."

My gaze slid to him. I used to love when he called me by my full name, the sound lyrical to my ears, but at this moment, all I wanted to do was tell him to *shut up*.

Chapter Twenty-Five

 When our marriage lay hemorrhaging, I continued to cling to the promises we'd made by cooking lush dinners each evening, hoping those efforts would somehow patch the torn remnants. I read cookbooks and researched recipes on the Internet, buying the proverb that *the way to a man's heart is through his stomach,* and some days were better than others.

In reality, Len and I ate dinner together less than once per week, because most nights he didn't make it home until the heat had long dissipated from the meal. And by the time he did arrive, I was already deep in the throes of my maternal duties of feeding, burping, and diapering, far too lost in turmoil.

Tonight marked the second time in a row I would sit across the table from my ex-husband and share a meal. As we waited to be seated for dinner at the RAG, the irony of it all needled me.

Mimi slapped her rubber-soled shoes across the linoleum floors and grabbed a couple of menus. "Hey, Suz. I'm thinking of putting a sign on your regular table. Right this way."

I eked out a wan smile at Len. "I come in a lot."

She seated us at the same table where Gage, Callie, Jeremiah, and I had dinner last night. Mimi was right—I often found myself at this same table at the center of the diner. I made a mental note to switch things up next time and ask for a seat near the window. At least I could watch the door from here. *And plan my escape.*

"Chai for you tonight, Suz?" Mimi's pencil stood poised over her order pad.

"Actually, I'll have an iced tea with lemon."

Mimi nodded, smiling. "Living large tonight. I can appreciate that." She turned to Len. "And something to drink for you, sir?"

I straightened. "Sorry, Mimi. This is Len, Jeremiah's father."

She peered at him above flat-rimmed reading glasses. "It's about time. A boy needs his father."

Len managed to pull his mouth into a smile, but his eyes had hardened. I could tell. He tipped his head. "Ma'am."

She didn't blink. "What can I get you?"

"Nothing yet."

She stuck the pencil above her ear. "I'll be back in a few for your orders."

She rocketed away from our table and Len watched after her. "She always a crank like that?"

"Not really. Maybe she's having a bad night. Let's figure out our order so we can talk. I've got a busy night ahead of me."

"Busy night?" He furrowed his brows. "Thought Gage and his fiancée were coming to your rescue and taking the kid off your hands."

I paused. "It's true—they are taking care of Jer, but I promised my boss I'd try to stop by later with some drawings."

"So you're going up to the cabin you mentioned."

I glanced around the diner, taking in tables occupied by animated people talking with each other. Everyone looked happy to be here in this stark but aroma-filled diner, sharing a meal with another soul.

Len grimaced. "Lost you there for a second. That's not familiar or anything."

I crinkled my eyes. "Did you ask something?"

"Just if you're going to that cabin you told me about."

"Cabin? Oh no. Not tonight." I checked the time on my cell phone. "The plan was to stop by my boss's home this evening, but it may be too late for that by the time we're done. Let's hurry up and order."

He raised both palms. "Fine. What's good in this dive?"

"Salad. Salad's good." *And doesn't take any time to cook.*

He pursed his lips. "I shouldn't have asked." He shut his menu with a *phwat*. "I'll have a bacon burger and fries. Not much they can do to mess that up."

I slid my menu to the end of the table, waiting and wondering again why I had agreed to dinner out. Then again, I knew. Guilt, or the big "g" as my mother used to call it, elbowed its way into my life the minute I saw Jer's reaction to Len's arrival. Add to that the bite Moondoggy took out of Len's leg, and I was a goner.

Mimi delivered my tea, took our orders—this time without comment—and skittered away with a promise to return "real soon."

After she left, Len straightened his arms, clasped his hands together, and dropped them onto the table in front of him. "So you found work as a painter."

I quirked my head and slid a sideways look at him. "That's random."

He leaned forward, which caused me to push myself away until one of the ridges in the vinyl-upholstered seat dug into my back. "Not at all. I've been hoping for a chance to hear about your career. You were always so good with that kind of stuff." He nodded. "I'm glad you found a way to make money with it."

I wagged my head from side to side, as if weighing his assumption. Sure, I made money, but would it be enough? That was the question that had me lying awake at night, contemplating my future with my son.

"It's a good job." I gave him a small smile. "And, um, I'm glad I found it too."

He watched me with eyes like dark chocolate. I'd always found that such an interesting contrast: dark eyes, tan skin, bleached-blond hair—only after time in jail, his skin had lost some of its glow and the streaks of sunlight in his hair had faded.

"This isn't just small talk, Suz. I remember the way people would say you were a 'natural' artist. 'Course, you didn't spend all that much time pursuing it." He lifted both shoulders and let them relax again. "Maybe if you had, I would have realized how important being an artist was to you."

"If you'd been home, you would have known how much time I did spend on my art. Or at least the amount of time I *tried* to spend on it." I batted a sore hand in his direction. "We're beyond this now. Let's not argue."

He shook his head. "You're right. If I'd been home instead of beating down doors, trying to earn a better living, I'd have known. It's my fault."

I stared at him. *Trying to earn a better living? Like selling a more sought-after illegal drug? Or filling up bigger bags of weed?*

I swallowed back the tirade that threatened to go public. "You know, you never took any interest in my love of art before this. Finding those classes was a godsend, but whenever you got home and I'd try and show you my work?" My head shook, as if trying to disassociate from the memory. "Well, you never seemed to care. I might as well have been showing you the results of my yearly blood test."

He hung his head, groaned, before raising his chin to look at me. "Sure I did."

I held him in an unwavering gaze. "You said watching paint dry wasn't your idea of a good time."

A patronizing look—or was it regret?—crossed Len's face and he reached out to me, his fingertips grazing my crossed arms. "Come here."

He touched my good hand and I let him. I don't know why I did. It's just that for once in a long while, Len appeared regretful, and it didn't seem right to squelch an emotion that had been a long time in coming.

"From what I heard, you're working to restore priceless art. They don't trust just any old hack to do that kind of work."

I slid both hands off the table. "Thanks . . . I think."

"You know what I'm getting at. You're trustworthy and honest, and I bet they love you over there."

"And you know all this how? In fact, how is it that you were able to find the studio, as I don't recall ever mentioning its location?"

"Some character named Timo." He laughed. "That a real name?"

Timo. "I'm afraid it is. And you're right; he's a character for sure. How do you know him?"

Mimi arrived, dividing us by sliding two plates—salad for me, hamburger for him—in front of us. "Ketchup?"

Len wrinkled his brow at her. "You had to ask?"

She rolled her eyes upward and sighed. "Be back in a flash."

I munched my lettuce, waiting for him to answer.

"Right, Timo. She, uh, my parole officer's secretary got your work number from the preschool, but when I called, you weren't in. The guy's a real romantic, though. When I told him I was planning to surprise you with flowers, he gave me directions."

Something tells me he was more than happy to tell my formerly incarcerated ex-husband where he could find me. "I'll have to thank Timo later, then."

Len smiled and I regretted my comment, realizing he hadn't heard my sarcasm. He bit into his burger and savored it for a moment, causing me to wonder if he was comparing it to jail food. We continued to eat in silence until he set his burger aside, wiped his mouth, and took a tall sip of water.

He implored me with those chocolate-colored eyes of his. "I suppose this is as good a time as any to bring up the dog incident."

I bit back a sigh.

"You know that I just wanted to protect my son."

I pressed my lips together, weighing my answer. He had to know that protecting our son had been my number one goal since he left us. It's what brought me all the way here to Otter Bay. Then again, he's already said that this is what brought him here too—or at least, one reason he came all this way.

I opened my mouth to speak, then let it flop shut as the door to the diner swung open and in walked a party of five women, laughing and gesturing and talking all at once. Holly was among them. She noticed me right away and came charging over. *Could she see the guilt wearing down my face?*

I slid out of the booth to greet her.

"Well, if it isn't the girl I needed to see. How're you doin', Suz?" She turned to Len before I replied. "I'm Holly. My aunt owns the place and I work here but I'm not on duty tonight." She turned back to me. "Havin' a little party with my sisters and some friends." She thumbed in the direction of the women shoving tables together across the room.

On alert that Holly may have something a bit stronger to serve up after the greetings had concluded, I found my manners. "Holly, Len is Jeremiah's father."

She brightened. "Oh, my, well don't you have just the most precious son? Jeremiah and I are good friends. Happy to meet you, Len. Hope you won't mind but I'm gonna steal Suz away from you for a few minutes." She linked arms with me. "Come on over and say hi to the girls."

I gave Len a tight smile and followed along, half expecting Holly to tell me to stay away from isolated hilltops—and her boyfriend while I'm at it.

Instead we hovered near the edge of the party. The "girls" were women celebrating a birthday, and if I bet money, I'd say the honoree was the one wearing a princess crown and sitting in the center of the row of seats. I recognized her as the wife of the town's new fire chief.

Holly patted the inside of my arm as we walked. "I wanted to thank you for what you said to Seth. That boy's been hurting something awful, but you set him straight and got him thinking. Don't know exactly how the good Lord's gonna use it all, but I see him startin' on Seth already."

This is not what I had expected her to say. *Stay away from my boyfriend.* Or *keep your opinions to yourself.* But serving up a thank-you? My head swayed side to side, unable to believe it. I took in her beaming face. "Holly, I wish I knew what you meant . . ."

"All I've gotta say is you shared your faith and that man really needed to hear it." She bent sideways and gave me a hug. "You're a sweetheart."

Oh, don't say that . . .

She straightened, her eyes popping wide. "Look who's here now." She unhooked my arm and waved a lithe hand toward the door where Seth stood in work jeans looking like he'd just spent the better part of this good day on top of a ladder.

The smile he had for Holly froze when he noticed me standing next to her. I whipped a glance around, like a cat searching for her escape. It didn't matter. He approached us, strolling with confidence toward the growing party atmosphere in the middle of the restaurant.

"Hey, Holly." He gave her a hug and a kiss on the cheek, then bent over and kissed my cheek too. He pulled away, as if he'd startled himself.

"Aw, sweet." Holly kept grinning and I began to wonder if the town's cherished waitress had eaten too many of her rum muffins.

"Good to see you, Suz."

I blinked more than necessary. "You too, Seth." *I guess.*

"Joining the party?"

Holly cut in, her boisterous head of curls bouncing as she spoke. "You know you'd always be welcome, but Jeremiah's daddy is probably missing you some by now. Tell him I'm sorry I stole you away for so long, would you?"

Fade to Blue

I swallowed and took a step away, retreating. "Of course."

She hugged me again before allowing one of her sisters to yank her back into the fold of chattering women again.

The color in Seth's face had deepened, and the confident air he'd walked in here on vanished. His robust shoulders dipped forward in a slight slump, and he spoke, not taking his eyes off my ex-husband, who downed a burger across the room. "You didn't mention he was coming for a visit."

I licked my lips. Would this be the appropriate time and place to mention that the man had found God, been released from jail, and traveled across the country to find his son—and me? "I didn't know it at the time. He told me he'd be in Otter Bay soon; just didn't tell me when exactly."

He gave a slight nod and glanced down at me.

I tilted my head to one side. "What?"

"Nothing. It's just that . . ." His gaze dropped to the floor, and I held my breath as I waited to hear what he had to say. "I'd gotten used to thinking of you without him."

"I am without him." *Not that it matters or anything.*

His brows flickered, his smile less than genuine. "And yet there he is."

Oohs and aahs crackled the air as two men in uniform joined the table of women. One of them, Josh Adams, the town's new fire chief, swooped down on the birthday princess and gave her a loud smooch on the lips.

The other one stirred up the women with, "There's more where that came from, honey."

More "oohs" filled the air, and I swiveled away from the

party atmosphere. Len stared back at me, eyes narrowed, as if a fire of another kind had just flared. I crossed my arms and hung my head back, wishing on the ceiling for that quick escape I was so fond of imagining.

Seth shifted. "Listen, Suz, I'm not going to lie. Seeing that guy makes me want to hit something."

I lifted my chin, expecting to see anger in Seth's face. I planned to tell him that this wasn't any of his business—nothing of my life was anymore. But he surprised me. Instead of a flat line, the corners of his mouth drooped. "So I'm not about to go over there and shake his hand."

"I wouldn't expect you to do that."

"You told me he betrayed you." He lowered his voice, the deepness becoming intimate. "If you *ever* need someone to rely on, you know where to find me."

I slid a look toward Holly who hugged another partygoer, her pretty hair bouncing as she laughed. "You know, under the circumstances, I should find someone else to rely on."

He cracked a smile. Never mind what it did to my insides. "At least you're talking to me now. You hung up on me earlier tonight, you know."

I gave my head a tight shake. "Couldn't be helped. And I wouldn't exactly characterize that as a hang up." I nodded toward Holly. "Don't you think you should go to her?"

"In a minute." He paused. "I've been thinking about our conversation from the other night, Suz. A lot." He reached out and brushed wispy bangs from my forehead. "Had me thinking about the way I've gone about my life these past few years, about the way I've crowded God out of the picture—especially when life didn't go as I planned it out."

His honesty had a melting effect on my heart. "Easy to do, Seth."

"But you didn't do that. You were a faithful girl, and now, even after what you've gone through—although I've missed so much of it—you are a faithful woman."

I allowed myself to linger on his words until the din of the crowd reached my ears. I'd been staring. He stared back. *How long could we stand in the middle of this diner and talk about serious things?* If Len's eyes wore laser beams, they'd be cutting through my back about now.

It took significant strength to pull my eyes away from his, but if I didn't, I feared he might see pools of emotion, the kind I wanted to avoid, forming behind them.

"Th-Thank you," I stammered.

Seth glanced over my shoulder. "Hope we get the chance to talk again soon." He gave my shoulder a brief squeeze before turning to join the party.

When I made what felt like an arduous walk across the diner to the table, Len sat back, crossed his arms, his mouth taking on a sarcastic smile. "Didn't take you long to hook up with that guy, now, did it?"

"Quick to make assumptions, don't you think?" I slid in across from him, my eyes averted.

"I'm not the quick one, apparently."

My appetite had vanished like a rock tossed into the sea,

and I allowed my eyes to face his. "I think we'd better keep this conversation focused on our son."

It took a while for his poker face to crack, but it did. If he wanted to accuse me any further, he neither showed it nor tried. Maybe, just maybe, he realized that putting me on the defensive was neither kind nor his place.

He lowered his gaze to his burger and then back up at me. "You're right, Suz. None of my business what you do now, although I'd like it to be." He watched me, as if gauging my reaction, but when there was none, he glanced away again. "Anyway, let's figure out this thing with Jeremiah. Least we can agree on that."

I nodded, this time in complete agreement.

Chapter Twenty-Six

"I prayed for you for hours last night."

"You did?" I rubbed a generous amount of moisturizer into my palm, taking in Letty and her paisley skirt and gypsy-style blouse, her hair knotted into a silky turban-style bun. The woman was walking art.

"What can I say? You were on my mind and I always take that as a sign from God that he wants me to pray. Why else would I be thinking of you so much?"

I laughed. "Oh, I don't know. Could you be jealous of my sneakers?"

She huffed. "Please. You should incinerate those." As I squirted more moisturizing cream from a tube, Letty moved closer and grabbed my hand like an angry school principal. "What did you do?"

I winced, unable to curl my fingers without pain. "Had a little kitchen accident. No biggie."

Her black eyes bore into mine. "You can't paint with a scorched hand! This needs medical attention and time off. No wonder the Lord had me praying for you last night."

Among other reasons. I extricated my aching palm from Letty's grasp, not doubting her assessment yet unwilling to forego work—and pay—to stay home and dwell on my predicament with Len. "I'll be fine, Letty. You worry too much. See?" I held up my palm and bent three fingers forward, trying not to allow the depth of pain to show on my face.

She shook her head. "You're a terrible liar."

"Well, you may get your wish. Fred will be coming in soon, probably by midmorning, and he wants to see some drawings I've been working up for him."

"Drawings?" Letty's forehead bunched.

"Yes, the ones for his cabin. I was supposed to bring them by his home last night, but . . ." I sighed, not wanting to divulge much about Len and the great big dog bite. "Some things came up that prevented me from getting over there."

Letty fell silent but her face took on a certain wistfulness. Had her mind wandered to memories of her husband? I wanted to ask what bothered her but never knew how far to probe. She held on to her privacy, unlike me who jibberjabbered much too much. I resolved to work on that.

I attempted a smile while hiding my hand at my side. "So what kind of duties could you give a maimed woman like myself to do?"

Her mouth stretched into a smile, even if her eyes did not agree. She handed me a delivery list. "Here, please call our delivery service and get an estimated time of arrival on all these items. Think your forefinger can dial all right?"

"It's greased up and ready to go. I'm all over it." The studio contained state-of-the-art tools and some of the world's greatest art flowing through its doors, and yet the phone stuck on the wall with the rubber cord attached to its receiver showed the old-fashioned attitude still much alive here.

I picked up the receiver, but Timo appeared in front of me. "So." He laid one hand casually onto the phone. "The ex is out of the pen now, eh? Bet he's got stories to tell."

"Then you'd win."

I made another attempt to reach for the phone, but Timo continued to block my way, a creepy smile pressed into his face. Did he not realize that his skinny self could do little to conjure up fear in normal, balanced human beings?

"So I bet you're glad I told him how and where to find you." In a really bad imitation of Inspector Clouseau, he pretended to examine his fingernails while pursing his lips and raising his eyebrows.

"Timo! I hope my ears do not deceive me. You did *not* give out the whereabouts of this studio to a stranger." Fred had arrived without my knowledge. He stood before us, his cheeks red.

Timo hunched his shoulders and looked to me for support. Realizing that a lost cause, he stuck his hands into his pockets and dropped his head forward, as if to inspect the colorless ground.

"Fred, you're back!" I reached over and hugged him, hoping to wash away any tension Timo's macho act, however lame, had brought on. I cupped his shoulders with my hands—trying not to wince from pain—and held my arms out straight. "You look amazingly well, boss. The rest suited you."

This time the tinge of his cheeks resembled a blush.

"Stop badgering the man." Letty flounced over and gave Fred's face a thorough inspection. "Suz is right. You look good, Fred. We have much to discuss, so come with me." Awkwardly, she linked her arm through his and pulled him away.

Timo released a sputtering sigh, like a helium balloon with an untied knot.

I gave him an innocent smile and slight shrug. "What can I say? You live right." I paused. "Don't expect to be rescued on a regular basis."

He slunk away as my hand reached for the phone.

"Suz!"

I whirred around and hung it back up as both Fred and Letty waved me over.

"Show the man your hand," Letty said as I arrived at our workstation.

"Would you please stop worrying? I'm absolutely fine. See it feels just—yow!" I yanked my hand away from Letty, who had taken it into her grasp and accidentally poked a blister with one of her manicured nails. I think it was accidental.

"She burned it in her kitchen. I don't think she is able to hold a fine paintbrush for a few days."

Was I invisible? "Fred. It's your first day back. Please don't worry about me—I'll be fine. Besides, if we give you too much to worry over, Sherry will string all of us up."

He gave me a fatherly smile. If he didn't just remind me of a big ol' teddy bear sometimes.

"Leticia is correct," he said. "You cannot work with an injury such as that."

Letty beamed.

Fred fished around in his pocket and pulled out a key. "Take this." He dropped the key into my good palm.

"What's this for?" My eyes examined it but I had no clue.

"It's the key to the log cabin. Take the next few days to wander around it a bit; take your boy and stay if you'd like. Get a feel for the blank walls and what the old place says to you."

I stared at him, speechless.

"Oh, I know we've already talked over one idea and it's lovely, but the walls are many." He scooted his chin toward the door. "Go on now. You're still on the clock."

I closed my fingers around the key, hungry for a chance at independence, if only for a few days. My hand felt heavy with the possibilities, my lungs nearly breathless. I looked up and nodded. "I'll just run home for my sketchbook and our overnight things. Thank you, Fred." My voice cracked and without much deliberation I rocked forward on my toes and planted a kiss on his bright pink cheek.

Letty stood behind Fred, unsmiling and silent, as if unusually tongue-tied. *My dear friend, Letty. If only I knew what you were thinking . . .*

"SURPRISED TO FIND YOU here."

"Hey, Gage." I stepped into his beach bungalow. "I could say the same about you. What's up?"

Gage continued to call out through the doorway to the kitchen. "Home for an early lunch. I'm meeting with a couple of prospective clients this afternoon . . . have to get my strength up."

"That's so great." I flopped onto the overstuffed chair and kicked off my sneakers. "Business going well, then?"

After the microwave bell dinged, he joined me in the living room with a bowl in his hands. "It is." He blew on the hot chili. "You going to tell me why you're here?"

I exhaled and dropped my purse at my feet, my head flopping back against the chair. "Fred gave me the key to the log cabin. Said Jer and I could stay a few days while I got a feel for the place."

Gage swallowed the bite he'd been savoring. "You were kind of glowing so I figured it was something good."

I laughed. "Glowing?"

He shrugged. "Don't laugh. I may be a dumb guy, but I know what glowing is."

"Especially since Callie's been doing so ever since taming

you. Ha ha." I pulled myself out of the chair and gave my brother a brief hug.

"Taming *me*?"

I wandered toward the hall, still laughing. "That girl's a miracle maker in my book. Thought you'd never settle down."

"Hey, where's my credit in all of this?"

His voice trailed after me as I reached the room I shared with Jeremiah. "Can't hear you!" I spied an overnight bag and began tossing in clothes and toys Jer and I would need.

"So." Gage appeared in the doorway. "Heard from him?"

"Who? Len?"

He took another bite, his face serious, almost stoic. He tried to act nonchalant, but a little sister knew better.

Jeans, extra socks, a pair of flip-flops . . . I shook my head. "Nope. We talked it out last night and he promised to call this morning to set up a time to see Jeremiah, but"— I dug my phone out of my pocket and held it up for Gage to see—"no calls."

"And what did you and he decide about, you know, the two of you?"

I stopped packing to look up at him. "I don't understand."

"C'mon, Suz. The guy came here for more than Jeremiah."

Toothbrushes. Don't forget the toothbrushes! Oh, and tooth-paste too. Sometimes my brother knew me too well. Instead of this being a blessing, at the moment, his uncanny ability resembled a curse. For if he continued to read my thoughts like this—thoughts I didn't care to confront—I might just have to banish the man. Or at least pretend I didn't hear a thing he said.

"Suz?"

I dropped a set of Jer's undies into my bag and took in Gage's face, his lips pursed, his brow furrowed. "Our marriage is over. We're divorced. Why do you continue to hint that there could be anything other than mutual parenthood between us?"

He stepped into my room, something he had not done since Jeremiah and I arrived unannounced on his front porch those many months before. Now as he set his half-eaten bowl of chili on the dresser and approached me, I saw something pleading in his eyes. With one emotion-filled look, Gage was asking for a promise of some type.

"I understand that you and he are legally divorced. And I believe with everything in me that this was the best decision for you. For Jer."

I frowned. "It wasn't my idea. You remember that, right?"

He reached for me. "Of course. You would never have asked that man for a divorce, no matter what kind of jerk he'd been to you."

"So why do you keep bringing up the divorce?"

"Because, you're you and he's, well, he's him." Gage let go of a sigh. "I'm afraid he might try to talk you into something that you haven't . . ." He looked up. "Please, Suz. Think everything through here. Don't let him sweet-talk you, not without talking it all out with Callie and me. Will you promise me that?"

I shut my overnight bag and scooched next to it on the bed. He was right, at least partially. I had been struggling, not with my feelings for Len per se, as the love I'd had for him was long gone. But I wondered, at times, if perhaps God wanted me to do the unthinkable and invite Jeremiah's father back into my life in a more real way. I'd wondered that ever since overhearing the women outside of Jeremiah's Sunday school class.

"You worry too much," I tried to assure him.

Gage sat on the rumpled bed next to me, playfully bumping my hip. "That's what big brothers are for."

"Is that right?"

"Yeah." He paused, as if formulating what to say to the little sister with a mind of her own. "Do what *you* really want to do, Suzanna."

All I wanted to do right now was pick up Jeremiah from preschool and head up to the cabin. I imagined us warming up yummies for dinner and sitting cross-legged with a game of dominoes in front of the old stone fireplace. While he slept on a feathery soft rug, I planned to walk and pray and contemplate the best placement for artwork on the walls. For a few days, at least, I hoped not to have to think about Len or what the future might possess.

"What is it you want to do about Len?" My brother wore anxiety like a closely tucked T-shirt.

I leaned into him and rested my head on his shoulder, hoping to calm his fears. Instead, as I gave him the most honest answer that came to mind, it occurred to me that those fears might just turn up a notch.

"Maybe life's not all about what *I* want."

Chapter Twenty-Seven

Len never called. Not that I checked all that often or waited by the phone as in those years during our marriage, but the truth is, Len said he would call and he didn't.

This shouldn't have surprised me, but it did. I glanced at Jeremiah, his body melted into his booster seat, his face a picture of contentment as he gazed out the window at passing pines. Light through the trees skipped and darted across his precious face.

Jeremiah was the main reason Len's silence bothered me.

"We're almost there, Mama. I can tell!"

I glanced at him again in my rearview mirror. "You can? Then you are a smart boy all right."

He nodded two times for emphasis.

After picking up Jer from school, we stopped at the grocery store up on the hill, the one overlooking the town of Otter Bay, and bought vacation food: fresh fruit, chips, sandwich fixings, and makings for a pie. I hadn't baked in six months, and although the dough was ready made, I snatched it up from the refrigerated case on a whim.

Jer had wrinkled his nose at that. "You gonna make a pie? I thought you only did that at our old house."

This was a problem. I tweaked him on the nose and pushed my cart away from the cold case with its foggy glass doors and enticing offerings. "I'm starting up again—just you wait."

He held on to the cart, the one he was getting much too big to be sitting in, and threw back his head. "I! Can't! Wait!"

Now as our car pulled into the drive, the afternoon sun moving toward the horizon, I realized that Jer was not the only one who couldn't wait. I whipped the key out of the ignition, dashed over to Jeremiah's door, and opened it up, watching him spill onto the pine needle-strewn driveway.

He dashed off, calling over his shoulder. "I'm gonna go play on the jungle gym!"

"Not so fast!"

He skidded to a halt.

"There'll be time for that. First, come help me with our bags. You don't want all that food we bought to spoil, do you?"

He picked up the pace at the mention of food and wrapped his arms around a bulging bag. Together, we made our way to the front door, and with a quick uptick of my heart, I slid the key into the lock and twisted until it opened with a click.

Gently scuffed wood floors ran the length of the long, narrow living room, but Jer had no time for the quiet admiration

I felt for the old place. Seeing an indoor playground every bit as enticing as the one outside, Jer plunked the grocery bag on the floor, kicked off his shoes, and slid around on his socks.

A contented smile warmed me as I bustled inside with the rest of the bags, pulling the door shut. This place, with its soot-stained fireplace, cozy rooms, and white walls looking every bit the blank canvas, felt like home. Seven hundred and fifty square feet of home.

In the ultrawhite kitchen, I began to unpack our groceries, piling everything onto a round glass top. Jer padded into the room and climbed onto a chair. "Wow! That's more food than an army."

"You mean we have enough to *feed* an army, right?"

"Right!" He nodded dramatically. "Can I go outside now?"

"Go put your shoes back on then, yes, you may go outside."

He scrambled off the chair and back into the living room, just steps away. He must have jumped into his shoes because he whipped past me in the kitchen and careened outside through the narrow kitchen door.

My eyes took in all the food I'd brought for the two of us, and I shook my head. *No way can we eat all this.* When we moved in with Gage, I'd decided the least I could do was cook meals and store the leftovers in one of the Tupperware containers Mom had left me from her side business. No wonder I had no idea how to shop these days, though. Between working and mothering, I'd done the shop and dash more often than not. And half the time, my dear brother insisted on filling in the wide gaps in my budget by stopping twice weekly for the important things, like ice cream for Jer and half-and-half for our morning coffee.

I pressed my nose against the backdoor window and watched Jer send dust and pine needles flying in his wake. *Lord, you provide enough for us to eat—and somewhere for Jeremiah to play. You are amazing.* I let the flimsy curtain drop and turned back to puttering.

Several hours later, as Jer played along the hearth and I contemplated the transformation of bare walls, my cell phone rang. I hesitated. What if Len was calling? Would I be obligated to tell him where we'd gone? What if he wanted to join us here? The thought dulled the excitement fluttering within.

A glance at the screen did not indicate the caller's name. Tentatively, I answered. "Hello?"

"Suz, it's me, Letty."

I collapsed into an armchair, relief at hearing a friendly voice. "Hi there."

"Hello there yourself." She cleared her throat. "I'm wondering if you could tell me where you left the delivery list I gave you earlier. You did not have a chance to make those calls and I would like to do that myself when I get back to the studio."

I cringed. "Sorry, Letty. You're right; I never finished. Never got started, actually. I dropped the list into my personal drawer beneath our workstation, figuring I'd pick up with it when I returned. But you know what?" I glanced around the bright kitchen, a new sense of purpose within me. "If you read the names and numbers to me, I'll make those calls from here."

She paused. "So, you are already in Fred's cabin, then."

It was more of a statement than a question. "We are. This cabin is a magical place. Oh, but I'm sure you already know that."

"On the contrary, I have never seen it."

An awkward silence followed. I rocked forward in my chair, sensing she had more to say. "Letty? Was there more?"

"Yes."

When she didn't continue, I prompted her. "Okay then. Why don't you tell me?"

A mixture of groan and sigh released from her. "I need help, Suz. Your help with something quite personal."

I straightened, intrigued. "Anything, Letty. Name it."

She chuckled, a welcome sound interjected into a mystifying conversation. "You don't know what I am about to ask."

"Doesn't matter." My hand gave an involuntary wave into the air. "You're my friend and I'm here to help. What do you need?"

She hemmed. "This is not comfortable for me to say."

"But we're friends. You should be able to tell me anything. Well, maybe not *anything*, but most things."

She hawed. "Okay, well . . ." Her voice sounded winded.

My face froze in anticipation. "Yes?"

"Okay, Suzanna. My car broke down and I need assistance."

"Of course." I swished my head around looking for a pen and paper, knowing the chances were nil considering the spotlessness of the cabin. "Just tell me where you are and I'll be right there for you."

"I am accustomed to fending for my own needs."

"I know that."

"How could you know? Have I ever told you?"

I squinted at her impatience—and at mine. "Are you going to tell me where you are?"

Her breathing became more pronounced. "I am outside."

"Outside . . . where?" I padded into the living room and peeked out the window. No Letty in sight. "Are you on Wickham?"

"Yes, Wickham, like that dastardly man in *Pride and Prejudice*. I am only halfway up the hill."

"Stay where you are." I grabbed my keys from the coffee table. "I'll be right down to get you."

"Absolutely you will not." Her voice had gained some strength, like she'd reached the first plateau. "I called to make sure you were there before making the climb. Don't come for me; I am almost there."

Letty was a hard woman to cross. I dropped my keys into my purse and waited for her by the window. Jer pressed his nose to the window, his body wrapped in a robe and slippers after his bath in the antique claw-foot tub. In hindsight, Letty's order to stay inside was a blessing.

When we caught a glimpse of her at the corner of the property, Jer ran to the door and hung on the handle.

"Wait a minute, buddy. Don't go outside—you'll catch a

chill." My own smile led the way to the door. *Did I just sound like my mother?*

I unlocked the latch and Letty wafted in, smelling like vanilla with a dash of nutmeg. "Glad you could make it."

She flashed weary black eyes at me. "If art does not work out for you, try the comedy shop."

"Ha. I will."

Although I motioned for her to rest on the couch, Letty stood in the middle of the sparse but bright living room, taking it all in. Her eyes softened and changed, beginning to sparkle in the flickering tongues of light coming from the fireplace. Having grown up back east, gathering wood around the cabin's perimeter and lighting a fire had been cathartic for me.

"Good thing you're here, my friend. I bought far too much food and had just been questioning myself about that. *You* must be my answer." I clapped my hands, feeling pretty proud. "You're staying for dinner and I will drive you home later with a care package."

"You are a pushy girl."

I laughed. "*Right.*"

"Okay, I will rephrase that: You *can* be a pushy girl."

"Is your car in a safe spot off the road? 'Cuz we could call a tow service, if you want."

She shrugged. "It's fine. I was able to coast to a spot beneath a tree."

I walked the few steps into the kitchen and she followed. "So, do you live near here, then? I thought your home was closer to town."

She dropped into a kitchen chair while I hunted for dinner. "I was spying."

"Spying?" I froze, a can of soup in each hand. "On who?"

She grimaced. "I had never been invited to this log cabin and wanted to find it."

"Wait, so you were spying on me? Why didn't you just tell me you wanted to come over?"

She gave a dramatic shrug, her hands landing with a bounce on the table. "Either way I would be in this predicament."

I went back to perusing the cabinet, avoiding the obvious questions in my mind. "Hmm. Car troubles again. Same thing as last time?"

"Yes, I think. There is a leak so I put in some fluid and hoped it would do the trick. It did for a while."

"Sounds like it's time for a trip to the mechanic. Gage knows a good one, and if you'd like I can get his name and number for you."

She gave me a rather vague answer of yes. Jer broke into the room. "Come over here," he said. "I wanna show you my puzzle." Jer dragged Letty by the hand out of the kitchen and over to the fluffy hearth rug where he had started putting together a thirty-piece kid-sized puzzle of a bear before losing interest. He let go of her hand and plopped onto the rug.

I stayed out of it except to watch Letty collapse onto the rug, her flouncy skirt spread out like a tapestry. Now did not seem like the right time to prod Letty more about her thirst for espionage tonight.

"I'll finish up with dessert while you two play." In the

kitchen, I retrieved the roll of dough from the fridge and laid it out on the cutting board, stretching and massaging it flat. I'd already peeled and sliced apples and washed a basket of berries. From where I stood, I could hear their laughter and the sound brought something warm to my heart. This little house must have been lonely in the quiet after its inhabitants moved out.

Two pair of feet clomped into the kitchen and surrounded me at the small island. I smiled. "That was quick."

"We want to know what's for dessert!"

I widened my eyes in surprise. "Oh *we* do, huh? Well, I'm making an apple and blueberry tart, although I hope these berries are sweet enough this time of year." I plopped one into Jer's mouth. "What do you think?"

He smiled with shiny pink lips. "Good! But what happened to the pie?"

I gave a dramatic sigh. "Well, I forgot to buy a pie plate and couldn't find one in the cabinet. Nor a rolling pin either." Secretly I was relieved. I hadn't made a from-scratch pie since before Len's incarceration. Had lost interest and never quite gained it back. Still, I made the attempt, and wasn't that something?

Letty looked intrigued. "So you're making a tart instead? Bravo. I would not have thought of that."

I tried to keep my smile from wavering. "My mother was a genius, always able to make us dinner and dessert, sometimes from scraps. Money was scarce. Lots of medical bills, you know? Anyway, she would never let a thing like a missing pie pan keep her from whipping up something fabulous for dessert."

My audience watched in silence as I piled sliced apples, blueberries, and generous servings of cinnamon and sugar onto the mix, much like Mom used to do. I blinked rapidly against building emotion until my cell phone rang and slashed through the quiet. I looked up, my fingers lined with dough.

"I'll grab that for you."

Letty picked up my phone from the kitchen counter before I had the chance to stop her. *Probably just Fred checking up on us.*

"Hello? This is Suz's phone."

I rubbed my lips together, waiting, pinching the ends of dough harder than they deserved.

"Just a moment. I will see if she is willing to speak with you."

My brows froze in an arched position. "Well?"

"Go! Clean up your hands." Her voice hissed. She covered the mouthpiece and motioned toward the sink with her head. "It's that charming window washer on the line for you."

Seth.

I doused my hands with sink water, dried them with a couple of pats on a towel, and took the phone along with an inconspicuous breath. Letty winked at Jer, put her arm around his shoulders, and guided him out of the kitchen.

I put the phone to my ear. "Seth?"

"Hi. Did I interrupt something?"

"Not really. Having dinner with a friend."

"So I did interrupt."

I found a chair and lowered myself into it. I'd missed the familiar sound of his voice, its effect balmlike. An involuntary smile jumped to my face and I snatched a look around the room, hoping no one caught that.

"Guess you're wondering why I called."

"I, well, yes." I tried to unloosen my tongue. "Why did you, Seth?"

"To officially apologize to you. Wanted to the other night but it was kind of . . . awkward."

My pulse revved a little. "Agreed. I was afraid Holly was going to knock my head off."

"Fat chance of that." His voice rumbled through the phone.

I leaned my chin on my hand. "I wouldn't have blamed her for being angry. I know we're just friends, but it might've looked to her like something . . . more."

He allowed silence to settle before answering. "Except that she broke up with me."

I sat up straighter. "Why?" *Tell me it wasn't because of me.*

"Guess she just wasn't all that into me."

I crinkled my forehead. "Oh, she was too."

He chuckled. "You don't believe me."

"It's not that. I wouldn't want to have played some part in your, uh, breakup." My stomach twisted just saying the words.

"You didn't. It was inevitable. And anyway, that's not why I called. Remember?"

My mind flitted around to various thoughts. "I know. I know."

"I'm ashamed of myself for the other night. You didn't deserve to have your faith and your outlook questioned the way I did. I let my personal problems, things from my past—things you don't know about—blur my judgment."

An image of the old Seth popped into my mind—his chin lowered, his gray-green eyes drooping at the corners. I longed to reach for him, to comfort him, yet how would that be perceived?

"And I'm sorry."

My heart pounded in the quiet. Seth's apology stood out like a lush red rose against the white walls and cabinets of the tiny kitchen. *Len has never apologized to me—for anything.* Seth cleared his throat, and I chased away my random thought.

"I've had a rough few years," he continued. "Not many people know about it, and well, maybe I've let it change me. And not in a good way."

My eyes shut, compassion pouring over me, my mind jostling with old emotions that suddenly became fresh again.

"What you said about your parents, well, you have every right to those beliefs. At one time, I'm sure I shared them. But then . . ."

"But then . . . what?"

He paused. "Could . . . could I come over there?"

"Now?"

"If that's all right with you. I want to see you, to talk . . . to explain my position."

The homemade tart lay half made on the kitchen island. Macaroni salad chilled in the fridge along with sandwich fixings that still needed prepping. In the next room, my son played happily with Letty, and I'd yet to learn the depth of her troubles.

Holly had said that my tirade—although that's not how she characterized it—had somehow affected Seth's faith. I wanted to know more. Longed to, really, but a cacophony of giggles erupted in the next room, and I shook my head. "I'd like to talk more with you, Seth, but can't tonight. Jer and I are actually on a sort of working vacation at the moment."

"You're not with your brother?"

"No. We're not. Maybe next week?"

He stayed silent long enough for me to wonder if he read more into my refusal than necessary. As if by putting him off I'd made him feel like his experiences didn't matter. Truthfully, they mattered to me more than I knew they could.

He sighed. "Sure, Suz. Whatever you want."

We clicked off the line, the dial tone resounding in my ear, making me wish I had been less hasty.

Chapter Twenty-Eight

 "What would it be like to have nothing more pressing to do than strolling along a foggy British moor while reading a book?"

Letty did not hesitate. "Depends on the book."

I laughed. "Is there anything you don't have an answer to?"

"Hmm. I will get back to you."

I sighed and turned my attention to the pastoral scenery rolling across the screen, my feet plopped onto a rugged coffee table, my mind happy to have something to fixate on other than Seth's call. After dinner, followed by a rousing game of Go Fish and a few more minutes admiring the gigantic puzzle in front of the fireplace, Jer and I convinced Letty to stay the night. It took some prodding, but when I agreed to let her have the couch, she relented. We then ushered my exhausted son to bed, and it took only one trip to the kitchen for water, plus an extra nighttime prayer for him to saunter off to dreamland.

Afterward, Letty put my copy of *Pride & Prejudice* into the DVD player. I couldn't resist stashing it in my overnight bag, considering this sweet cabin resided on the namesake street of one of the story's characters. From scene one, we'd been mesmerized by the British landscape and romantic story, rehashing it as it moved along.

"I've watched this a dozen times and still never tire of all that melodrama coming from Lizzy's mother. Any time, any day, I can shut my eyes and hear her cry out, 'Oh, Mr. Bennet!'" Laughter erupted from me. "That woman gets me every time."

"He's a sly fox himself, that Mr. Bennet." Letty wagged her head, then rested it against the back of the overstuffed leather couch, the most relaxed I'd ever seen her. "Sometimes I think his cleverness in the face of poor financial decisions and loony offspring is often overlooked."

The man lived with six women, including his wife who always seemed to have a severe case of "the nerves." Maybe Letty had a point. Mr. Bennet had a lifetime to create witty comebacks, and yet who do we remember most when thinking of that story?

Letty looked at me. "Do you know what my favorite part of the movie is?"

"When Mr. Collins proposes to Lizzy? Or maybe when Lizzy and Mr. Bingley's sister take a turn about the room?" I said that last bit in a terrible British accent.

She batted a hand at me as if to say "silly girl." "No. It is when Jane rescues Mr. Bingley from his own twisted tongue."

I narrowed my eyes, thinking.

"You don't remember? It happens during that first dance when they meet. He begins to tell her about himself but thinks better of his phrasing and backtracks. Only he makes a mess of it all, and his face shows his embarrassment. This is when Jane smiles agreeably and answers him, as if his words made every sense in the world." Letty glanced at me, her eyes reflective. "That is when I knew she loved him."

"Such a romantic you are!" I smiled at her from my relaxed spot on the couch. "I hadn't thought of that before, but yes, I can see that now. I suppose I've always been more caught up with Mr. Darcy to notice the nuances of any other love match in the movie. He can be such a rogue, but she gets what's beneath his surface facade. Oh, to have someone say to me as Darcy does to Lizzy, 'You have bewitched me, body and soul!'"

Letty snorted. "I have always thought that line somewhat over the top."

"Not me. If a man looked at me like that and said those words, I'd be a goner."

"So this is what it would take for you to fall in love again?"

She might as well have poked me with a pitchfork. I raised both hands in surrender. "I wasn't serious, you know. Been there, done that, know what I mean?" I withered against the nervous laughter coming from me.

Letty watched me, dark lashes accentuating her large eyes. "You do not want to talk about it. I can accept that. For now."

She stood and stretched her back. "We should talk about these walls. Are those sketches what you are planning?" She pointed at my sketchbook on the coffee table.

I brightened at the adept way she changed the subject. I'd hoped to get her talking about her financial need, but at this point, I'd take any topic other than my love life. Or lack thereof.

"One word: anemone."

"Spell that."

"I'm serious. Can't you picture a giant sea anemone, fluid and glowing on this wall over here?" I swept my arms wide in front of the whitest wall in the room. "After that, I don't know. Probably more tidal life. Sometimes I work better with a spark of an idea that grows as I paint."

She picked up the book and thumbed through the pages. "These are stunning, but you don't work from a plan? How can you not work from a plan?"

I shrugged. "It's how I'm wired. Weird, I guess, but I'm told that my designs are pleasing, so . . ."

"And when people tell you this, do you believe them?" I leaned my head left then right, weighing her question. "Usually."

"Good. You should. Obviously Fred sees your gift, even if you have not fully accepted it yourself." She sized up the wall again. "Did you know that sea anemones are often referred to as windflowers?"

"No, but that makes sense. They are gorgeous creatures with graceful, long petals. I could sit on the rocks and study them for days, if I had the time."

"Perhaps you should study them more, learn what they are like, how they react to predators and where they flourish most. This can only help you in your design, yes?"

"Yes."

Silence like a weight dropped between us.

I stuck a fist onto my hip. Now, suddenly, I'm the direct one in this relationship? "It's too early for sleep. Let's go in the kitchen while I get together some of tonight's leftovers for you to take with you tomorrow."

"I do not need your charity."

I waved her off. "And I do not need all this food." Something in my gut I couldn't quite capture, like a gnat buzzing around my head, drove me to haul out a large grocery bag and begin filling it up.

We'd left the kitchen in disarray, evidence everywhere of one fine meal shared together. Letty had wanted to clean up before the movie, but I shooed her out of there, corralling her to help me put Jer to bed. She never mentioned ever wanting kids of her own, but I could tell by the way she'd sung to Jeremiah and wrapped him in his blankets "like a burrito"— she rolled her *R*s when she said it—that she would make a beautiful mama someday.

I rifled around in a drawer and found quart-sized bags as she stood there, forlornly watching me. "You going to tell me what's going on with you, Letty?" I kept on with my bag filling and all-around eye avoidance. The clock ticked against the silence.

"I could not stand you when you started working at the studio."

My chin jerked up. "What?"

She sat in a kitchen chair, her usual confidence faltering. "Okay, maybe that's part fabrication. I *wanted* not to like you."

I stiffened.

"You came in for your interview looking chipper and put together like Pollyanna—only with brown hair. You did not have the credentials some of us have, and yet Fred hired you on the spot."

I expected honesty, maybe even some kind of painful confession, but criticism? I hadn't expected that. Sadness pulled down the corners of my mouth and I went back to packing up groceries for her, only slower than at first.

"I saw why he did almost immediately."

My eyes flashed, defiantly. "Why?"

"You do beautiful work. There is no doubt about it. And I believe Fred had another reason for hiring you."

"This cabin?"

A slight smile reached her lips. "Yes, of course, this cabin. Already you have inspired ideas for it, and it is obvious this type of work is your forte."

"But there's something else."

"It is probably not for me to say."

I shifted and sighed.

She flashed her long eyelashes toward the ceiling. "You are a petulant child!" Her teasing tone sounded forced.

"Whatever it takes."

"Fine. Sherry confided in me once that she and Fred have a daughter. As far as anyone knows, they never see her. They have been estranged for years."

I took a seat across from her. "Wow . . . I can't imagine that happening to dear Fred and Sherry."

"Nobody can. Sherry told me they believe they were too harsh with her when she was young. When they tried to force her to attend college, she left—and rarely ever has she called or visited."

We sat there, Letty and I, floating on silence. This news about Fred and Sherry's estranged daughter drew the deflating evening only lower. I wanted to know about this mystery daughter, and yet Letty's news that she "couldn't stand" me continued to run like a ticker tape through my mind.

"I was wrong about you," she finally said. "When you first began working for the studio, I attempted to needle you, but it never fazed you until I had to give up and admit that you, Suzanna, are impossible not to like." She said this like she'd made some great discovery, such as how the moon and the tides are tied together. "I understand now why two men fight over you."

I slapped the table and shook my head. "Not true. No way are two men even half interested in me—nor I in them."

She chuckled, chipping away at the flimsy barrier that had begun to grow between us. "Okay, Suzi-Q, whatever you say. I am not here to fight with you, but I know what I see."

I clasped my hands on the table in front of me and leaned forward. "Do you want your groceries or not?"

Letty began to laugh, her two elegant hands cupping her mouth. "You cannot even be spiteful. How could I not love you from the start?"

I sat back and crossed my arms, unsure of how to take this. "Letty!"

She continued to rock, laughing until tears fell from her eyes. She used her manicured fingers to wipe them away, the attempts mostly unsuccessful, which caused her to laugh more until all I could do was roll my eyes and offer her a napkin.

"Thank you." She grinned while wiping, sighing, and rocking away. The more she struggled and flopped about, the more the kitchen filled with the scent of her perfume. "I am so sorry, Suz, but you don't know how long it has been since I have truly laughed." She blew her nose like a trumpet, which sent us both into fresh peals of cackling.

I smacked a hand over my mouth, my eyes on alert, and gestured toward the doorway where Jeremiah—hopefully—still slept.

She pressed her forefinger against puckered lips, trying to add a "shush" but unable to without more tittering. Her chuckling grew more muffled as she steadied herself, napkin to mouth.

I shook my head, wiping my eyes with the back of one hand, and blew out a slow, steady breath, my voice unable to hide its sarcasm. "Wow. So sorry to be such a thorn in your side. I had no idea."

She reached over and grasped my hand. "Do not apologize,

Suz. You don't understand." She sat back. "My problem with you stemmed from my own fears."

"What do you mean?"

She looked about the kitchen, then at me. "My husband— his name was Alexander—he worked all day, every day, on his art. He taught me more than I learned in school." Her eyes misted again, this time not from mirth. "It was his dream to work solely in the Hearst Castle, restoring the ceilings and walls throughout. He studied art for many years and could tell the difference between sixteenth- and seventeenth-century carved ceilings just by viewing them."

"He never had the chance?"

"I am afraid not. He was much older than me and had been ill for years. He was in remission when we married, and we thought that perhaps this would finally be his time to reach his goal." She shrugged then, her smile almost shy. "But this was not the case."

"I'm so sorry, Letty."

She nodded in quick bursts.

I tilted my head, watching her. "How does this relate to your fears and how you felt about me?"

"I long to fulfill my husband's dream. I've worked hard. I have tried to show Fred that I am qualified and capable, hoping he will recommend me for the next promotion into the castle. There is a rumor it will be very soon." She glanced away. "Fred took such an immediate liking to you, always sending you for special trips up the hill or on isolated jobs like this one here at the log cabin . . ."

"You thought I was your competition?"

"Don't give me that wide-eyed expression of yours. That is exactly why I did not like you that first day you walked into the studio. I thought you were a . . . a charmer."

I squinted at her, not liking the direction of this conversation. "Really."

She dropped her head back and raised her chin, as if the answer she sought could be found in the knotty pine ceiling above. "After only one day, I saw your character and knew I had misjudged you. You were honest about how much you do not understand about the world of art restoration—most others would have hidden that information. Some in this business have even been known to steal ideas from others. Still, I stayed close, watching, hoping Fred would find in me what he found so appealing in you."

"Oh, Letty."

She raised a hand. "Do not feel sorry for me. I understand that some people were born with charisma, while others were not."

I grunted. "Please."

"Laugh at me if you like, but there is much more at stake than my pride." She paused, seeming to gather strength with the pull of one deep breath. "What money Alexander left me did not last long, nor did it cover all of our debts. Without this promotion, I cannot survive on what I am making at the studio now." She looked me square in the eyes. "But if I leave now to find higher-paying work, before possibly being recommended for that promotion, I will never be able to share my husband's dream of working at the castle."

Understanding filled me. The *cabana* she doesn't allow anyone to see, the near-constant poor state of her car, Sunday visits to the town's thrift store—Letty's broke, and for whatever reason, she chose this moment to share that revelation with me.

"Then don't leave. I'll help you with the incidentals, you know, like food." We both smiled at this. "But do not leave until you talk to Fred about that promotion. Promise me."

"He may have you in mind for it."

With a promotion like that, I could afford to rent this cabin for Jeremiah and me. We could extricate ourselves from Gage's busy life and give him the privacy he'll soon need. But could I be content? No. Not if it meant taking the position away from Letty, who had yearned and toiled and dreamt of spending her life restoring the castle's unending supply of irreplaceable art.

The idea to turn *down* a position like that—audacious as the concept was—gave me an astonishing lift, like the sudden flutter of finding just the right shade of lipstick to go with a new dress. I, too, had dreamt of working inside the castle walls, surrounded by all that art, but the reality now . . . after spending days and days *and days* on one minute section of an ancient door? Far from the appealing high I'd thought it would bring me.

I stared my friend down, the one who possessed both the patience and skill for this type of work, imploring her not to give up hope. "For someone who has fought adversity while working to learn her craft, you worry too much. There is no doubt in my mind—not one bit—that when the time comes, yours will be the first name to come to Fred's mind."

I didn't add that I'd make sure of it.

Chapter Twenty-Nine

Saturday morning sun drew Jeremiah, followed by groggy me, out of our cocoons of piled-high quilts and blankets and into the task of gathering our things for the ride home. My son's idea of helping out, though, meant multiple rounds of jungle gym climbing. "I'm staying out of your way, Mama."

Ah yes, I'd taught him well.

Letty left the day before, after our night of heart-to-hearts. Gage drove his mechanic, Andy, up to jump-start the stalled car. Afterward, Andy gave Letty a ride home, with the promise to take her car back to his shop to "noodle" around the engine awhile, as he put it.

I *knew* what it felt like to have empty cupboards. I understood the depth one must plunge in order to do the only thing that's left: ask for help. So, despite her protests, Letty strolled out of here with a hug and grocery bag bulging with apple-blueberry tart, fixings for sandwiches, cans of soup and tuna, a jug of lemon iced-tea, and a half bag of oranges.

In three days, not a whisper from Len. Although only minutes from town, Jer and I had holed up in this cabin the entire time, not leaving for anything other than walks in the nearby pine forest or hot chocolate breaks in the evening on the back porch. I'd begun to wonder if seeing Len after so many months of separation had been an aberration of sorts. Time away from the routine and from work made me cling harder to the dream of a quiet life without complications.

"You ready?"

Jer bounded out of the house, the one I'd spent much of last evening scrubbing and straightening, across the patch-sized front yard, and into his booster seat. The ocean grew large and wide as we descended the hill, all buckled in. "Know what, Mama? I think we should go to the beach today. I don't think you want to be done with your vacation yet."

"You know me well, kiddo."

"That's *right*. I do!"

I laughed. "Maybe after I unpack our stuff and put in some laundry first." No white caps appeared anywhere in sight, the sea rolling rather lazily onto shore. My son's suggestion grew wings. "I suppose we could eat up the rest of the sandwiches at the beach."

"Picnic!"

"Okay, sure. We'll take a picnic with us."

Gage's cottage sat empty when we arrived. I had to remind my growing boy to come back and help me unpack, which he did with a noticeable frown. *Let's hope that's not a glimpse into the teen years.* Once inside, I hurried to finish up a few chores, then change out of my jeans and long-sleeved cotton shirt and into a swimsuit, my favorite mesh-blue coverall, and squishy flip-flops. I stuck a floppy hat on my head.

"You ready, Jeremiah?"

He slapped down the hall from the bathroom wearing swim trunks that reached to his puffy knees, and with large goggles over his eyes and a snorkel hanging from his mouth.

I bit back a laugh. "Guess you are, then. Let's go, hmm?"

I hadn't planned on playing more today, but with a sun shining this bright and a newly refreshed heart, how could I resist? We walked along the road, past the other cottages, most of them occupied on this dazzling day. Three women, Holly's relatives, lounged in Adirondack chairs and waved at us as we passed by, Jer skipping with gusto and me trailing behind.

The tide looked lower than usual, offering hope that I might have a chance to tread across uncovered rocks and search the pools for more inspiration for the cabin's walls. Letty had taken it on herself to teach me all she knew about the soft and pretty creatures that intrigued me so. She said that though anemones looked like underwater blossoms, they moved about and ate like other sea animals. News to me. I'd watched them several times and they never budged, their bodies stuck to undersides of rocks like they'd stepped in peanut butter before heading out to play.

I laughed at the image, remembering the time I'd been repapering the drawers in my old kitchen. Only three years old at the time, Jeremiah stepped onto contact paper in his stocking feet, then danced around like a wild creature, unable to tear it off.

"What are you laughing 'bout?" he asked, one hand on the railing.

A handwoven beach bag swung from my arm. "Just happy, kiddo. Feels like summer, you know?"

"I'll race you to the beach!"

"You're on!" I kicked off my flip-flops and hooked them with two fingers, but by the time I reached the top step, Jer had jogged down the stairs and jumped into the pebbly sand below. I hardly recalled being so reckless and free, but it wasn't all that long ago that summers had meant scorched hot dogs and weak tea, followed by swatting at mosquitoes until well past dark.

I reached Jer at the same spot we always played, intuition telling me the value of routine in his life. It's how memories were made, the kinds one wanted to treasure and uncover over and over again for a long, long time. Sitting on the bath sheet I'd brought, we scooched our fannies deeper into the sand. Jer began to stack smooth rocks called moonstones while contentment drew my mind and sight out across the vast sea where flying fish skittered and popped and pelicans glided in formation, scouring for lunch.

I'd hardly noticed the gathering of beachgoers to our left until one of them, a familiar guy with a slight paunch, waved in our direction. Funny how people you see in church, wearing their Sunday best, look so out of place with so much skin hanging out of their beach clothes.

After acknowledging them with a friendly smile and wave, I laid back on the blanket to peer into the baby blue sky. Had I not taken that moment to raise my eyes to the heavens, would I have seen the dark clouds form as I did?

I shaded my eyes with one hand. "Hello, Len."

He bent over me, blocking the sun now, examining my face. Did he hope to find fear in my expression over his three-day disappearance? Or anger, perhaps? Or maybe he hoped I would throw my arms around his bleached-blond head and welcome him back?

"Daddy!" Jer leapt to his feet, apparently unconcerned with my ruminations. "You coming to our picnic?"

"That sounds like a fine idea, little man." Len held Jer to his bare chest and glanced down at me for some kind of encouragement. "If it's okay with your mother, that is."

Jer's wispy blond hair defied gravity as he arched his back so far he nearly tumbled from his father's grasp. "C'mon, Mama. Let him stay. He must be stah-ving!"

"Sure, of course. He's your father." I took another glance at the blue-green sea and shrugged, my smile less than full. The church man wrapped a Velcro strap around his thick ankle and grabbed a surfboard. A teenage boy with a similar shape—gut included—did the same, and the two made their way across the rocky beach to a wide clearing in the sea.

Len watched the men traipse into the ocean, their ribs pronounced from sucking in against the cold water. "You want to go see the surfers, Jer?"

He struggled out of Len's grasp and pulled his father closer to the water's edge. I let my eyes trail after them, my body stiffening. The older man in the water shook his head, turned around, and began jogging in big leaps out of the surf, that long board still stuck under one arm. I watched as Len struck up a conversation with the shivering man and Jeremiah hopped like a bunny at his father's side.

While the activity piqued my interest, waves and wind and bubbling wet sand coaxed me in a different direction, lulling me to forget my worries and bask in this moment. This was how it should have been: Len, Jer, and me, on a beach, living a full life.

The church man dropped his board to the ground and bent, hands on knees, until eye level with Jeremiah. He spoke to my son and stopped, his face reacting in ways that made it look like he was truly listening. For his part, Jeremiah's head bobbed like it did whenever he shared one of his many opinions.

Without warning, Jeremiah spun around and sprinted in my direction, leaving sand clouds in his wake. "Mama! Daddy's gonna borrow that man's surfboard!" He yanked me by the hand, no match for my laziness. He pulled with all the might of a four-year-old until I relented. "Come on. Come watch!"

By now the church man's family lined the shore, sending fat plovers scurrying away in Chaplinesque fashion. Did Len expect that the board he borrowed would include an audience?

The man's son paddled back in and spoke with Len amidst the rising tide, offering directions we couldn't hear. Was he explaining the metaphor of surfing as art? That the board represented a brush, the wave a wide, blank canvas, and the surfer, the painter? Each stroke of the painter's brush, it was believed, represented the artist's mood, creative expression, and *experience*.

The latter of which, Len had none at all.

On the other hand, he'd always looked the part of the stereotypical West Coast surfer, so score one in the image department. We watched as Len nodded, those locks of his rustling in the sun, then threw himself over top of the board on his stomach, his legs bent at the knee, his feet writing on the sky. A wave bounced over the nose of his board, salt water spraying his face.

I'd forgotten until now about Len's balance. He could squat flat-footed on the edge of a diving board without falling in, while I always tottered there, forced to roll up on the balls of my feet to avoid wobbling. And sometimes even that didn't work. I'd witnessed his adeptness at balancing several times at a neighbor's pool, well, before life gave way to secrets and other dangers.

I hauled Jer up and held him to my side, noting that his days on my hip were numbered. We watched Len as he paddled out using a crawl stroke behind a teen we'd learned was Steven Jr., the man's eldest boy.

"He's gonna have to be careful not to cork the board." Steve Sr. gave Jer and me a step-by-step surf lesson. "Yeah, he's good. He's got his body centered, so he oughta be all right. Steven'll make him sit on the board out there first to get a feel for it." Arms crossed across his belly, he glanced down at us, quite fatherly. "The key is staying calm. 'Specially the first time on a board."

I nodded, half listening, half wondering how life could feel so ordinary all of a sudden. Beyond the breaker, Steven Jr. made a spinning motion with his hand, as if to instruct Len to turn around. Len pulled the board around, rose onto his knees, then dropped into a sitting position, just the slightest wobble left to right on the landing.

From the shore, Steve Sr. gave Len an exaggerated thumbs-up, despite the fact Len was oblivious to it. "Your husband there has some talent. 'Course, he's not standing yet, but just getting that far without upending himself is a big accomplishment."

I didn't correct him. Not that I didn't try. But when I opened my mouth to utter the truth—that we were divorced—my mouth shut so fast it rattled my teeth. The awkwardness of it all caused my heart to feel as if it had dropped to the hollow of my stomach. Would I always feel as though a scarlet *D* were sown into my blouse like a modern-day Hester Prynne? My mind revealed the ridiculousness of the thought, but my heart, where it continued to roil in the pit of my stomach, sunk even more.

"Well, would you look at that? That guy's got *some* talent." Steve Sr. and the rest of his family all hooted and cheered, as if Len was out there "shootin' the pipe" like some Hawaiian hotshot surfer. True, he looked strong standing on that board like he'd done this all his life, but he also reminded me of a bent-kneed sumo wrestler, his feet death-gripping the board at either side.

"Woo-oo, Daddy!" Jer kicked his legs and pointed, and I had to admit he looked impressive out there, gliding on that never-ending wave, riding it onto shore. For a second time, life felt ordinary and new all at the same time.

Jer scrambled from my arms and splashed into the water, twisting that heart in my gut a little more. Len scooped him up, licks of white foam glancing off their legs and arms, and into the air.

Steve Sr. whipped him with several man pats to the back. "You're a natural, all right. We were expectin' you to take the polar bear plunge out there, but man you surprised us."

Len grinned and shook his locks like a long-haired dog after a dip in the pool.

I flinched. "Great. Thanks for that."

"You're welcome." He laughed and swiveled his face to Jer's. "You wanna try surfing too?"

I lurched toward them, reaching for our son. "No way."

Steve Sr. scoffed. "You have to start them young, Mom." He poked his hand into the air above him, motioning about who knows what, and waved his wife toward him. She'd already gone back to their beach setup to pick up her knitting, and I cringed at the way she hastily set it back into her bag and jumped from her chair.

"Here you are." She caught up to us, her voice slightly winded, the tiniest life vest I'd ever seen dangling from her forearm. "This one should fit him just fine."

"That a wet suit?" Jer scrambled to the ground and took it from the woman's grasp.

Len squatted next to him and guided his arms into the slots. "Nope. It's a life vest and it'll help you since you probably don't swim yet."

Was that pause at the end of his sentence directed at me and my parenting skills?

I lowered myself into the wet sand, unconcerned that its mushiness took no time in working its way past the elastic of my swimsuit. "You may wear the vest, Jer." I took over dressing duties. I snapped the plastic latches shut at his chest and implored him with my mommy eyes. "But you may not go out farther than you can stand. Do you understand me?"

"Aw, c'mon, Suz." Len removed my hands from my son's vest and pulled Jer close to him. "You gotta relax. You saw me out there. I can handle this."

Alarms rang in my head. "Out *there*? Are you insane?" I jolted my head side to side. "You are *not* taking Jeremiah out into deep water!"

Steve Sr.'s wife patted my shoulder. "Steven Jr. can go with them. Don't worry; he's done it with all the boys." She cast a serene smile at the rest of her ragamuffin clan. "Besides, he knows better than to take a little boy out into too high of surf."

I thrashed a look at the family of gangly, sand-crusted kids encircling me, their faces quizzical, egging me on to allow my young son to get on a surfboard with his father—*an ex-con!*

Shame heated my face for thinking such thoughts. *The man had reformed, Suz. Have some compassion!* But still . . . take Jeremiah, who could barely blow face bubbles in the bathtub, out into the ocean? I couldn't breathe, couldn't fathom what I would do if anything were to—I obliterated the thought with a flick of my head.

"Fine." I stuck one stick-straight finger in Len's face. "One ride and you must guard him with your life."

He laughed. "Or what?"

"Or I will kill you."

The way their mother ushered them all away from me like a befuddled hen, I got the feeling that Steve Sr.'s family members were literalists. So maybe announcing that, should the need arise, I would not hesitate to do away with Jeremiah's father wasn't the most appropriate thing to say. And yet, it made the point. Isn't that what mattered?

I stood, hands on hips, eyes squinting into the afternoon sun. It calmed my fears a bit to stand unwavering, a beacon of sorts, almost like a lighthouse shining the way for Jeremiah and his surfboard to follow home. Of course, it soon became painfully clear that neither Len nor Steven Jr.—nor even Jeremiah—paid any attention to me whatsoever.

No matter. I wouldn't leave my post. In this moment, as the surging tide slapped my shins and bounced off my knees, and as I braved the blazing sunlight to keep my gaze zeroed in on my son, I realized more than ever that there was nothing I would not do for that child.

Nothing.

Chapter Thirty

 "You had a phone call."

I dragged myself to the overstuffed chair across from where the two lovebirds sat side by side, Callie leafing through *Brides* magazine and Gage holding a fat pencil over a large sketch pad. With my thick white robe wrapped about me and my feet stuck into fake UGG slippers, all I wanted to do was sink into the chair and watch something brainless on TV.

Callie glanced up from a shiny page. "Don't you want to know who it was?"

I shrugged. "Oprah?"

She frowned at Gage. "Aw, hon, you told. Thought you were going to let me do the honors."

Gage kept working on the drawing in his sketch pad. Probably the design for the camp's new mess hall.

"Seriously, Seth called on your cell phone. Hope you don't mind that I picked it up for you." Callie beamed. "Sounded like he *really* wanted to speak with you."

"He told you that?"

"He has such a nice voice." She glanced at Gage. "Isn't that what I told you?"

Gage shot me a look. "She said he had a voice that could coax a screaming kitten out of a tree."

Callie slapped him on the thigh with her magazine. "Well, it's true." She laughed. "You mock me so!"

He slid closer and threw his arm around her, kissing her mouth. "I would never mock you. Tease a little—maybe. Mock—never."

They nuzzled and cooed and forgot all about me. So I dragged myself back up, willing myself not to make my dramatic eye roll too obvious, and headed into the kitchen. I took my phone with me and slid it onto the island, giving it the once-over as I paced the room, chewing on the idea of calling Seth back.

Men, it appeared, were at the root of all my problems.

Earlier Len had brought Jeremiah back to shore giddy from the ride, and I took that opportunity to grab our uneaten lunch and skedaddle home. After offering a cursory thanks to Steve Sr.'s large family, I took Jer by the hand and led him to the rickety staircase with Len following behind. He knew he had annoyed me, so he cracked a few jokes.

"So the preacher says . . ."

I shot a "why me" look into the abyss-like blue sky.

The phone mocked me from that kitchen island, daring me to pick it up. I turned a cold shoulder to it, though, and filled the teakettle with water and switched on the burner. Chai waited for no one.

Unfortunately, the phone proved me wrong. An incoming call caused it to buzz and bounce on the island. I yelped and grabbed it up before glancing at the screen. "Hello."

"Suz? It's me. Your stalker."

I hesitated. "Seth. Hi."

"Hi."

"I heard you had called and was just about to, uh . . ."

"I was just calling back to say that I'll be up at the warehouse tomorrow, fixing some beading around the top row of windows." He paused. "Was going to suggest that we take a lunch break together."

"I don't know if I can."

"We never finished our talk. I was hoping we could do that tomorrow."

I nodded as if we stood face-to-face, my breath suctioned right out of me. "Okay, yes, maybe midmorning or so."

"Yeah, sure, midmorning."

The whir of heating water drew my attention and I lowered the flame beneath the kettle. "Seth? Is there something . . . something going on?"

"What do you mean?"

I forged ahead, tired of the drama that had characterized my existence lately. "I don't know. True, we haven't really been friends for the past six years or so. But"—I pulled a mug out of the cabinet, then a box of tea from the drawer—"we were once very close."

"I remember."

"And now we're either dancing around subjects or annoyed with each other."

I plopped the tea bag into a mug, poured some boiling water, and waited for Seth to formulate his thoughts. In my mind, I saw him knitting those brows together, gathering the words to say, his mouth twisted in that usual way of his. Strange how the image conjured up expectation in me.

"Boy. You tell it like it is now. That's new for you."

"How so?"

"I don't know, Suz. Sometimes I remember times from when we were young. All the times I dragged you to things you probably didn't want to do. You were a good sport, but you could have told me no occasionally." He exhaled into the phone. "'Course, you finally did that, didn't you?"

I despised confrontation when I was younger but learned that sometimes it had to be done. My eyes shut against the memories of the days and weeks after Len's incarceration and all the growing up I had to do, all the people I had to ask favors of or explain my position to.

"Please, if you could give me a couple of weeks, I'm sure I'll be able to make that payment . . ." *"We must have our cleaning deposit back . . ."* *"We'll just need the assistance for a little while . . ."*

I let far too much honey ooze into my tea, watching the

sticky substance dissolve in the heat. "Maybe you're right. I've changed in that respect—kind of had to."

His voice grew low, earnest. "You had to face things most daughters never do at that age. Change was expected."

Tears spiked the back of my eyes. "I never meant to hurt you, Seth. Everything I knew was spinning. I just had to take control of it."

"I know you did."

Of course he did. Seth knew me better than most back when my world was ever-so-steadily edging away from me, even better than Gage did. When Mom had died, my attempt to take control of my life led me to choose the wrong path. Was I in further danger of misreading God's direction and making more perilous mistakes in the days ahead?

I didn't know the answer, but the idea lingered.

I did realize, though, that hearing Seth's voice and bumping into him around town, even for only brief moments, affected me in ways that intrigued me. And his words of late—an apology, explanations for his attitude—brought comfort like my daily tea yet frightened me too, as if I'd been handed a harness and asked to bungee jump over the sea. I didn't know whether to hug him like an old friend or choose to keep my distance.

"So we're on for break time tomorrow, then? I'll bring bagels."

My eyes squeezed shut, forcing out the voice of warning in my head. "Okay. And I can grab a carafe of coffee on my way out."

He uttered a "See you" and hung up, and I continued to stare off into nothingness.

"Fun call?" Callie stood in the doorway, a mug in her hands. "I was just going to grab some water. You okay?"

I slid away from the island, dropping the phone with a thud, and leaned back against the stove, cradling my mug in my hand. "I'm fine, but give me something to think about other than myself. How was your meeting with the minister tonight?"

She filled her mug with water and took a sip, her beaming face shining across the room.

"That good, huh?"

Her dimples deepened when she smiled. "I never thought of myself as a froufrou girl, but oh, Suz, it's going to be a beautiful wedding!"

"Of course it will be—even if you're not all that froufrou." I laughed, the emotion bringing relief to my shoulders.

"But we've been talking about things other than the wedding, of course. Pastor Erik has covered every topic you can imagine related to marriage—money, kids, resolving conflict . . . sex." She said that last word in a whisper. "He's leaving no stone unturned, that one."

"And it's not weird talking to the pastor about all those personal things?" I drained my mug and set it into the sink. "I mean, marriage is such an intimate place for two people. I'm just wondering if it's strange talking it out with a third person."

"Not at all. I am really glad we're doing this, actually.

Especially with someone like Erik who's been through so much turmoil of his own."

"Like what?"

One of Callie's eyebrows shot up. I'd only seen her do that when angry with Gage way back when. "You don't know? His wife had an affair about four years ago."

"The one he's married to now?"

She nodded. "Yes—Andrea. It was this huge scandal in the church, people divided over it, but Erik decided to take a stand for his marriage—and God healed it. Eventually."

"She really cheated on him?" I'd probably never be able to look at the pastor's wife the same way again.

"Really did. A lot of people never could forgive her and left the church, but Erik proved that forgiveness can bring about the miraculous. I'm surprised you've never heard him talk about it—they're both very open about what happened. But then again, it was a long time ago. Anyway, he talked to us about that time in his life and how much easier it would have been to walk away. Nobody would have blamed him, but he chose to believe that God could do the unbelievable, so Erik trusted him to fix both his marriage and his heart in the process." She leaned back, looking up to the ceiling. "Good, good stuff."

"So, you believe they're healed now? Completely?"

She cocked her head. "I do. Not only because I've witnessed them together, but I also know the Holy Spirit's power that's been promised to us. God restored their love and made it stronger, even. Something to remember." She shook her head. "Not that I think Gage and I would ever get into that situation."

"You mean having to forgive each other for committing adultery?"

Callie paused. "Suz. I wasn't talking about your situation. You know that, right? No one blames you for what happened with Len. That was all his doing."

"I know that."

"If anyone's been more than kind and giving considering the mess he put you through, I'd be surprised. You've been the epitome of forgiveness. Most women wouldn't have allowed a man who had done those things back into their lives."

"Ha—I'm not a saint, Callie."

"No, but you look at dark things in the most positive light possible. A person doesn't have to know you long to see that. You helped me so much to look at things that way. Remember when you painted all those verses on the walls in my house?"

I smiled. "How could I forget?" Outside of helping out in Gage's office, Callie had offered me my first paying job in Otter Bay. "I was afraid you'd fire me for taking such liberties with your bare walls. A temptation I had difficulty resisting."

"Well, no worries there. That was such a low point in my life, but those beautiful words painted freely took hold of my heart and made me realize the preciousness of this life and how much I had to be thankful for. Don't sell yourself short, Suz." She set her empty mug into the sink and wrapped an arm about my shoulder. "I think Len realizes the huge error he made and how it's too late now. He's lucky you've allowed him the grace to be a father again to Jeremiah."

Gage poked his head into the kitchen. "Am I interrupting?"

Callie gave me another squeeze. "Nah. Just girl talk." She slipped across the room and landed a smooch on his cheek. "I'm going to go—lots of cabin assignments to wrestle with tonight."

Gage pulled back, surveying his fiancée's face. "Thought you delegated that responsibility to your assistant."

She pressed her forefinger to his protesting lips. "Some things are hard to give up."

I puttered around the kitchen, trying not to notice the way Gage captured Callie's hand in his own and pulled it to his mouth, kissing it softly. Until now, I hadn't wanted to admit the appeal of a relationship like that. Even during my marriage, before I noticed the deep chasms forming, I had longed for that kind of intimacy. Had I ever known it?

Gage ushered Callie out of the kitchen, and I heard the screen door slam shut as he accompanied her to her car. Maybe what Letty said the other night at the cabin was true. Maybe Len, in his own clumsy way, was attempting to woo me back to him. Maybe his acceptance of faith had given him hope that, if only I'd forgive him, things could be like they once were. No, scratch that, that things could be like they had never been before.

I dried the last dish and stuck it into the cabinet, my mind and heart divided over what to think about that and what to do next.

Chapter Thirty-One

 Monday morning brought Letty into the studio with a new mission. Fueled by a desire to pay me back—so not necessary, but whatever—she sidled up next to me with a stack of books and an exuberant mouth overflowing with information.

"Feathery, intertidal blossoms, another term for sea anemones, often withdraw their petal-like tentacles and fold themselves inward until the swirl of activity around them subsides." She read from a marked page. "But they are not wimps!"

My personal tidal-information provider went on. "Although the sea anemone may look delicate and flowerlike, in reality they are hardy creatures that trap their own food, move and hide for survival and—get this—they *reproduce* in the energetic waters along California's central coast."

"Um, Letty? It was only a bag of groceries."

She snapped the book shut and dropped it onto my workstation. "Oh, but you did so much more than that, Suzanna. You talked me out of my own dreary misery. I will not rest until I have paid you back in full. And part of that is providing you with information about the project you are about to embark on."

She leaned in close, her perfume curling up my nostrils and causing me to tense lest I sneeze in her face. "A true artist must have in-depth knowledge of her subject. This is Art 101 and I, Leticia, am your teacher."

"Yes, ma'am." A snicker trailed through my lips, but I clamped my mouth shut when she gave me the evil eye.

"We will move on—for now." She slipped an apron over her head and motioned for me to follow.

The project lay across the table, shrouded by a sheet. I peered at Letty. "Is it . . . dead?"

Timo guffawed.

Letty clucked. "So now you are a comedienne? Shall we unveil it for her, Timo, or let her simmer in her curiosity?" She sent him a wave, as if to say "oh, never mind," then tugged one corner of the sheet, pulling it away with a flourish. Letty looked at me. "What do you think?"

"It's . . . gorgeous." I ran a finger along the molded edges. "It's completely intact—every bit of it. And primer's been applied too."

Letty crossed arms in front of her and nodded like a proud mother. "That's Timo's work. He molded and replaced the broken sections, then applied the primer. It's why we keep him around." She dipped toward him, those arms still crossed. "The *only* reason why."

"Ch-yeah." In a not-so-debonair move, Timo stuck a pencil atop his ear only to have it slide out and hopscotch down his back. He bent to pick it up and, upon rising, bumped his head on the workstation. Letty leapt forward and grabbed a jostled jar of brushes to keep it from overturning.

With a look that would wilt fake daisies, Letty dismissed Timo, then turned to me. "Is this not the most beautiful almost-restored door?"

I patted her upper arm, warmed by the glow in her eyes. She loved her work and who could avoid getting swept up in her passion for it? "Oh, Letty, it is. Truly. Maybe someday you will visit Monaco and see it hanging proudly in place."

"You mean other than in my dreams?"

I laughed and set off to find my own apron. With the door's finish line in view, Letty and I would work straight through the morning. We still needed to in-paint where needed and apply gilding in strategic spots.

I prepped my station and got back to work, with Letty sending only an occasional comment or instruction my way. I would not allow my mind to travel the labyrinth of thoughts that had awakened me through the night. Instead, my mind and heart stayed focused on the painstaking restoration of this wounded door, my energy better spent here than on my worries. Whoever claimed to dislike good, hard work had obviously never had his or her heart broken.

Nor had she been faced with the challenges of forgiving the one who broke it in the first place.

My back ached, but I didn't let it bother me, each pull of my muscles another sign that progress was being made, each shot of pain a reminder that I was learning a skill that may one day grant me the independence I sought.

A clap resounded against the studio's din. "Enough! I am going for coffee. Want some?"

I glanced at the clock, shocked by how much time had passed. "Actually, I'm meeting someone."

Letty squinted at me.

"Okay, fine. I'm meeting Seth."

"The one with the voice—and the squeegee."

I grabbed a wadded-up paper towel and tossed it at her. "Have your fun. We're friends, Letty, and he just wants to talk to me about something." I shrugged. "He's been trying to make amends lately."

"Sure he has." She held up her pointer finger to stop another protest. "You don't need to explain yourself to me. He has brought you breakfast and that is more than enough explanation." She flicked her chin toward the door.

Seth stood behind me holding a large bag with a handle, a goofy grin on his face.

"You're here. Hang on a second and I'll grab some coffee for us." I moved quickly away from him, annoyed that my face had grown hot.

Filling up the thermos I'd brought from home gave me time to recover. If only I could dash into the restroom and pat some cool water on my face, take a few deep breaths, and start over. Instead I willed away the heat from my face, even as my heart began to beat a little louder. *Rats.*

"Let me hold that for you." He took the carafe from me, his smile wide. "Ready?"

We slipped out the door and walked up a narrow, undulating path behind the studio. I didn't have to ask where Seth was headed—the path led to a spot above the studio's roofline that exposed the wide arc of the sea.

The path tightened, going from smooth to rocky soil. Seth stopped, stuck the thermos under one arm, and reached for me. "Give me your hand."

I let him take my hand in his, and together we pushed our way up the steep incline. We continued on like that until reaching the lone table and bench beneath a fragrant pine with umbrella-like branches stretching out for shade. The ocean sparkled like crystal in dappled sunlight.

He set the coffee and bag of bagels onto the table, but his hand lingered on mine. With a start, I withdrew my hand and made some innocuous comment about how beautiful the ocean looked, realizing the redundancy in saying "beautiful" and "ocean" in the same breath.

He thrust a hand into the bag. "So I brought you cream cheese in three different flavors: blueberry, strawberry, and the plain stuff. You still like blueberry?"

I reached for the small white tub. "I don't know. Haven't had any in . . ."

He quirked a smile. "About six years?"

"Yeah." I had once bought a tub of it for a picnic and when there were no takers, I ate the whole thing myself. Disgusting, but at eighteen who really worried over their fat intake? "Quite the memory you have."

He tore a piece of fresh bagel and stuck it in his mouth. "Not something easily forgotten."

"Tsk, tsk. Even Jer's finally learned not to talk with his mouth full." I mumbled something unintelligible, pointed at him, and laughed.

He swallowed his bite and laughed back. "What can I say? You bring out the little boy in me."

"Caring for one child is enough, thank you very much."

"Ah, from what I can tell, you love being a mom. And your boy adores you."

I smiled at that. "He's my life now. Wouldn't change that for anything."

"I'd like to get to know him."

"Who? Jeremiah?"

Seth swallowed his bite of bagel and stopped before taking another. "If that's okay with you . . ."

The idea sounded comfortable, like iced tea on a warm day. Yet a trickle of something—anxiety, maybe?—attempted to wriggle its way up my neck. "Of course it's okay. Maybe we can meet for ice cream some weekend." There. A noncommittal, simple answer.

"Ice cream it is, then." He paused. "Actually, I was wondering if you and Jer would like to drive over to the zoo in

Atascadero with me on Saturday to see the monkeys. I'm sure we could find some ice cream nearby."

Just the three of us? I imagined us standing in front of the monkey exhibit, mesmerized by the wild creatures whooping and swinging high above our heads. A perfectly whimsical idea from the Seth I once knew. And yet his idea sounded anything but spur of the moment. Something about the way he suggested it, while watching carefully for my reaction, gave me the impression that it was premeditated.

I kept myself focused on the half bagel before me, smearing it with blueberry cream cheese. "Sure. That sounds nice. Do you want to drive back up here or . . . ?"

"Of course. I'll come by and pick you up around noon."

"Great."

An awkward silence settled between us. I chewed my bagel slowly.

He reached for the plain cream cheese. "When all is said and done, the purist in me prefers the old-fashioned kind. Does that make me sound old?"

I smiled, thankful for broken ice. "Is that why you cut your hair? Because you're getting 'up there' and thought the style too young for you?"

"Nice segue. No, I cut it because it reminded me of my grandmother's mop—after she'd spiffed up the whole house."

"Spiffed up?"

He grunted a laugh. "Cleaned, washed . . . whatever." He took another bite of bagel and let his gaze wander out to sea before swinging it back to me. "You think it's too establishment for me, don't you?"

I shrugged. "Wouldn't say that. Haven't noticed too many men in suits wearing spiky hair."

"They're short spikes and Holly's hairdresser, Dora, says they're not too much."

A small snort escaped me. "You have your hair done by a hairdresser named Dora?"

"What? You think that's weird?" He leaned on his elbows, a piece of bagel suspended before him. "A lot of guys go in there."

"It's just that I always thought of you as more of a barber kind of guy." The giggles came and I pressed the back of my hand to my lips, forcing them closed. "Not like you ever actually went to one back then."

He gave me a mock glare. "Laugh all you want. I'll have you know I get plenty of compliments on my hair."

"I bet you do." He exuded strength, not in a bulky, he-man kind of way, but he looked fit and healthy and cut in all the right places. I glanced away, pulling myself from that kind of admiration—the kind long since buried, but oh so remembered.

I cleared my throat. "So. You said on the phone that you had something you wanted to tell me."

His eyes shrunk a little, as if his thoughts had moved from lightness to something more serious. He dropped the remaining piece of bagel onto a napkin and dusted the crumbs from his hands.

"I did. But I don't know where to start exactly." His lips twisted and I caught myself fixating on them.

"Sounds serious."

His face, raw with sudden emotion, caught me off guard. I twiddled with my fingers, lacing them in and out of each other as he gathered the steam he needed to continue.

"Here goes. I know I've already said this, but I came barreling at you the other day, and you didn't deserve it, Suz. We hadn't seen each other in years, so where did I get off mentioning your parents—let alone criticizing you for how you remembered them?" He reached for my hand and rubbed the back of my fingers. "I am sorry, and I hope you will forgive me for being so stupid."

Emotion whirled through me. He shifted, piercing eyes focused on me, waiting, and I knew that my lack of response unnerved him. My gaze dropped to where his fingers drew circles on the back of my hand and I mustered up the courage to speak. "Forgiven. I'm sorry, too, for overreacting." I didn't move my hand away, irresponsibly leaving myself open to a man's heart again. Was I ready for that?

"Can I tell you something that I've observed?" he asked. "Your faith has changed; it's deeper now. You always had a hopeful outlook on life. Shoot, when we were kids you could turn down my crazy ideas but do it so positively that I didn't even realize you were saying 'no.'"

I smiled at that.

"I shouldn't have expected anything less in regards to your parents, but somehow I did. I remember how *I* felt about your parents' passing. It didn't seem fair. So, of course, when you spoke about them in that glowing way of yours, only this time with more conviction than I'd ever known, I balked." He shook his head, staring at me. "It made me angry."

"Angry? But why?"

He shrugged one shoulder. "Because it opened up a wound in me that wasn't done healing."

A drawn-out silence hovered between us and I wanted to probe, to find out what troubled him enough to say such a thing. I was at a loss.

"Suz, I've done more in the past six years than travel across this country from job to job." A determined set to his chin told me he was ready to continue. "I met a girl. Thought she might be the one—after you."

My expression fell.

"But then . . . I broke her heart."

I bit my bottom lip. "Seth, you're not the first guy to—"

He shook his head, silencing me. "It didn't end there. This is where it gets tough." He gathered air into his lungs and clasped his hands together, squeezing them as if gathering strength. "She became pregnant—with my baby." His voice, usually so soothing, sounded jagged, broken.

"You're a father? I–I had no idea."

Instead of joy on his face, though, his eyes brimmed with tears and the edges grew pink. "I tried to straddle both worlds, still flitting around and taking jobs I didn't care about while also promising to set up a life with Ginny. By the time I made up my mind to get serious and make a commitment to her and the baby—she was gone. She found someone else, someone who wanted to marry her and give her everything I'd been too selfish to deliver."

"She left you?"

"She did."

"I'm sorry."

"Me too." His breathing was pronounced. "One day they were going out to dinner and a car ran a red light."

An invisible forced wrapped around my lungs and squeezed. I waited for him to finish his thought, and all the time hoped that he would not.

He looked up. "They were broadsided. Ginny and her fiancé made it through, but the baby died in her womb. She was almost to term. I spent the last couple of years blaming everyone—me, Ginny, God—for allowing that to happen."

A tear dribbled down my cheek, landing on my forearm. "Seth, I don't know what to say, other than I am so very sorry . . ." I had no words, nothing but sadness in my heart for him and the child he never knew.

"I've wanted to talk with you again, ever since the other night when you laid into me for bluntly judging you. What you said speared me." He shook his head, a tiny smile pulling at the corners of his eyes. "Instead of allowing my faith in God to comfort, I've been using it to condemn myself, completely forgetting everything I believe to be true about eternity. And about his grace to forgive."

I reached for Seth's hand and cradled it between mine.

"So much of my confusion has been about my struggle with God. Not that he failed me." His eyes found mine. "But that I had failed him."

"Oh, Seth. I can't imagine losing a child." An ache lurched in my chest. "But I understand what it's like to think you've failed God. That's giving us way too much credit, though."

He nodded, his lips rubbing together as he thought. "I've felt a barrier between God and me for a while, but I have been realizing something more and more."

"What's that?"

He shrugged. "That I'm the one who put it there. He's been offering me forgiveness and healing all along, but my hard head wouldn't accept it. I couldn't forgive myself, Suz."

I watched him. "And now?"

"Now I'm like God's stalker." He leaned closer, his face animated like the Seth I once knew. "I've been reading and studying, trying to catch up on everything I've missed for so long."

I smiled, pulling our entwined hands close and pressed my lips to his fingers, the familiar smell of his skin awakening our past. Sorrow retreated from his eyes and it did a number on my heart and in my soul.

His voice drew me in more. "Suz?"

"Hmm?"

His forehead shifted. "I've missed . . . us."

My heart and head overflowed with responses, but only one made it out. "I've missed our friendship too, Seth."

His brows dipped and his eyes darkened.

Why had I chosen this moment to define our relationship? After years of mistakes, wouldn't it be better to base a relationship on something more reliable than emotion?

My head tried to make its case. My heart, however, wasn't listening.

I continued to hold his hand, watching a frown develop across his face. "Seth, I—"

"Am I interrupting?"

Seth's hand jerked from my caress, and my chin swung sharply to the side. "Len." I winced, and not only because of the throbbing pain at the base of my neck.

Len stood in the tall grass, a kid-sized pair of size three slip-on shoes dangling from one hand, the other propped onto the hard edge of his hip.

If I wasn't mistaken, by the pouting expression on my ex-husband's face, he had much more than a pair of lost shoes on his mind.

Chapter Thirty-Two

 We had nothing to hide. So why did Len's unexpected presence make me feel as if my father had caught me in a compromising position with Seth?

He wore that man-pout better than ever. "Was just going to return our son's shoes to you. Took a run out on the beach today and found them there, half covered in sand."

"Thanks." I reached for them, dazed.

Seth shifted and began to gather up our makeshift breakfast.

He wouldn't make eye contact, no matter how hard I searched his face. "Don't leave," I whispered.

He stopped and gave me a halfhearted smile. "Duty calls."

Len cut in. "If he has to go, I'll walk you back. I've been thinking about Jer ever since teaching him to surf the other day. The boy's got good balance. We should talk about developing his skills. I could help him with that."

I both nodded and wagged my head, confused. As Seth moved to leave, I touched his arm and looked into his face, my voice still a whisper. "You sure you have to go?"

"Yes."

"Sorry. Let's talk again soon."

He shrugged that one shoulder again. "Sure."

"I will pray for you, Seth."

The caress in his eyes melted me. It was all I could do to hold myself back from following him down that hill, even though I could in no way keep up his pace.

Len took a seat on the bench, the same place Seth had just vacated. It didn't seem right.

I crossed my arms. "Wouldn't it have been easier to just drop Jer's shoes onto the porch?"

"You're angry."

I rubbed my lips together. "It's complicated."

He raked his tousled hair. "Honestly, Suz. Didn't plan on interrupting anything. If you want to blame someone, take it out on Timo. He pointed out the way for me to find you."

I exhaled and darted a glance to sea, a place of instant relief. Of course, Len couldn't have known that Seth and I were up here together. Not that it mattered.

"When I found the shoes, I took it as a sign that I should come find you. You seemed pretty peeved at me yesterday, and in my gut, I knew I shouldn't have left things that way." Len opened both palms, like in surrender. "This faith thing is all new to me, but when I get a feeling like that, I can't ignore it."

I eyed him. "You haven't mentioned much about your, um, newfound faith, Len, and I've been wanting to ask you about it."

He motioned to the opposite bench. "Then sit down and I'll spill my guts."

My gaze switched to the distant studio. Letty would be pacing, watching the clock by now.

Len came around the bench to stand beside me. "I get it. You have to go back to work. I can respect that." He offered his hand. "C'mon. I'll tell you all about it on the way down."

For the next several minutes, I listened as Len spoke about the chaplain who wouldn't give up on him. The man's visits were relentless, apparently, and in Len's words, "He prayed me into the Kingdom." He was there for Len when the parole board considered his release and helped him purchase a ticket to fly all the way out here to reconnect with his family.

I flipped him a brief smile. "Guess I owe him a thank you." I would not soon forget the pure happiness on Jer's face when he saw his father again.

As we stepped and slid down the rocky hill, I lost my footing more than once and stumbled into Len. I never fell, and by the time we reached the level area behind the studio, my annoyance had vanished. Maybe I'd been too hard on him, judging the new Len by what the old Len had done. I flashed on the two women outside of Jeremiah's Sunday school class. They chattered blithely about divorce, indifferent to those around them, and I shuddered recalling how their judgment felt.

Len was trying to show me he had changed. Was my doubt standing in the way of his spiritual progress?

We reached the back door to the studio just as Fred appeared.

"Well, hullo there, dear Suzanna." My boss smiled in that cherry-cheeked way of his, no sign of illness on him.

"Fred, you're here!" I gave him a hug, and he blushed. "Good to see you. I'd like you to meet Len, Jeremiah's father."

They shook hands, Fred's mouth no longer smiling but pursed, like he suddenly had something on his mind. "Good to meet you." He turned to me. "You coming in, Suzi-Q?"

I nodded. "Sure thing. If I don't get back to the door project soon, Letty'll mount my head on it."

He chuckled, entered the studio, and held the door open for me. He directed a congenial smile at Len. "You know the way down from here?"

Len nodded, then looked to me. "Are we done?"

Fred stayed in place, waiting patiently and holding that door. I held up my hand with the shoes dangling from them. "Thanks for returning Jer's sandals. I'll call you about setting up a schedule for visitation."

He chucked my chin with his fingers. "Aw, we're going to be as formal as all that?"

His words sounded light, but the disappointment in his face threw me. I hesitated. "I'll call. Promise."

After he'd gone, Fred and I weaved our way slowly through

the studio. "I didn't want to ask in front of Len, but did you enjoy your weekend at the cabin? Were the accommodations to your liking?"

I placed a hand on his shoulder. "It's a dream, Fred. I can't thank you enough for allowing us to stay. Oh, and I worked up more drawings and would love to show them to you and Sherry, when you're ready."

"Did you happen to bring them?"

Letty appeared before I could answer. "Fabulous. You are here. I was about to pull on my hiking boots and break up your little love nest out there."

Fred frowned. "Is that what I did, Suzi-Q?"

I blinked. "What? No." I threw a daggered gaze at Letty. "Please."

My boss stood between Letty and me. "Before I forget, the missus and I will be touring some restored areas of the castle in about a half hour. Why don't you join us, Suz—and bring along those drawings of yours. Can you do it today?"

I kept my eyes from Letty's face. "Uh, sure. I signed Jer up for after-school care, so that should be fine. If Letty doesn't mind me flaking on the door again, that is."

Letty only shrugged, her warm skin turning pink.

My brow furrowed. "Wait!"

Two sets of eyes focused on me.

"Can Letty join us?"

Fred appeared startled, and a look of dawning crossed his face. "If she'd like, then she is welcome."

"Oh, she would like."

Letty grimaced. "*She* is right here."

Fred peeked at her over his glasses. "If you're ready to tear yourself away from the door project, then you may certainly come with us today, Leticia."

"I would like that."

"Good." He glanced at us both and offered a salute. "Sherry and I will meet you outside in one half hour."

ON MY PREVIOUS JOURNEY to Hearst Castle I rode in the back of a commercial van with carefree college students—while hiding from Seth. Today could not be more different. Although that last predicament had been altogether strange and funny, I remembered the day as bright and beautiful. Today, dark clouds formed on the horizon, threatening to blow one way or the other, and I guessed they'd head in our direction about the time we arrived for a stroll around the Neptune Pool. The outdoor pool, of course.

"Of all the days!" Inside the car, Sherry pulled the collar of her wool coat tighter around her neck. "The morning held so much promise too."

Fred sniffed the air through an open slit of a window. "Doesn't smell like rain, though. Probably just a gray day." He turned to his wife. "Glad I have you to look at. Like a rainbow against the blah."

Sherry tittered. "Such a charmer." She turned from her seat up front. "The man has poetry in his soul that just leaks out everywhere. Find yourself one like this, girls, and you will never be bored."

I held back my laughter while Letty kept her face still like stone. "You are one lucky woman, Sherry." Did Letty's eyes just flip upward ever so slightly?

"Here we are!" Despite the drop in temperature, Sherry's excitement at visiting the castle overwhelmed her desire for a brighter day. "Where's Clem?"

Letty and I unlatched our seat belts as Fred patted Sherry's hand. "He'll be here. His car died this morning so he's getting a ride up with a worker." Fred turned to us. "You ladies probably remember him. Tall guy . . . runs the window-cleaning business . . ."

"Seth?"

He snapped his fingers. "Seth. That's him. Clem called to say that Seth would be driving him up in his truck." He craned a look out through the windshield. "Thought they might have made it up by now, though."

The rumble of engine and crackling of driveway arrived on cue. Through the window I caught a glimpse of Seth's face behind the steering wheel of his work truck, his smile congenial as his passenger carried on about something. His eyes, though, bore straight ahead, as if lost or thinking some far-off thought.

I opened the car door and stepped out. Whatever had captured Seth's attention vanished and when he smiled at me, it reached his eyes.

Clem hopped out of the car, ducking from a day that had turned blustery. He greeted us all quickly and then led the way up the stairs. Fred, Sherry, and Letty followed him while I stayed behind.

Seth hung back too and leaned against the passenger side of his truck, both hands shoved into the pockets of his faded jeans. He'd changed into a nubby plaid shirt but still shivered against the swirl of cold air. The divide between us had grown between the morning and afternoon.

"We didn't get to finish our conversation."

He shrugged that one shoulder, never pulling his hands out of his pockets. "No big deal."

I shifted from one foot to the other and exhaled. "Well, it is a big deal. To me."

"Why?"

I took two steps closer, then tilted my head. "Because until recently, I've been mad at you."

"At me? Why?" He shoved away from the truck.

"You've been ornery and somewhat bitter, more often than not."

He raised an eyebrow in defiance and took another step forward. "Really."

I straightened my shoulders and walked right up to him, swallowing the heady sense his closeness brought. "Really. But now you're not and I understand why. I misjudged you. And I'm sorry about that."

A tiny smile pulled at his mouth. "So you say terrible

things about me, then offer me a 'sorry about that' and it's supposed to be all better?"

I paused. "Yes."

He shrugged, but this time with both shoulders. "Well, okay then."

At this moment Seth resembled the man—or rather, the boy—I once knew. The stress lines I'd noticed earlier, the ones that tightened his eyes, had softened and lengthened as if molded by laughter. I longed to reach up and brush away the tendril of hair that stroked his temple and threatened to hide those sea green eyes of his. And when had he begun to grow out his hair again?

"Did everything work out with the ex?" His forehead shifted and his eyes narrowed a fraction.

"Yes. Fine. Sorry he interrupted us."

He pulled one hand out of his pocket and raised it, allowing it to hover in indecision before awkwardly laying it on my shoulder. "Would you have preferred that I stayed? If you would have let me know in some way, I would have . . ."

"Would have what?"

"Stuck around. Looked like you two had some things to discuss, so I left."

I reached up to my shoulder and placed my hand over his. "He's Jer's father, and until recently, I didn't think he'd be a part of his son's life." I released a deep breath. "Lots to decide now."

"Complicated?"

I shrugged. "I don't want to put it that way. Jer and I have done better on our own than I expected. Well, thanks to my brother. It wasn't my plan to shut out Jer's father; he managed to do that all by himself."

Seth's brow furrowed. "You've never told me what happened between you two."

I tilted my head to one side. How had I not told Seth about Len's incarceration? If I blurted out the whole unseemly story now, every negative thought Seth had about Len would set like concrete. Did I need to dredge it all back up again, especially with Len's newfound faith growing on baby legs? And what about Jer? Older kids back home teased him mercilessly about having a jailbird for a daddy. Thankfully at that age, he hadn't a clue how deep those claws dug.

I glanced away, waffling. "Like I said once before, he wanted out, and I had no choice but to let him go."

"And now?" Seth's eyes searched my face, my skin searing from the intensity.

"Now . . . what?"

"What's happening between you two now?"

"We're trying to figure out the whole single-parenting thing." I rubbed my face, a gust of wind tugging at my hair. "It's not easy."

"Might be, if you took him back."

My chin jerked up and I stepped backward, stifling a gasp. My heel landed on uneven pavement but Seth reached out and caught me, one warm hand a support to my lower back.

His mouth moved stunningly close to mine. "Just saying

that the guy obviously wants you back, Suz. He's trying to make you see how tough it is out here alone."

I pulled out of his grasp. "We can make it just fine."

And yet I knew that Seth, like Letty before him, had only spoken what he'd witnessed. Len had said as much in the letter he sent from prison, only I'd chosen to ignore that sentiment and stick with the safer one about wanting to be a good father to Jeremiah.

Accepting Len as a parent to our son I could handle. Anything more, I could not.

Seth held me steady with one long stare. "Is that what you want, Suz? To be alone?"

A sudden thought, clear as a cerulean sky after a windswept day, produced a catch in my throat that made it difficult to breathe. I dropped my gaze to the ground, afraid of what my eyes might reveal.

No . . . I want you.

Chapter Thirty-Three

 "There you are." Letty stood at the top of marble inlaid steps, both hands in the air, her face animated. "You are missing out."

Seth bent, his lips tickling my ear. "I don't want you to be alone." Slowly he removed his hand from my back. "Guess you'd better go."

I nodded, still unable to look at him, except fleetingly. "I'd better."

Letty waved me up the steps. "They are waiting for you in the Doge Suite. Have you seen how well the restored ceiling has held up? And the blue drapes are to die for!"

I took the steps two at a time, in step with Letty's exhilaration.

"Oh, and if only I could find a knockoff of that enormous antique blue perfume bottle—I would only have to fill it once and be set forever!"

Involuntarily, I sniffled.

She slowed to a jog. "Will lover boy be joining us?"

I flinched. "Stop that."

The joyful smile on Letty's face disappeared.

"Never mind. Let's go. Come on."

She grabbed my arm. "I am sorry I teased you. You know I didn't mean you any harm."

Poor Letty had no idea the turmoil racing like a luge through my insides. "Yes, I knew that."

She stepped up the pace again, her heels clacking against the red brick tile entryway. I followed her, but her speed—and perhaps a touch of that over-the-top enthusiasm—had waned.

By the time we reached Fred and Sherry, we both sounded winded, but a flicker of Letty's enthusiasm had returned. She spread her arms wide. "Does this room not make you want to immediately board a plane to Venice? Or at least settle in for the night?"

I glanced around, viewing the ornate room a second time. I could appreciate its historical significance and its flagrant Italian roots, but if I were to be honest, it dripped with gaudiness, its furnishings overbearing. Instead of inspired, I imagined a night where ghostly images carrying lanterns drifted by and the heavy bedding became my closest friend.

Sherry and Fred stood before the windowed doors, admiring the attached balcony and the restored wood ceiling that braved the elements day in and day out. "There are many more projects like this one to be handled."

"Tell me about that, Fred."

He turned, a smile holding up his cheeks. "They'll be looking for a project manager soon, someone detail oriented to stay on top of a steady stream of restoration jobs."

I slid a glance to Letty who had become stoic, her skin paling a little.

"Someone like Letty?"

Fred pressed his lips closed, his fuzzy eyebrows shifting as he squinted against the powdery light pouring into the room. He turned and winked. "Well, now, the cat has been let out of the bag."

Letty's eyes popped wide open. "Do you mean you will consider recommending me for the position?"

He grinned. "Who else? Not Suzi-Q, I hope." He chuckled heartily until it began to sound more like a roar.

My jaw dropped open and Sherry patted me with a motherly "there, there." I recovered and reached over to give my friend a hug. "Such great news!"

Confusion narrowed Letty's eyes. "I am honored, Fred, but why haven't you said anything before this?"

"Frankly, Leticia, I wasn't sure if you'd take the position even if it was offered to you. You have become the quintessential mother hen of the studio, keeping us on time and organized. I'm convinced you could take over the project manager position." He peered at her over the top of his spectacles. "Would you?"

"In a heartbeat."

"Very well, then. I'll make the recommendation. I cannot promise, of course, but I believe you will have a very good chance."

She held back, but I could tell she wanted to burst from the news. "Thank you, Fred."

"Before I do, however, I need you on another important project—"

Sherry sidled up next to her husband and poked him in the side with her elbow. He grunted, then looked to me. "So, what do you think of this room, Suz?"

I delayed answering by taking a deep breath and allowing my eyes to flit around, looking at nothing in particular. "Oh, well, it's so . . . blue . . . and, uh, historical."

Letty winced.

Fred only nodded. "And if it were up to you, you would remove the drapes, paint the room in a base color, and let your imagination roam free. Would you agree with that assessment?"

Is this a trick question? I searched the ceiling for just the right word, but oh, to be a wordsmith instead of an artist at a moment like this! "Honestly, Fred. This room is not my style, but you know what? I respect the artistry behind it. Passion shows, I think. I've often admired certain works, even when I knew they would never make it to my walls." I grew bolder. "If asked outright, lots of people would admit they'd never sleep here, but many of those same people if asked whether the room was beautiful, would say, 'Absolutely, in its own way, it certainly is.'"

Letty cackled. "Pollyanna, you never stop amazing me."

"I'm just sayin'."

Sherry nudged Fred again. "Tell her, dear."

"I've thought long and hard about this, and I have decided to move you to part time at the studio. At least temporarily."

"I . . . I don't understand." My mind crunched the numbers, and Jer and I could not survive in California, particularly the West Coast, on a part-time income. "Is it the quality of my work?" I swished a look at Letty. "Has it been subpar?"

Sherry's head agitated. "Nothing like that, dear. It's because we have such big plans for your work." She clapped her hands together. "Big ideas!"

Fred lowered his chin toward his wife. "I take it you'll be filling her in."

Sherry slapped him on his shoulder. "First, we want you to take over the painting of the cabin. The whole kit 'n' kaboodle. We'll pay you for your time, of course. And when you are through with that . . ." She caught her breath, her face aglow. "Fred wants you to make over that bleak studio."

Fred rocked on his heels, his hands folded across his portly belly. "Fred does, does he?"

His wife settled both hands on her waist, her elbows sticking in the air like chicken bones. "Yes, you do. We both understand the outside must look so dull and unremarkable for security, but there's no reason on earth not to create a veritable showroom inside. No wonder the artists come and go like flies in that depressing place of yours."

Letty gasped. "Make over the studio? It's been lifeless for as long as I have worked there."

Fred tilted his head, his rimmed glasses slipping further down his nose. "You don't approve?"

"On the contrary. I wish I had thought of it myself. The place could use some color and style, and who knows? Perhaps our ordinary studio will one day achieve the status of this castle and attract visitors from all over the world."

Fred chuckled. "In that case, we would certainly need to ramp up our security, but you are thinking big, Leticia. I like that. You'll do well as project manager too." He turned to his wife. "Are we ready to move on?"

"Not until Suz says something. Well, dear, what do you think about our plan? Did I mention that you and your precious son are welcome to stay in the cabin?" She folded her hands, squeezing them together over and over.

She needn't have expended the energy. I knew, almost from the start, that the life of a conservator was one thing in my mind, and quite another in the day-to-day grind of restoring classic art pieces. I'd come to admire people like Letty whose patience surpassed mine at every stroke of the brush, but I also realized that my climb in this business could only go so far. It had become a niggling worry scuttling about my mind, but something I'd been unable to fully face considering my need for survival.

Even though it would wear on me like a pair of cardboard flip-flops, I would in-paint molded crevices for the rest of my life if it meant that doing so would provide food for my son.

"I'm overwhelmed and I won't let you down. Thank you both so much for your support."

Sherry's earnest expression faltered and she slid a glance to Fred, who blinked several times, his eyes reflecting the outside light. Had I disappointed them? Before I could find the courage to ask, Fred reached for Sherry's hand and they rallied from their momentary show of emotion.

"We are pleased, Suzi-Q," Fred told me. "Very pleased indeed. Perhaps we'll start early next week? We have a shipment coming in that I must deal with first."

"Oh, tell the girls, would you, Fred?" The last tremor of disturbance faded from her face.

The breath he took added nearly an inch to his height. "As you know we receive curiosities from all over the world, and lately their value has been more or less sentimental." He gazed at his wife. "We will need all hands available for the pieces that will arrive early Monday."

"They're from Germany's fairy-tale castle!" Sherry blurted.

Letty's face registered intrigue. "Neuschwanstein?"

Fred nodded. "That's right. A variety of pieces including damaged candelabras and the pièce de résistance: a lost mosaic."

I tilted my head. "Lost?"

Letty tapped my arm, a mesmerized look in her eyes. "As in 'just found.' Fred, is this true? They have found a lost mosaic and are shipping it all the way here?"

He glanced around as if the walls had ears. "It's safer here with us, far away from the raiders in Europe. You will handle the project for me before moving up in the world, I take it?"

"Anything, boss. You know that I will."

A tingle ran up my arm at the sound of the cloak-and-dagger project. I'd never heard of this fairy-tale castle, but whose interest wouldn't be piqued by the idea of some long-lost German art piece showing up on California soil?

Sherry fanned herself. "Is it hot in here or is it just me?"

The headiness from the past hour nearly overcame me too, and I moved toward the window, hoping for some fresh air. Had I really learned Seth's secret, had a surprise visit from Len, and discovered that my life as a conservator was short lived—all in one day?

Sherry slipped out of her wool coat and draped it over her arm. "There. My, that's better. My goodness the excitement in here has me nearly sweltering!"

Fred offered her his arm. "Shall we go?"

Letty and I trailed behind them, watching Fred lead her from the suite. We giggled together, Letty and I, and listened as Sherry's voice reverberated through the hall. "Let's go take another look at that golden suite that Hedda Hopper always enjoyed so much . . ."

The past few months made me feel as if I had slipped into a bikini and waded into the frigid ocean, the cold strangling my lungs. I'd determined to fight my own resistance to it, to warm up against the ever-decreasing temperature. Now, even though part of me felt dumped by my boss, the rest of me relaxed, as if the tide had waned, until it lapped only as high as my knees.

I only hoped the sensation would last.

Chapter Thirty-Four

"So after the top-secret shipment arrives, Fred will be sending you off to that remote location to work alone?"

We strolled through the grounds of the zoo, Jer, Seth and I, animal sounds filling in the gaps of our conversation. I shucked off the bite in Seth's tone. "You sound like my brother. It's not like that. It sounds like a demotion, but really, Fred's done me a favor. Restoration work is tedious and backbreaking. My esteem for those with the patience for it has tripled."

Jer swung my arm hard. "That bird is speeding, Mama!"

Seth stopped and hoisted Jeremiah onto his shoulders. "There. You can see it better now."

I stepped up and read the plaque. "It's a scarlet macaw. And you're right, kiddo—it can fly up to thirty-five miles per hour."

Jer's eyes widened. "Wow!"

We watched the bird a long while, until I looked away at one point, dizzy. How strange and comfortable to be here with Seth and Jeremiah. So much had happened in the past few years, and yet this day felt so simple. So easy. It should have struck me as odd seeing my son riding on Seth's shoulders. It didn't. I wished the feeling could last.

Seth winked at me. "Bet the colors of those birds in there inspire you."

I snapped out of my meanderings. "Definitely. Fascinating how many bright colors God thought up for those feathered creatures."

Seth let Jer down but took his hand while we continued strolling along the winding path. "So what'll you do after the cabin's finished?"

"Dream bigger, for one thing. Open my own freelance painting business maybe." I shrugged. "Callie's already planning to hire me to do some painting up at the camp. She's thinking about a mural for the new Kitteridge Clubhouse."

"Well, then, I guess I have something to disclose to you."

I raised my chin. "Go ahead. Disclose."

"Callie asked me to bid on window cleaning for the camp. If they accept my bid, we'll likely be bumping into each other up there since it's a big job. Wouldn't want you to think of me as your stalker."

I laughed. "Too late for that."

Seth stopped and opened his mouth in mock surprise. His hand wrapped firmly around Jer's. "I'm shocked."

I grimaced. "Whatever."

Screeches ricocheting through the air indicated we had reached the monkey exhibit. The only visitors to the area, the white-eared monkeys swung high in the air, from branch to branch, giving us a private show. Jer bobbed his chin and grinned at Seth. Without hesitation, Seth knelt to let Jer once again climb aboard his shoulders.

He hoisted Jer up for a closer look. "Can you imagine swinging through the air like that, Jeremiah?"

"Maybe when my arms grow bigger!"

We all laughed.

Seth glanced at me. "So are you excited to see the shipment from the magic castle?"

"It's a German castle, and yes, I am." I kept my voice low, like on a reconnaissance mission. "I may not be the best conservator candidate around, but I do love a good suspense. Apparently the castle's owner, King Ludwig II of Bavaria, was quite the eccentric."

"Kind of like Hearst."

"Touché. Anyway, the Disney castles actually are based on Neuschwanstein."

"Disneyland!" Jer's heels kicked into Seth's chest.

I winced and reached out, stilling my son's feet. "Sorry."

Seth stood there, unfazed.

"We going to go to Disneyland with Daddy?" Jer bent his head down, his hands cupped beneath Seth's chin. "You can come too, Seth." His voice sounded so sweet and earnest.

I reached up and patted Jer's arm. "I don't know about that, son, but maybe Gage and I could take you."

Jer barked out a "Yes!"

Seth's brows bunched together, and his eyes searched my face.

My heart dulled. "It's still very confusing to him," I whispered.

He flexed those brows again and nodded. "I understand."

"It's not that going to Disneyland with you doesn't sound fun."

He smirked. "Of course. The Magic Kingdom with me would be amazing."

A laugh dribbled out of me. "And there's the Seth that *I* know."

A jumping monkey clung to the fence, inches away from us. I stepped back but Seth stayed steady, nearly eye to eye with the animal. With his constant movement, Jer massaged Seth's chin, his eyes fixed on that monkey. "My mom's afraid of the fast rides," he said, surprising me. He dropped his gaze to Seth's crown. "You could hold her hand or something."

No doubt I turned crimson.

As that monkey hung there, vying for attention, Seth slid a glance at me. He grinned. "I'd hold her tight, Jeremiah. Real tight."

Chapter Thirty-Five

"The shipment is on its way up the highway!" Letty hung up the phone, alerting the crew—and the additional presence of plainclothes security—of the imminent arrival of our new and top-secret assignment.

The pieces arrived, brought packed in heavy, rugged wooden crates, just as Fred had described them. My boss motioned for the head of security. "Secure the doors, and we'll have a look, shall we?"

Much like that moment, the rest of the week zipped by like a blur. After five days' worth of nonstop hours on my feet, most without lunch, I limped home on Friday night and headed straight for the sand. Callie had picked up Jer from school with a promise for a movie with Moondoggy, along with ice cream for dinner and hamburgers for dessert. How could he or I resist?

Fall had come, and yet telltale signs of summer continued to hold fast. Wild lupine sprouted in craggy places between rocks and under the weathered stairs to the beach. Though the air held a nip and the clear seawater felt like melted snow to the touch, I slipped off my shoes and tread across exposed rocks, careful not to step on pillows of anemones that lined the way. Despite their blameless appearance, they were known to become quite belligerent, squirting seawater at offending tide poolers.

Safe on my perch, I watched the waves crawl in lean and low and offer an occasional drenching to the creatures needing water to live. Unable to resist, I brushed the tentacles of an open anemone and delighted as it suctioned itself to my fingertips. It released me once it realized I wasn't dinner. I remembered what Letty told me about anemones shrinking when undernourished. Did that apply only to food? Sometimes when confusion reigned and doubts overshadowed me like fat rain clouds, I too felt myself shrinking.

Despite the breeze and the darkening sky, both my mind and body longed to stay out on this rock. *Just a little while longer*, my mind seemed to say, like Jeremiah might upon visiting a park filled with shiny new toys. Voices drifted in the distance, broken only by the increasing crash of waves. Reluctantly, I unfolded myself and stood, carefully making my way back to shore.

A couple strolled by as I stopped among a scattering of moonstones to slip my feet back into my shoes.

"Hey, Suz."

Still bent over, I looked up to find Holly standing next to a guy wearing long swim trunks and carrying a short board.

"This sure is a favorite place of yours." She smoothed back wayward curly locks against the breeze. "This is my friend, Duke."

"Hi, Holly. Duke."

Worry dimples sunk in around Holly's mouth. "I don't know if you've talked to our Seth lately, but this is not what you might be thinkin'."

I gave a quick nod. "He told me that you two, um . . ." I glanced at Duke. "That you decided to be friends."

Holly threw back her mess of curls and exhaled toward the sky. "I am so relieved!" She looked at me, her face still a bundle of nervousness. "I don't know what I'd do if you thought I was some kind of two-timer. Seth is a good man but too serious for me. Know what I mean?"

I hesitated. "Yes, I think I do."

"I mean, if anybody's perfect for him that would be *you!*"

I opened my mouth to answer, but it stuck there, frozen. Holly was exactly the fun-loving type Seth once wanted me to be, but the passage of time had brought change, making us both more cautious, thoughtful. After those first few startling moments of spotting Seth in Otter Bay, I'd believed that rekindling our friendship would be miraculous. Now I stood here, thinking about Seth, no longer a boy but a man. *Could there be something more?*

"I wish . . . oh, I wish . . ."

I tilted my head, waiting. "What do you wish?"

Holly searched my face, and she had something big on her mind. You could not sit at this woman's table as many times as I had and not know when she had something she wanted to share. She inhaled, her shoulders rising, but visibly shook off whatever thoughts pressed on her and released her breath.

After a beat, she nodded toward the stairway, her forehead etched with worry lines. "Somebody's been watchin' you, Suz."

I squinted in the fading light. Len leaned against the rickety railing and gave me a slight wave. How long had he been there?

"That your ex?"

"Hmm. Yes."

"Well, then. 'Night, Suz. Thanks for understandin'."

"Sure. Of course."

She wandered away and I took my time wiggling pebbles out of my shoes, knowing that as Holly and her surfer friend made their way up the staircase, Len would probably pass them on the way down.

"Figured I'd find you here."

"Hey, Len. Tried to call you earlier . . ."

"I was on a job."

I nodded. "I bet you came by to talk to me about Jer. He's

with Callie right now, so I suppose this is as good a time as any to hash out some kind of visitation schedule."

"Suz."

I crossed my arms, tensing against the cold. "Yes?"

He cupped my shoulders with his hands. "I'm not here to talk about Jer. I want to talk about us."

I wrinkled my forehead. "What do you mean 'us'?"

"You know . . . the letter I sent? I came back here for more than Jer—I came back for you too. You understand that, right?"

There it was. What everyone had warned me about, the intentions I had suspected but never openly acknowledged nor embraced. Some small part of me may have wanted to believe we could turn back the hands of the clock and love each other again. That wispy belief dissipated, however, the second Len appeared at the studio, the first time I'd seen him in months. I couldn't even accept the wilted flowers from his hands.

Even so, I tried a little. For Jer's sake, I tried to stay open to possibilities far outside my comfort zone. Although I hadn't known about them, my pastor and his wife had weathered the unthinkable in their marriage—and emerged strong and healthy and whole again. Should I have tried harder to look for a similar miracle in my own life?

Guilt tweaked my insides but not enough to make me change my mind.

"You said something like that in your letter, yes." I rubbed my lips together, unable to allow my eyes to connect with his. "But it's too late."

His hands slid down my arms, stopping at my elbows. "Too late? No, Suz, it's not too late for us to put what we had back together. Weren't you the one always telling me to have faith? Where's yours now?"

I made myself look at him. I didn't have all the answers, but I remembered the tears I cried when those divorce papers came. Len had lied, he cheated on me, but I never filed for divorce. He had done that. For months afterward, I obsessed over whether my signature on those papers effectively denied God the chance to do some kind of supernatural healing of our marriage.

"Len, my faith is in God, not marriage. I can forgive you for the past—I already have, but I can't be with you again, not in the way you're talking about."

He dropped his hands to his side and clenched his jaw. "Why not?"

I stood there as spray from the rising tide began to mist our feet. My eyes grew heavy and sad, and my insides shivered against the cold. Our relationship lacked more than a romantic spark. "I'm sorry. I don't trust you anymore."

He drew back, his face incredulous. "Like I ever asked you to."

I jerked my head. "Excuse me?"

He smirked, a familiar, unwelcome side of him emerging. "Never mind, but this conversation isn't over, Suz." Len ran one hand roughly through his hair, clearly agitated. "Not by a long shot."

Chapter Thirty-Six

 I couldn't sleep at all that night. Nor the night after that. Callie and Gage, each in their own way, tried to find out what had happened to cause me to become a poster child for insomnia. It didn't matter how often I attempted to deny it either—the dark circles gave me away.

So wouldn't you know it? Sunday morning arrived and a knock on my bedroom door woke me from the soundest sleep I'd had in days.

"Jer's up. Come to church with us?"

Although I heard my brother's voice, the actor Simon Baker appeared in my head. I must have been dreaming about the Aussie with the sly smile and magnetic eyes. I blinked and threw off the covers. "Give me half an hour."

Forty minutes later, as I sipped coffee from a travel mug, the three of us arrived at church. Callie ditched camp early and joined us. She swooped down to Jer's eye level and gave him a smooch. "How's my bud? Having a nice weekend with your mama and Uncle Gage?"

"Yeah." He grabbed my hand and dragged. "Have to get to my Sunday school class now."

Callie smiled and smoothed a stray hair sticking from his head. She glanced up at me. "I'll take him, if you want."

I let go of Jer's hand, plunked a kiss on his feathery head, thanked her, and left with Gage to find seats. The sanctuary brimmed with people of all ages hugging on each other, waving across the aisles, grinning at softly uttered niceties. I frowned at my coffee mug. Obviously not as leaded as the coffee served in Fellowship Hall.

Callie caught up with us and slid into the pew just as the first note of worship began. Something about the strum of a guitar, the lifting of voices to God, the shut-the-world-out attitude of Matt, the new worship leader, transported me out of my fatigue and worry and into his presence. I stayed there all morning, through the music, then the sermon, and even past the announcement about the covered-dish gathering on Thursday afternoon. Dragging myself from the muck and turmoil of my confusing life and focusing on God's mercies instead calmed the ruckus in my insides.

After service, Gage and Callie left to pick up Jer while I wandered into Fellowship Hall to fill up my travel mug. Although my soul had received a jump start, my body, still lacking sleep, needed assistance from caffeine. I found a hot carafe and pumped the top to fill my cup just as Pastor Erik strolled in and began greeting the dribble of parishioners milling about.

His wife, Andrea, entered from a side door, snuck up behind him, and gave him a peck on the cheek. I watched him reach back and whirl her to within inches of his face, his eyes animated.

Ever since Callie told me about their marriage troubles, I'd chafed at seeing them together, thinking I couldn't *not* judge Andrea for her past. But at this moment, seeing them carefree and out in the open about their relationship, that trepidation gave way to hope. In them I saw a breathing miracle, and though I couldn't seem to find one for myself, their story bolstered my faith.

"Mama!" Jer bounded into the hall and threw himself against my legs. "I had a donut!"

"You did? Isn't that fabulous?" I wondered how my sarcasm would translate to a four-year-old.

Gage smothered a smile. "He had two. Happy day. If you girls want to linger awhile, I'll take him out to the playground to run off some of that sugar."

I touched Callie's arm and nodded to my brother. "That'd be great. Give us a few minutes?"

"Sure thing."

I spotted a quiet corner of the room and nodded to the empty space. "Can we sit?"

"Sure, honey."

Callie and I commandeered the two comfortable chairs far away from the after-church stragglers. "You've been lost in your head for days. Something you want to talk about?"

"I was just noticing Pastor Erik and Andrea. They look so happy. I'd never have known about their problems if you hadn't mentioned them."

She nodded.

"And it got me thinking . . . Do you think I should have fought harder for *my* marriage?"

The edges of her eyes drooped and she let out a sigh. "Oh, Suz. When I told you about them, I wasn't trying to put something onto you."

"I know, I know."

She wiggled forward in her chair, as if readying for battle. Or at least an old-fashioned pep talk. "You weren't around then, but Pastor Erik did a whole sermon on divorce. It's a touchy topic with us church folk, and I think he wanted to clear a few things up. I remember it well because a high school friend was going through a nasty divorce at the time. When she heard Erik and Andrea worked things out, she also worried that she'd given up too soon."

"How'd she come to terms with that?"

"She didn't, not at first. She stepped right back into an emotionally abusive relationship, and it was a very dark time for her. For all of us who stood helplessly by. Erik and some of the church elders finally talked her into leaving him."

"Really?"

"Suz, God doesn't like divorce, but sometimes it is

necessary. We can't say that it's good or his will, because we know it hurts his heart. The point is, it may not be his desire, but he gives his permission for it in certain circumstances. He offers grace for your healing too."

She hung her head and breathed deeply before riveting her gaze back on me. "Len treated you and Jer terribly. He cheated on you. Stole from you. Lived a life of crime that put you in great jeopardy. I've watched you accept him back into your lives, and you've been noble and caring about it." She paused. "But his newfound faith doesn't mean you have to give him full access to your heart again. As your friend and your sister in Christ, believe me when I say that God loves you fully the way you are and where you are in your life. He wants to give you the desires of your heart—and we all want to see you set free of guilt and drama."

Lately I'd begun to feel suffocated by decisions as if they were enemies. The lowly sea anemone pinched off its tentacles to disengage from predators. What might it be like to have this ultimate defensive move in my repertoire?

"Does what I'm saying make sense?"

With a gratefulness welling from within, I gave my sister-in-law-to-be a hopeful smile. "It does. Thanks so much, Callie." Her reassurances shook me in a way, reminding me that it did no good to dredge up the same weary battle over and over again.

Especially one that I'd already won.

"DON'T FORGET TO PACK your pillow this time, Jer!"

Last time we stayed at the cabin, Jeremiah groused about having to lay his head on a pillow made from feathers. I tried to explain to him the value of down but he wouldn't believe me. "I like Uncle Gage's pillows better."

My brother cringed when I'd told him this on Monday morning. "Those pillows you've been sleeping on are an embarrassment. I meant to replace them but . . ."

"Hey, beggars can't be choosers. We showed up on a bachelor's doorstep and were happy to get four walls and a roof." I laughed. "And milk in the fridge that hadn't passed its expiration date."

Jer traipsed into the living room where I sat organizing my purse and Gage read the newspaper. "Okay, Mama. I got my pillow and my Giants blanket."

"Great. Anything else?"

"Yeah. I put cars in my suitcase."

"You didn't take out all your clothes, did you?"

He wagged his head fast, then slower, and then stopped all together. "Uh-oh." He spun on sock feet and slipped back toward the hall.

I looked to my brother who resumed his reading. "Did he think I wouldn't notice that he had no clean underwear in his suitcase?"

Gage smiled weakly.

"What's the matter?"

"Nothing really." He folded the paper and tossed it into the magazine rack next to his chair. "You know you're welcome to stay here for as long as you need. Even after Callie and I get married."

I nodded. "May have to."

"So wouldn't it be easier to stay here and just spend the days painting at the cabin? The light's better during the day anyway, and besides, won't Jer make it tough on you?"

"We've been over this, big bro."

He grimaced. "I know. You'll call me if you need anything?"

"Of course."

He sighed. "I'll hold you to it. And if I don't hear from you, I might have to take a drive up there."

"I'm shakin'." I laughed and tucked lipstick into the side pocket of my purse. After locating Jer's wayward sneaker and wrestling it on to his foot, I gathered our suitcases and headed to the car. I planned to drop off Jer at school, then head up the hill to move in, assess the walls, and pull together a shopping list for the art store.

I arrived at the cabin later than planned, an unending list of errands slowing my pace—one of the perils of being a full-time working mom. Soon enough, I'd find myself in my car on the way to pick up Jer from preschool.

When I stepped into the little cabin, I shivered. The past few days had left a chill in the place, and I sucked in a breath while quickly digging through my bags for a sweater. The wood floors moaned as I padded around, unpacking and placing important items—such as fuzzy socks and boxes of chai tea—in plain view.

The scent of dry wood stacked on the living room hearth drew me to the floor where I kneeled and tossed slivers of timber into the fireplace. I could see Jer and me happy here, playing games by the fire or working on homework in this cozy room as he grew older. Some might say that the old place smelled musty, past its prime, but I loved it. It smelled like history to me. I wondered about the people whose feet had passed through these rooms, wearing the wood smooth in places.

Seth once dreamed of building a log cabin in the woods, an A-frame in particular. I sat up on my haunches, my bottom pressing into my heels. Where had that memory been hiding? Soon after we met, I remembered walking along the river's edge with him. He grabbed a branch shaped like a *Y* from the weeds and pointed it across the surface of the water.

"There," he said. "That's where I'm going to build my cabin some day."

I scrunched my face, trying to picture his imagined Shangri-la. "Will this be before or after you travel the world?"

He flipped the stick upside down and leaned into it, the Y portion digging into the earth, his eyes studying the sky. "Depends."

"On what?"

He grinned and leaned over, kissing me softly on the mouth. "On you. It all depends on you."

My throat caught at the memory. I broke a twig in two and tossed it onto the stack of wood in the cold fireplace, my mind hovering between the past and the present. Had those two worlds merged inside my mind? I rocked on my heels. Nothing stood between Seth and me now. Not Holly, or Len—so why couldn't I allow myself to dream bigger when it came to us?

You've been afraid.

Fresh tears pricked the rims of my eyes. I've made mistakes before and let my emotions get the better of me. How could I be certain I wouldn't make any again?

My grace is sufficient for you.

Shame attempted to coil itself around and through my ribs, constricting my breathing. *But . . . when I married Len, I did what felt safe. I was blinded by grief and fear and did what seemed right in my own eyes.* I forced myself to breathe. *And I let you down, Lord.*

My power is made perfect in your weakness.

My heart surged. Jeremiah. Despite my failed marriage, I'd been blessed with a beautiful son. How could I continue to hold on to fears, to my mistakes? A tear trickled down the side of my cheek and dribbled off my chin. I tossed a final stick into the fireplace and stood.

Why wait another minute to tell Seth how I feel about him? How I . . . love him?

A creak echoed through the kitchen, silencing my thoughts. I swiped my cheek with the back of my hand and moved to investigate. I stepped over the narrow threshold into the kitchen, and it happened again. The wind had found a way to rattle the back door's scarred window.

With a shake of my head, I slipped back into the living room, then down the short hall to the bedroom. Our suitcases lay on the bed, half emptied, and I determined to finish unpacking, still dreaming of moving into this old place. When my cell rang, the beat of my heart sped up. I glanced at the number on the screen, but it wasn't Seth. "Hey, Letty."

"Are you covered in glowing green paint yet?"

"Ha ha. I'm going to try to keep the paint on the walls this time. Of course, once Jer's here with me . . ."

"Then no doubt you will be washing paint out of your hair."

"Funny. Did you want something?"

"If you are asking whether my car is running, it is." She laughed. "I only wanted to check on my friend. Are you good?"

"Let me see. I'm surrounded by blank walls, nestled in the pines, and dancing around on wooden floors in my stocking feet. Yeah, I'm good."

"And you are planning to stay there for a time today?"

I tilted my head to one side and squinted. "Ye-es."

"Good. I am happy for you."

"You sure you didn't want something in particular, Leticia?"

"My, you are a suspicious lady. I have to go now. Ta-ta."

Ta-ta?

I dropped my phone onto the bed, finished unpacking our clothes, then went in search of my paint supplies. Thanks to that job Gage found for me soon after moving here, the one painting the walls of Callie's house, I'd been able to embellish my paltry supply of brushes and other tools. Sadly, I hadn't touched them since.

Wisps of light carried in through the filmy curtains in the living room, casting the space in a filtered glow. A creak rang out through the kitchen again, this time causing me no concern.

I found my supply box and settled into the couch, barely noticing that another creak from that kitchen door groaned louder than before.

When a click followed, I looked up, startled. "Fred?"

No answer.

I craned my neck toward the doorway but saw nothing out of order. I set the box onto the cushion next to me and stood when the familiar sound of floorboards shifting pricked my ears.

"Hello? Is anybody there?"

A trickle scurried up my ribs. I froze. Another creak, another shift in the floorboards.

Len appeared in the doorway.

Chapter Thirty-Seven

"You scared me to death."

"Couldn't be helped."

"How did you . . . ?"

He crossed his arms and leaned against the door frame. "You're easy."

"Meaning?"

"I've been watching you for weeks. Not very observant, Suz."

I swallowed. "You didn't need to spy. All you had to do was ask." Déjà vu. Hadn't we had this conversation before?

He puffed out his lips and glanced around. "Nice place. You must be doing all right."

I faced him. "Next time knock. And use the front door while you're at it."

He coughed out a laugh. "You've gotten to be a pushy broad. Can't say that I like the change."

"What's wrong with you, Len? Why are you here, creeping around my house?"

He tucked his chin toward his chest, his eyes wide. "*Your* house? Well. You're doing better than I thought. *Much* better."

I shook my head. "The owner hired me to decorate the walls. Maybe some day, if I make enough, I'll be able to live here full time. For the time being, I'm just staying while I work."

"Or you could stay in the shed as I've been doing. You could afford that now, couldn't you?"

My blood chilled, coursing its way through my veins like finely crushed ice. I opened my mouth to speak, to lay into Len, but no words would come. Instead of the repentant man I'd come to expect, Len had boldly stepped inside these four walls, his face an image from the past. Had he really changed at all?

"The shed? Is that where you've been sleeping?"

He flicked his head toward the back door. "It's not much, but it kept me somewhat warm at night. Discovered it that first night when I followed you and Jeremiah up here. You were having yourself a girlie party with that woman from work; otherwise I might have stopped in to say hello."

"You're scaring me."

"Good."

"What do you want?"

"I tried to do things your way, Suzanna. I brought you

flowers, played with the kid, sent you a love letter, but you're impossible." He unfolded his hands and reached behind his back, retrieving a pistol. He spun it in around his finger. "So now we play it my way."

I rocked back on my heels. "Just tell me what you want."

He gave me an exaggerated shrug. "Fine. I want access to the studio, and all those priceless works of art."

The past and all its ugliness stood before me. The coldness that had fallen through me in sheets began to simmer. "I'm not the owner. I can't get in there any time I want."

"You have a key."

"I don't." It wasn't exactly a lie.

He stepped closer until only the small living room couch separated us, a gun shining in his hand. "Then you'll have to figure something out. You won't see Jeremiah until you've figured out how to get me into that studio."

If he had thrown a punch to my windpipe, the blow wouldn't hurt this much. I gasped for a breath. "What . . . have . . . you . . . done?"

"He's fine, of course. You didn't think I'd hurt a child, did you?"

I blinked. "I left him at preschool this morning."

He smirked. "With stupid people who couldn't protect a bowl of fruit."

I remembered the day the receptionist so easily gave away information about Jer's whereabouts. What if what Len told me now was true? Why didn't I pull Jer out of that school right then?

"He's with my girlfriend now. You know her as my parole officer's secretary." He cackled.

"Your . . . girlfriend?" My eyes fought to stay open, faintness attempting to overtake me.

"She just got into town. Under other circumstances, you two might have been friends." He shrugged, oblivious to the pain his careless words caused. "I won't tell you where she's taking him until you've taken care of what I want."

Panic replaced my initial shock at Len's announcement. The space behind my eyes and my nose began to fill. As I willed myself not to cry, the sound of crackling pine needles and the crunch of tires on the driveway wafted in from outside. A car door shut and footsteps approached. Len came around the couch and stood uncomfortably close. Too close.

"Expecting company?"

I gave a vehement shake of my head. A knock on the door threatened to prove otherwise.

Len shoved the gun under a couch cushion, then leaned close, his voice a harsh whisper. "Remember, you won't see Jer unless I get what I came for. Now, answer it."

I tried to steady my heart with a quick breath. No use. I opened the door and stepped backward. Seth stood there, his eyes bright, mischievous almost, his smile quirked up at one corner, just like it used to do . . . when we were in love.

"May I come in?"

No wonder Letty had been so giddy and secretive on the phone—she must have told Seth I was here. I cracked a weak smile and he stepped in. He noticed Len standing behind me and faltered slightly, that grin of his shrinking until his mouth resembled a flat line, one brow lifting in question.

Len looped a lazy arm around my shoulder. "You didn't tell me we were expecting company, Suz."

"I–I didn't know." I tried to smile again, but my lips wouldn't cooperate. The change in Seth's eyes, from bright to brooding, told me he'd interpreted my discomfort as guilt. "It's good to see you, Seth."

Len reached to shake his hand. "Yeah, man. Good to see you. What can we do you for?" His wisecrack roiled my insides.

Seth glanced at me, his face guarded. Or was he hurt? "You've chosen him. Again."

"Seth, don't." My hands, rolled into fists, bore the brunt of my fingernails cutting into my palms. His accusation surprised me. It took me becoming engaged to Len for Seth to speak up last time, for him to try to change my mind. Today he seemed groomed to fight.

I slid a look at Len standing next to me, smirking. One word and my ex-husband's scheme would be foiled. Yet I couldn't risk it. I would never jeopardize my son's well-being. Not for anything. Nor could I risk Seth's.

"You don't deny it, then." Seth's eyes dulled considerably from when he first arrived.

"I . . ."

Len cinched me closer. "If you haven't noticed, she and the kid and I are tight, like the Three Musketeers. You trying to break up a family?"

A million emotions traversed Seth's face, but I would not provide the answers he sought. I couldn't. "We were just, uh, going to have some tea. Would you like to join us?"

I hated the expression that took over Seth's face, like he stared at a madwoman. "Tea? Really, Suz? I shouldn't be here. You've made that obvious." He shook his head. "Games then, games now, huh? What were you going to do? Keep playing us both until you finally made up your mind about which guy to toss away like one of your old paintbrushes?"

"No."

Len twiddled with a strand of my hair. "She's not interested, pal. Not then, not ever."

"Wouldn't matter if you were, Suz." Seth's mouth twisted. "I'm taking myself out of the game." He whirled around, shoved the screen door open, and left me there to watch him stalk off, rigid, angry.

This time, Seth would never come back.

I CROSSED MY ARMS and did some spinning of my own. No time to nurse a broken heart, not with Jeremiah's whereabouts foremost on my heart and mind. "What are you planning, Len? To keep me captive here? Will you be adding kidnapping to your list of crimes, then?"

He guffawed and pinched my cheek. "Funny girl. You make me laugh." He flopped onto the couch like a college student after an exam. "You don't scare me, you know. You've got all the toughness of a candy bar."

I dropped my arms, my fists still clenched, and headed for the front door. Len flew off the couch and landed in front of me. He yanked the screen door shut, slamming it hard against the old wooden door frame. "Don't be stupid."

"Just wanted some fresh air."

"Right. And I'm about to get the award for Otter Bay citizen of the year."

I swallowed back the fear that attempted to rise in my throat like bile. "I'm not going anywhere, Len."

"That's right. You're not. Oh, wait. You'll be taking me to the studio tonight. Guess you will be getting out . . . after dark."

"Where is Jeremiah?"

He smiled that sickly smile again. "Having ice cream with a beautiful woman."

And there it was. This wasn't about Len's desire for his child, but a way to hurt me. Despite his past with drugs and crime, I knew Len cared for our son. He wouldn't do anything to hurt him. Hurt me? Yes. Jeremiah? Never. A whirl of cool air slipped around me like a flimsy cloak and I shivered for the second time today. What if I helped Len commit a crime . . . and then he stole Jer from me anyway?

I made a move toward the kitchen, hoping to shield him from my fears.

"Going somewhere?"

"Tea. I want a cup of tea."

"Just don't eye that back door or anything."

I stepped into the kitchen and robotically filled a kettle with water and set it over a lit stove burner. No matter how much I rubbed my palms together, they refused to warm up. Len hovered near the doorway, silently, but I did my best to ignore him. Or at least appear to ignore him.

With shaking hands, I put a bag of chai into my cup and poured scalding water over it, watching it float and steep into darkness. A swirl of cinnamon, cloves, and ginger reached my nose and I breathed it in, hoping to be enlightened. Maybe, just maybe . . .

If Len understood that his actions today would have grave consequences, he would back off and do the right thing for a change.

Stop trying to fix a broken life.

But if Len thought this through, wouldn't that make all the difference?

He has not learned his lesson yet.

But maybe this is his old life trying to overtake his new life in Christ . . .

You are not God.

Was this my fault? Had I wanted so badly for Len's soul to be fixed that I ignored the signs that little had changed? Had I done that in our marriage too?

Be still. Wait patiently.

I sipped the tea without cream, letting it warm my insides. My maternal instinct wanted to grab a sharp object from a kitchen drawer and plunge it into Len's side, but as I lowered myself into a chair and sipped the warm tea, I brushed aside the thought. Instead I let my gaze drift out through the kitchen window where the jungle gym waited for Jeremiah to give it a workout.

God, please, please, please *show me what to do.* I prayed and waited for answers to come.

Chapter Thirty-Eight

Len had ripped the phone from the wall, tossed my cell phone out the window, and ignored my attempts to reason with him. Time passed moment by excruciating moment. More than once he spoke quietly into his phone, but no matter how hard I strained to hear his conversation, it didn't work.

I turned to unpacking Jer's things, lining up his little shoes by the closet in the bedroom. I refolded his play clothes and tucked them into a dresser drawer, as if nothing was amiss. And I laid out the cars he had packed into the suitcase himself, the way he did at home.

I also obsessed on the moment when I'd have no choice but to unlock the studio door and let my ex-husband abscond with the treasures so lovingly being restored. Letty's crestfallen face and Frank's weak heart fought for places in my consciousness. Would they ever forgive me? Could I ever forgive myself?

Surely they would understand what my mother's heart must do.

I lifted Jeremiah's suitcase and began zipping up all the pockets when something dropped and bounced across the wood floors. I felt around for the object and stopped it with my fingers. A smooth marble—the same one I had taken away from Jeremiah weeks ago, convinced he was still too young to play with jacks.

Had he taken it from my drawer and packed it away in his suitcase? When it disappeared from my nightstand drawer, I'd asked him about it.

"No, Mama. I didn't take it."

My young son had lied to me.

Like father, like son.

With my thumb, I pushed the marble around on my fingers. God told his disciples to have faith like a mustard seed, but what was the converse of that? Might this tiny toy represent a pinch of trouble in my son's young life instead of faith? And might this speck of trouble grow into a mountain someday? My hand fisted around it, and I shoved it into my back pocket before heading for the living room.

"I'll take you to the studio on one condition, Len." I tried not to let my eyes search for the gun.

From his prone position on the couch, his arms crossed at his chest like he'd been dozing, Len scowled at me. "Good luck."

"I won't show you where the key's hidden unless you bring Jeremiah to me first."

He spat out a laugh. "Right."

Len saw all that art as his ticket to freedom. Having a son to care for couldn't possibly be in his plans, and yet for me, my son's life, the shaping and molding of it, *was* my future. I drew in a jagged breath. "Take it or leave it."

He stared me down, then shrugged. "Yeah, sure. The kid'll be there."

I watched him, wary, yet with no choice but to believe him. I only hoped that if he didn't follow through with my request, I would have the sharpness of mind to know what to do before allowing him to take off with whatever he wanted.

Len appeared neither bewildered nor thrown by my sudden boldness. He settled back into a sleeping position on the couch and shut his eyes—as if my presence, and my demands, meant nothing.

My eyes flickered on an almost-imperceptible change in light. A shadow had passed in front of the living room window. I glanced at Len on the couch, but he hadn't noticed. A second shadow passed by, followed by the slightest crackle of gravel and the faintest creak of the back porch steps.

Had Len's accomplice shown up?

I approached him and he stirred. "Not thinking of leaving again?"

I forced a roll of my eyes, as if his question felt natural. "Please. Just getting myself more tea."

He closed his eyes again. "Whatever."

Carefully, I stepped over the threshold and through the narrow doorway into the kitchen, and what I saw waiting for me, watching me from behind the glass, made me want to burst into tears.

Seth.

He watched me through the window, Gage only inches behind him. I gasped, then threw my hands over my mouth and shook my head. It took all of me not to throw open the doors and let the cavalry in.

But what would happen to Jeremiah if I did? And could they overpower Len before he overpowered them?

A voice called out from the living room. "I don't hear any tea pouring."

Seth motioned for me to stay quiet. He held my seething brother back with a steady hand. Any sense of bravery had left me and I stood rooted to lackluster linoleum, unable to move. *Just breathe . . .*

A pound on the front door caused my neck to jerk.

"Man! Don't your friends ever call first?" Len swore, and a thud on the living room floor told me he dragged himself off of the couch. "Get out here and answer your door."

Seth pointed at the knob of the back door and mouthed, *Open it.*

I couldn't take my eyes from him but called out to Len. "I burned my hand. Could you . . . would you grab the door for me? Probably just a salesperson or something."

He swore again and I heard him unlock the latch. The door swung open hard and Len shouted.

The urgency in Seth's eyes implored me again. A deep voice and the blare of a siren tore me from my stupor and I sprung forward, opened the back door, and allowed Seth to tackle me in the tiny kitchen of the log cabin on the hill.

HE HAD DONE IT again. Len had lied to me.

Gage held me at arm's length, his eyes unwavering. "Suz, you have to see that Len gets put away for a very long time."

My eyes popped open wide, like I had consumed a week's worth of caffeine with a pound of chocolate thrown in for good measure. I couldn't settle myself. "Jer . . . he's really okay? You're sure?"

"Don't worry. He's with Callie. She won't let anything happen to him. You know that, right?"

I nodded. "He said his girlfriend had taken him some-where . . ." My voice sounded foreign to me.

Gage groaned and pulled me to him. "She tried, but the preschool wouldn't buy her story—that Len had sent her to pick up Jer. When they couldn't reach you and the woman became belligerent, they stalled her and called the police. And they also called Callie. She was there in a heartbeat."

If only I hadn't believed him . . . If only I had forced my way out of here . . .

"You had no way of knowing if what Len told you was true. I don't blame you for being scared, Suz. The guy's a monster, he—" Gage swallowed his tirade as another officer approached.

Earlier it had taken a simple nod of my head for the police to cuff my ex-husband and force him into the back of a squad car. Whatever strength I'd shown then, though, withered into all-out shakes. Every part of me shook as more and more questions bombarded me, but Gage stayed close during every painful moment.

Seth did too.

Only he paced during much of the questioning, stopping occasionally to gaze at me, his eyes a caress, before resuming his steady march. My bewildered mind faded in and out of the present as Seth hovered so near.

You have to be strong. You have to see that his punishment fits the crime.

Despite all that Len had done, it hurt knowing that Jer wouldn't have his father in his life. Yet Len had come all this way, not to pursue his faith and his family, but to feed his greed. And he had done so willingly.

How ironic that Seth, too, had willingly moved across this big old country, but he did so for the adventure of it all. And when he hit bumps in the road? He manned up, faced his past, and set about making things right.

I had been looking for that kind of stability all my life.

My longing to see Len change would not bring it about. He might never find true salvation—although I vowed to pray otherwise, and in the end, it was up to God. Not me. Faith, I'd found, meant planting yourself where the roots needed the deepest watering.

I made up my mind. The officer searched my face, his pen

poised over his notepad, and I gave him everything he needed to know.

After the officer left, I gazed up at Seth, his gray-green eyes rooted on me. He stopped pacing. I reached out to him. He covered my hand with his, slid onto the couch, and pulled me into his embrace. "If my pride hadn't gotten in the way, I could have seen what was really going on in here."

"Shhh." I stroked his face. "How did you figure it all out?"

He gazed at me. "Holly."

My mouth dropped open.

"I was too angry to go home, so I stopped in the diner, stewing. Sidled up to the counter and ordered a large coffee. Black." He eyed our hands, intertwined with one another. "She asked about you. Said she'd seen you on the beach and offered you a sisterly hint about the two of us."

I smiled at the recollection.

"But she kept talking." He paused to look at me, a sad, lopsided smile on his face. "You know Holly. She told me that she'd seen Len watching you on the beach—and how it had given her the creeps."

"She said that?"

"Well, she said seeing him gave her the shivers, and that she didn't think she trusted him. It dawned on me then that maybe you hadn't rejected me after all."

"Oh." My heart dropped a little.

"I'd already left the counter, intent on coming back up here to confront the guy, when Gage flew into the diner like a madman, shouting that you were in trouble."

I gasped. I had not imagined the drama unfolding beyond the cabin's doors.

Seth tilted his head. "He was on his way to you when he noticed my truck parked in the lot."

A knot in my throat loosened, and I swallowed back tears.

Seth let go of my hand then and pulled me to him. "I've never run so fast in my entire life." His voice, raw and passionate, grazed my ear. "I've loved you forever, Suz."

I turned my face and peered at him, eyes glistening. "I know that now. I love you too."

Chapter Thirty-Nine

One Month Later

 I watched him through the window of the tiny log cabin where I now lived, his gloved hands smearing sweat and loamy dirt across his brow, a light mist falling onto his hair, his shoulders, his face. Every once in a while he'd stop, lean on his shovel, and send me a smile that fluttered my insides like butterfly wings.

Callie spoke into my ear. "He still out there working?" She hugged my shoulders. "Somebody's in love."

Gage stood next to his bride-to-be, craning to peer out the window. "Tried to help him but he wouldn't hear of it. Says it's something he's got to do on his own." He kissed me on the top of my head. "Seth's a good man."

You are too. If not for my big brother, where would I have turned? When we needed help, Gage accepted us into his home, no questions asked. He promised to be a father figure to his nephew, and he never turned away from that vow. The thought pricked my heart a little. With his father back in jail—for a long time—Jer would need his uncle Gage now more than ever.

He'd need Seth too.

Fred and Sherry and Letty joined us from the other room, and I pushed away old thoughts and brightened. "Did you ever think this kitchen would be so full?"

A serene smile stretched across Fred's face. "We had hoped to see it someday, Sherry and I. And prayed too."

Sherry stroked his face and leaned her head on his shoulder. She no doubt thought about their daughter and the reunion that had yet to be. Still, she told me recently, they had reason to hope. "Shannon accepted my phone call, and we have begun the process of restoration." She chortled. "No pun intended."

Letty pushed her flashy self through the small group of us crowding around the window and wagged her head. "How long will that man of yours slosh around in that muck for you?" She gave me an exaggerated sigh along with a sly grin. "It is true what I have said before—you are impossible to dislike."

I grinned back at her. "Again with the compliments, Leticia? What has gotten into you?"

"I will tell you what. This house and what you have done to it." The smile on her face was as genuine as the ring on Callie's finger. "When I walked into the living room I thought perhaps that I should go for a swim inside the tide. Vibrant and yet tastefully done. *This* is your calling, Suz. Those plain, white walls have come to life." Letty winked at Fred. "No offense."

He nodded, patting his belly. "None taken."

I smiled at Letty. "So you start at the castle on Monday?"

"Yes, indeedy, she does." Sherry clapped her hands.

"Fabulous," I told her. "Kind of like having my own season pass to Hearst Castle."

Letty clucked. "You wish."

I bumped her with my hip. "Uh-uh, I know!"

She threw an eye roll toward the ceiling. "Can no one resist her charms?"

Callie gasped and our gazes veered toward the kitchen window again. "He's done it! It's coming down!" She poked Gage's shoulder. "Oh, honey. Go help him."

Gage cracked a smile, kissed her forehead, and slipped out the door.

We all stared through that window, watching the men in my life tear down and haul off broken pieces of that rickety shed, the place Len had spent countless nights planning out his deception. They carried away ragged sheets of plywood until the only thing left behind was a mud-covered concrete slab and the two men standing over it, triumphant.

Callie checked the time on the sea-inspired wall clock. "Time for us to go. Meeting with the minister one more time tonight before the big day, so I'd better get that brother of yours home to clean up."

Sherry patted Fred's shoulder in a less-than-discreet way. "Us too. I've got a chicken in the Crock-Pot that's sure to taste like rubber if we don't get going ourselves."

Letty led the way out, calling over her shoulder, "You will not find me staying behind to be the third wheel—that is for sure!"

Jer trailed into the living room then, his eyes like slits from his afternoon nap. He yawned until his nose nearly jammed into his eye.

"Make that a fourth wheel." Letty cackled.

The whole gang slipped out the front until the screen door bounced to a close. I led Jer into the kitchen where he peered through the window, his chubby cheeks mottled and red. "That Seth out there?"

I nodded.

"Can I play in the mud with him?"

I laughed. "Look. It's raining hard now."

"Aw, why's he get to be outside in the rain?"

Seth swiped the sweat from his forehead with the back of a glove, leaving behind another layer of dirt. He caught us spying and beamed.

I swung the door open wide, breathing in the clean smell of wet pine and earth. "I made my famous chai tea. Come out of that rain and join us?"

With no arm twisting necessary, Seth hopped across the yard in long strides and bounded up the back steps. He shucked off his work boots and waded inside, his socks soaked through.

"Ew, you're messy!"

Seth tousled my son's hair, his grin wide enough to reveal dimples not seen in years. "You think your mother minds?"

I set his tea before him. "Not a chance."

In quite the grown-up manner, Jer suggested Seth take a hot bath. Then he wandered into the living room where his setup of cars waited for him on the hearth. As Jer played, Seth and I sat across from each other, idly sipping hot tea, neither of us caring one whit about the grime covering his clothes and skin. Lulls in our conversations once bothered me, as if not filling a quiet moment with words meant Seth didn't care.

Oh, but now I knew how much he did.

Seth reached across the glass tabletop and took possession of my hand. He brought it to his mouth and kissed my fingers, his eyes lingering on my face. In a move I would forever play again and again in my mind, Seth slid out of his seat and onto the floor, kneeling beside me. He pulled me toward him until his hands cupped my face and his lips found mine, and he kissed me hungrily. The rainy day outside did nothing to dull the explosion of warm colors in my head.

He eased his mouth from mine, his gaze scrutinizing. "You're a mess."

"You are worse." I giggled like a teenager. Again.

His mouth and his eyes sobered. "I might have been too hard on ol' Mr. Hearst."

"No kidding. You?"

"Didn't he say that dreams were meant to be shared?" He kissed my fingers again. "I couldn't agree more."

I thought about those dreams and how they provided the faintest of light in the darkest of storms. Unlike films of old played for Hollywood's A-listers in the famed Hearst Castle, our story didn't end in blackness splayed across a drop-down screen. Instead it picked up, not where we had left it, but at a more vibrant, poignant spot in our lives. It was as if our story had faded, then brightened again to a luxurious ocean blue.

As I reveled in Seth's touch and found peace in the quiet with him by my side, I let myself fall into his embrace, dirt and all, allowing all worries and guilt and self-recrimination to wash away.

Dear Reader,

The title of my third Otter Bay novel is based on the concept of "fade to black," the phrase that denotes a movie's ending. Instead of black, though, Suz's tender story is about new beginnings. Therefore the title *Fade to Blue*.

This book is for you dreamers, the ones who hold on and never let go of that dream—no matter what. You're the ones who look toward your dreams like a faraway star. Though the earth may move beneath you and that star fades from view, you hold your ground. Chin up. Eyes focused. Trusting God.

You know who you are. I've been there too. All too often, I find myself there again.

I'm thrilled to continue the Otter Bay novels with *Fade to Blue*, once again set in a favorite locale: the rocky central California coast. It's a place where glowing windflowers, dazzling seascapes, and—in this novel—God's grace abounds.

I hope that as you read Suz's story, you experience the Good Shepherd's gentle leading (Psalm 23), and fall in love with the concepts of forgiveness, sacrifice, and grace—as much as you do the breathtaking locale.

With love from the Central Coast,
Julie

Acknowledgments

Thank you, readers, for your encouraging notes about the Otter Bay novels. You inspire me to continue writing stories filled with *faith, flip-flops, and waves of grace.* I want you to know that I keep your sweet notes in a file and reread them often. We all need to be encouraged now and then, so thank you for doing that for me!

Thanks also to those who helped specifically with *Fade to Blue:*

Tami Anderson, Dan Carobini, Elaine F. Navarro, and Julie Gwinn, all who read and critiqued this story in various stages.

The entire B&H team who slave over the details of putting a book together, especially Karen Ball, Julie Gwinn and Kim Stanford. Many thanks also to Julee Schwarzburg for your skillful and gentle editing, and to Steve Laube for handling the business side of things.

Special thanks to "Otter Bay" locals for their insight into the Hearst Castle: Ted Moreno, Bruce Koontz, and Rich Bullock. Also to Kim Pummill-Talon who graciously loaned me her copy of *In & Around the Castle*, written by her grandfather Byron Hanchett. Mr. Hanchett worked for William Randolph Hearst for many years, and his account provided fascinating stories and insight.

I'm also grateful to my pastor, Rev. Dr. Mark Patterson of Community Presbyterian Church, who delivered a timely message of grace that helped me complete this story.

Kisses to my family, Dan, Matt, Angie, Emma, and Charlie the Dog, my constant sources of inspiration and love; and my parents Dan and Elaine Navarro, my ever-enthusiastic cheerleaders.

Most especially, I thank you, Jesus, for picking me up when I was at my lowest point and showing me the way to salvation. Thank you for the lessons you teach me with each and every book.

Discussion Questions

1. Which of the characters in *Fade to Blue* did you relate to most and why?

2. Suz and Seth's parting had been acrimonious. Yet when she sees him years later, she hopes the bitterness has faded. From your experience, does that sound like wishful thinking? Why or why not?

3. A traumatic experience caused Suz to pick up with her young son and move across the country. If you've ever had to start over, with a job or a church or a move, how did that turn out?

4. Letty is a curiosity to Suz, sometimes openly friendly, other times guarded. Yet they are thrown together as coworkers. How have you found it best to handle a relationship that's not easy to decipher? Were you able to overcome your unease, or did you walk away from the relationship?

5. When Suz's boss, Fred, learns she's never actually toured the Hearst Castle, he says, "There's curiosity in your eyes, and while that may be dandy and fine enough for some folks, no one can get work done that way. You need a tour to cure you of your wonder for the place." What brings you to a place of wonder and awe?

6. After watching a movie in the castle's old theater, Suz asks Letty if she's ever wished she could write her own life story. Have you ever wondered the same thing? If you could rewrite your life story, how would it look? (See Jeremiah 1:5; Psalm 139:13.)

7. By all accounts, Suz's former husband, Len, treated her terribly. Why do you think she feels so compelled to give him another chance? If you've ever faced a betrayal of trust, how did you overcome that?

8. While Suz feels otherwise, her brother, Gage, is adamant that she shouldn't trust Len again. Both Suz and Gage are Christians called to love one another, yet they are in conflict over the subject of Len. How can both be correct? Or are they? (See Galatians 5:15 for why resolving conflict is important.)

9. Suz is constantly conflicted, torn over wanting her son to have a relationship with his father and wanting to move on with her life. She wants to do the right thing in God's eyes. How have you handled internal conflict like this?

10. Seth has changed; he's not the carefree man Suz remembered from her teen years. What did you think of the way Seth acted around Suz?

11. When a sea anemone reacts to Suz's touch by curling inward, she has an "aha" moment—*Is that how I am sometimes, Lord? Do I reach out for you, then quickly withdraw when you offer me your hand?* Discuss some aha moments you've had by God's gentle leading.

12. Sparks fly when Seth and Suz discuss William Randolph Hearst. While Suz sees the former newspaper magnate and investor as a dreamer, Seth calls him a narcissist. Why do you think that was? How might their personal outlooks on life affect their opinions?

13. When Len insists on taking Jeremiah out on a surfboard, Suz is against it. Do you think she's being overprotective? Why or why not?

14. In the final chapters, discuss some of the tough choices Suz has to make. Do you think she made the right ones? Explain.

15. Throughout history, God has provided second chances for his people. Talk about a time when you felt the forgiveness of God and a second chance at restoration.

16. Why do you think the author chose the title *Fade to Blue*? What does it mean to you?

Other Exciting Titles by Julie Carobini

An Otter Bay novel

Sweet Waters

JULIE CAROBINI

A Shore Thing

An Otter Bay novel

JULIE CAROBINI